"COUNSELOR, WHAT ARE YOU SAYING?" PICARD ASKED.

"I'm saying we may be overlooking something important here, Captain," Troi said. "I've been monitoring Data's emotions all day, and I can say for certain that though he has been functioning under a great deal of stress, he's been managing it quite well. The only time he gave off an emotional response that truly concerned me is when he realized that you didn't believe him."

"Which means . . . what, exactly?" Admiral Haftel asked uncertainly.

"Data is trying to come to terms with some very complex concepts—among them mortality and isolation," Troi explained. "These are concepts that even organic beings have trouble understanding. But I believe that something else is happening simultaneously, something we've all been helping him to work toward for years, but perhaps never expected to see happen so suddenly. We just heard him tell us he came to a conclusion without any evidence to back it up, something the best Starfleet officers do routinely. Yes, in Data's case, it could mean a malfunction. Or . . ."

"Or?" Haftel demanded, clearly not liking where he thought the conversation was leading.

"Or he's finally developing thought processes that extend beyond the scope of pure fact," Troi finished, and she could see that the captain had already grasped her meaning.

"Intuition," Picard breathed. "Data has developed intuition."

STAR TREK
THE NEXT GENERATION®

IMMORTAL COIL

Jeffrey Lang

**Based upon STAR TREK and
STAR TREK: THE NEXT GENERATION
created by Gene Roddenberry**

POCKET BOOKS
New York   London   Toronto   Sydney   Singapore

This one is for Katie.
Forever.

An *Original* Publication of POCKET BOOKS

POCKET BOOKS, a division of Simon & Schuster, Inc.
1230 Avenue of the Americas, New York, NY 10020

ISBN: 0–7434–0592–7

First Pocket Books printing February 2002

10 9 8 7 6 5 4 3 2 1

POCKET and colophon are registered trademarks of
Simon & Schuster, Inc.

For information regarding special discounts for bulk purchases, please
contact Simon & Schuster Special Sales at 1-800-456-6798
or business@simonandschuster.com

Printed in the U.S.A.

ACKNOWLEDGMENTS

Acknowledgments, naturally, to Gene Roddenberry, not only for *Star Trek,* but for other worlds he created in his career, and one in particular. If I told you here which one I meant, well, what fun would that be? I would also like to thank the many writers, producers and other creative folk who helped populate the *Trek* universe, most especially to the following for the use of their ideas in this work: Robert Bloch, Richard Manning, Hans Beimler, Tracy Torme, Stephen Kandel, Dan Koeppel, Rene Echevarria, Melinda Snodgrass, Jerome Bixby, John Meredyth Lucas, Boris Sobelman, and John Kingsbridge. No doubt I have inadvertently omitted a few, so my apologies in advance to you all.

May I request a round of applause for the actors who helped create such indelible characters? In particular, I'd like to offer a tip of the authorial beanie to Mr. Brent Spiner. Many hands may have created his mind, but Spiner gave Data a soul.

A gracious thank you to friends, family, neighbors, colleagues and the occasional complete stranger who have listened to me alternately wax enthusiastic and whine bitterly about this project. Most especially hugs and manly expressions of affection (where applicable) to Heather Jarman, Helen Atkins, Helen Szigeti, Tristan

Mayer, Joshua Macy, my wife, Katie Fritz, and our son, Andrew.

And last (though most definitely not least), a toast to Marco Palmieri, who said, "I have this idea for a book about Data and the role of artificial intelligence in the *Trek* universe." If there was any justice in the universe (or a little more, anyway), his name would be on the cover, too. He'll modestly deny that, but I'm here to tell you that it's true. Thanks, dude.

SOMEDAY, THOUGHT NOONIEN SOONG, *when I have a choice in the matter, I'm going to live where it's always hot. Not warm. Not temperate. Hot.*

Checking to see that his lifeline was secure, Soong set his legs against the face of the cliff, raised his hands to his mouth, and, after lifting his breathing mask, puffed onto them in three quick, sharp breaths. The battery packs for the warming coils in his gloves were dying. When Ira Graves first mentioned this little expedition, he'd told Soong to pack gear for climbing in cold environments. But Soong had interpreted that to mean the sort of conditions you might find in the North American Rockies or, at worst, the lower reaches of the Alps. Nobody had said anything about *this*—sub-zero temperatures, practically no atmosphere and freakish rock formations. Soong had completed some difficult climbs in his not-quite two decades, but even with the antigravs, the conditions he was currently facing were a little more complex than anything he'd faced before.

Soong decided to blame everything on Graves. It was convenient. Just because Graves was arrogantly brilliant (or brilliantly arrogant—Soong wasn't sure which) didn't mean he was always perfectly in control of *everything.* Academia, Soong had concluded, was a pond where the little fish—students like himself—were gobbled up by the bigger fish—grad assistants like Graves—who were, in turn, gobbled up by even bigger fish like Dr. Emil Vaslovik, probably the biggest fish he was ever likely to meet.

He would have liked to flatter himself by thinking that it was his exemplary work in the artificial intelligence workshops that had brought him to Vaslovik's attention, but Soong understood enough about how the system worked to admit that his mountaineering skills probably had more to do with it. Maybe Vaslovik had heard about the time Soong had climbed the campus clock tower. *Going to have to work on curbing those impulses, Noonien ...* Whatever the case, when Graves had contacted him and told him—not invited, but *told* him—"You're going on a little trip next week," Soong knew he wasn't really in a position to refuse. So, there he was: halfway down a ninety-meter cliff while the two other men who had brought him here sat on a ledge twenty meters above him. *There has got to be a better way to get ahead in life,* he decided.

His scan had revealed that there was another ledge approximately twelve meters below him, but the lantern dangling from his belt wasn't powerful enough to cut the gloom. He was just going to have to trust his abilities and take it slow, the way his father had taught him. Soong activated the comm link inside his breathing mask with the tip of his tongue and said, "I'm going to continue my descent now. Does the tricorder show anything unusual below me?"

Too loudly, Graves said, *"No. Nothing. The cliff face is stable. You should be okay."*

Soong tapped the comm link again and said, "Not so loud, Ira. You're going to shake me off the cliff."

Vaslovik switched on his comm and asked in his grave, yet oddly soothing manner, *"Are you all right down there, Noonien?"*

Soong grinned. It was only the fourth time Vaslovik had asked him that in the past twenty minutes. Somehow, he hadn't expected the quadrant's greatest expert on machine intelligence to be quite so . . . grandfatherly. *But what did I expect? Someone who spoke in syntactically perfect sentences and glided like a mech on ball bearings?* He decided grandfatherly was good, grandfatherly was, in fact, just fine. It helped to make up for Graves who, by contrast, was condescending and just generally insufferable.

Soong shook himself. *That's a good way to get into trouble, Noonien.* His father would have cuffed him on the ear. *Think about what you're doing, about where you're placing your foot next.* The cold was getting to him. He could feel himself drifting.

Soong inspected his safety line, then checked the telltales on the antigravs. The right battery pack showed bright green, but the left one was blinking yellow. He did a quick test, pushing off the cliff face, and felt a slight wobble. *Not good,* he thought. The batteries were supposed to drain evenly and keep him stable. *Probably the cold,* Soong decided. The packs hadn't been rated for sub-zero work.

But I'm okay for now, he decided. *All the more reason*

to get this over with quickly. He set the antigravs for full, then squeezed the release on the guide rope, and slowly eased off the antigrav. Pushing off the cliff with his toes, Soong expertly rappelled down about six meters, then stopped and set his feet, flipped the antigravs back up to full. *Damn,* he thought. *These gloves are just not doing it.* He checked the view between his legs, waiting for his lamp to stop swinging back and forth. Nothing unusual. The ledge should be only another five meters, maybe less. *Wait. What's that?* Something odd below, something pointing in the wrong direction.

Soong tried to sidestep across the face of the ice to get a different angle, but the cliff face was too smooth. *It would help immensely if I knew what the hell I was looking for,* he thought disgustedly, but Vaslovik had been tight-lipped on this point. "You'll know it when you see it," he'd said. "*If* you see it. For now, just concentrate on getting to the bottom of the chasm so we can set up the pattern enhancers. If we can do that, we can transport down the workstations, set up a shelter, get the sensors going and do some serious work. I'll be more surprised than not if you see anything on the way down." It was, up to that point, the longest single speech Vaslovik had addressed to Soong and there was something about how the dour, silver-haired man spoke that made you take everything he said very, *very* personally. His eyes never left yours, though there was a definite temptation to try to let your own gaze slide away toward random objects. Listening to Vaslovik required willpower.

"So, why not just transport directly to the bottom of the chasm?" he had considered asking, but hadn't. If that had been an option, he knew Vaslovik would have done it. Checking the ship's sensor logs, it became clear: there was something very peculiar about the place. The sensors—and they were very *good* sensors, despite their age—couldn't penetrate the interference around the area. Might be mineral deposits or low-level radiation, or . . . Something else. Soong tried not to think about that option too much. Whatever the case, transporting without enhancers would be extremely risky. "Not that *this* isn't risky," he muttered to himself.

"What was that, Soong?" Graves asked.

"Nothing, Ira. Just catching my breath."

His attention was wandering again. *Okay, Noonien, concentrate. Do the drill, just like Father taught you. Check your levels, antigravs up, squeeze the release, push . . .* He pushed off and suddenly found himself with no support on the left side. The antigrav had failed. He released the pressure on the handgrip, hoping the autolock mechanism would stop his descent, but it was too late. He had already started sliding and tumbling.

Soong released the autogrip and grabbed the rope, then flattened himself against the cliff face, toes digging in for purchase. He'd been in this situation once or twice before, just like anyone who climbed regularly. There was no avoiding it; equipment failed. The difference here was that on the other occasions there had been someone above him, someone more experienced, someone he knew and trusted—usually his father—watching to make sure the safety lines were fixed and secure. Graves began to shout, *"Soong! Soong!"*—almost making him lose his grip on the rock because of the need to tear out his earpiece.

He felt a jolt as he cracked his knee on a rock. There was no pain, though he knew that would come if he survived the next couple of seconds. He could feel the bite of the cord as it slid through his gloves, but there was no sensation of his descent slowing. *Cord must be wet,* he decided.

And, then, another shock—up through both legs this time—and a sensation that he imagined must be how icicles feel after they've lost their grip on the eaves of a building and shattered on the pavement below. All sensation dimmed down for a moment and Soong realized he was slipping into unconsciousness. *No, no. Bad idea. Bad idea,* he thought and willed himself back to awareness, and all the attendant discomfort. Everything below his waist was screaming at him and he saw a bright light. *Has Ira already started climbing down?* he wondered, but then realized he was staring into the lens of his lamp. It had broken loose and was lying on the ground . . . no, not the ground. A ledge.

Fighting down panic, Soong gingerly felt to his side, searched for the edge of the precipice and found it. Maybe a meter wide where he was sitting, though it seemed to be wider to his left. It seemed stable, so Soong shifted his weight, then rolled off the handgrip that had been stabbing him in the side, and pulled himself up into a sitting position. His pants were shredded and there was a fair amount of blood smeared on the tatters, but he could move his legs so he knew they weren't broken. He pulled out the med pack, peeled an anesthetic dermpatch off the roll and applied it to his thigh. Soong was rewarded with almost instantaneous relief, the pain dropping down to a dull throb. A quick pass with the medical tricorder confirmed what he suspected—scrapes and some serious contusions, but nothing life-threatening. He set to work patching up the worst of it. Blood loss in such a cold place was a bad thing.

Soong became aware of a distant buzzing sound, so he groped around until he found his earpiece. He tapped the comm link and said, "Graves? Ira? Please stop shouting. I fell, but I'm all right." The buzz from the earpiece died away and was replaced by a dim murmur. Vaslovik was speaking.

"Noonien? You're safe?"

"For now, Dr. Vaslovik. I'm on a ledge maybe forty meters down. I'm hurt, but not critically. If you can wait a moment, I'm going to try to bandage myself up."

"All right, Noonien. Go ahead. If necessary, set up your pattern enhancer and we'll beam you back to my ship." Soong felt some of his anxiety drain away; he would get out of this place one way or another, assuming the enhancer survived the fall. Soong began to unsling his pack to see if it was undamaged, but stopped himself. He only had a little time before the cold totally sapped his strength. Better to concentrate on the task at hand.

Soong pulled the lamp closer and tried to set it down where he could use the light to inspect his legs, but the lantern wouldn't stay in an upright position. The ledge was bumpy and irregular, but Soong's attempts at finding a crack to wedge the lamp into were unsuccessful. Thinking he might chip out a small depression, Soong unslung his climbing hammer, took aim and swung. The hammer hit hard, but instead of the satisfying *chink* he had expected, all he got was a dull *thud.* He shone the light onto the ledge, then bent down to examine the spot where the hammer had struck. The surface of the rock was unscarred. He looked at his hammer and saw that the blade was dulled by the blow.

What the hell . . . ?

At first, he thought it was some kind of petrified plant

root, but looking more closely he saw that it wasn't a plant at all. Later—much later—he realized that it was the fingers that had confused him. They were extraordinarily long, almost like they had been melted or softened, then stretched like taffy. The arm and the upper body, too, seemed freakishly elongated, but it was impossible to say much else about it since the lower half of the body seemed to be dangling off the other side of the ledge.

Holding the lamp so he could keep an eye on the figure, Soong unslung his pack and began assembling the enhancer. As he worked, he tapped his comm link again and, as calmly as he could, said, "Dr. Vaslovik? Ira? On second thought, maybe you should come down here."

PART ONE

Chapter One

" 'IT WAS A DARK AND STORMY NIGHT . . .' "

Commander Bruce Maddox wasn't sure he had heard correctly, so he hauled himself up out of the maintenance hatch and said, "Excuse me?" He had been looking for a loose connection or a mismatched isolinear chip, *something* to explain the power fluctuations, but there was no reason to believe that Emil was thinking about that, too. Maddox sometimes wondered if *Emil* had a loose connection somewhere or a mismatched . . . well, a mismatched *something*. Whatever mismatched thing it is that makes a genius into a genius. And as far as Maddox was concerned, there could be no doubt about it: Emil Vaslovik was a genius, albeit, occasionally, a very *annoying* genius.

People had called Maddox a genius at various times in his career and he had always enjoyed it, but now, looking back, he wondered if sometimes they had been mentally inserting adjectives before they got to the noun. *What might those adjectives have been?* he wondered in a rare moment of introspection. But then he shook his head and the moment passed. *Not relevant to the project,* he decided and passed his tricorder over another set of connections. The word "relevant" featured very largely in Maddox's vocabulary, which was why Emil Vaslovik's habit of uttering non sequiturs was so galling to him.

"I said, 'It was a dark and stormy night.' "

"I heard you the first time," Maddox said, resting his back against the console. "But what does it *mean?*"

"It doesn't *mean* anything," Vaslovik said, more than a trace of amusement in his voice. "I was just looking out the window and watching the storm clouds gather. It made me think of the opening line to a novel called *Paul Clifford.* It's rather famous . . . well, infamous, actually.

" 'It was a dark and stormy night,' " Vaslovik recited. " 'The rain fell in torrents—except at occasional intervals when it was checked by a violent gust of wind which swept up the streets (for it is in London that our scene lies), rattling along the housetops and fiercely agitating the scanty flame of the lamps that struggled against the darkness.' " He stopped and regarded Maddox, who had once again pushed himself up out of the console.

Maddox, who rarely held strong opinions about anything literary, said, "That . . . that's *terrible.*"

Vaslovik chuckled. "Leaves a bad taste in your mouth, doesn't it? The author's name was Edward Bulwer-Lytton. Wrote reams of stuff just like that back in the nineteenth century. Became so famous for sheer badness that some literary society used to hold a contest in his honor. The object was to compose the worst opening sentence for a novel."

Maddox regarded the old man carefully to make sure

he wasn't kidding. Vaslovik had a peculiar sense of humor, but Maddox could see that he wasn't joking about this. "Why would they do that?" Maddox asked. "What value is there in writing a *bad* sentence?"

Vaslovik shrugged, but his eyes glittered merrily. "Don't really know. It was the twentieth century. Who knows why they did anything? Self-awareness—or even enlightened self-interest—didn't seem to be part of their makeup. I expect it just seemed like a good idea at the time."

Maddox rechecked his tricorder readings, mostly to give himself another minute or two before he had to crawl back into the bowels of the console. "And this has exactly *what* to do with me being waist-deep in isolinear chips and EPS conduits?"

"It's a dark and stormy night *despite* the fact that the planet is protected by a weather control grid," Vaslovik explained. "Maybe the problem you're trying to track down has nothing to do with anything inside the lab. Maybe it has something to do with the weather."

Maddox looked out the window. Vaslovik was right; it was dark despite being almost an hour before sunset. Like most people who had lived most of their lives on Federation worlds, Maddox was at once fascinated and intimidated by the idea of a *real* storm, the kind where lightning and wind could damage buildings, people and things.

The climate over much of Galor IV was generally quite moderate; it was one of the reasons why the Daystrom Institute of Technology had situated the Annex there, but violent weather was not entirely unknown, necessitating the weather control grid. There were too many delicate, intricately planned experiments taking place at any one time to risk a stray lightning bolt overturning the figurative apple cart. But in the past, whenever a storm system large enough to overwhelm the grid came along, the Environmental Control Center alerted all the labs so that they could take steps to ensure experiments were shielded.

But, Maddox realized, *sooner or later something was bound to get through.* Out loud he said, "Well, this is inconvenient."

Vaslovik shrugged and said, "But we weren't too far along. We can shut down now and resume when the storm has passed."

Maddox set his tricorder down on the windowsill and sighed, "I suppose you're right, but I was hoping we would be able to complete the tests tonight."

Suddenly, a bolt of lightning seared across the sky. Vaslovik stumbled back away from the window, but Maddox caught the old man before he could fall. "Sorry," Vaslovik said. "That caught me off guard." A moment later, a rumble of thunder set the window to vibrating. Another flash of lightning gave Maddox a momentary glimpse of the wind stripping the leaves from a nearby tree. Something crashed against the window, bounced off, and rolled away into the darkness.

"Haven't seen one like this before, have you, Bruce?" Vaslovik asked.

"No, I haven't—" Maddox began to reply, but then watched in stunned amazement as a blue-white bolt of lightning shivered down from the sky and slashed into the ground not ten meters from the lab. Maddox swore he could feel the ionized oxygen molecules prickling his skin as they swirled away, then rushed back in. A clap of thunder shattered the air and left Maddox momentarily breathless. Then, a second, even fiercer explosion tore through the courtyard and Maddox saw a sickening greenish flame leap up from the ground. He turned his head away and covered his eyes from the intense glare.

When he opened his eyes again, Maddox could see nothing except a red smear, a ghost image on his retina from the bright flash. "The power's gone out," he said. "That lightning bolt must have hit the main grid." He looked down and saw the tiny lights of the tricorder's control surface. Maddox picked it up, comforted by its familiarity. The instrument had been programmed to look for surges in microvoltage, the kind you find with poorly aligned isolinear chips, but the electromagnetic burst from the lightning bolt had caused it to reset. Maddox tapped the control to run a diagnostic function and, by the light from the display, saw that Vaslovik had silently moved away from the window toward the center of the lab.

"How did you do that?" Maddox asked.

"Do what?" Vaslovik asked.

"You walked all the way over there without running into anything. I didn't even hear you move."

"Counted my steps," Vaslovik said calmly. "Twelve steps from the window to the control console. Six steps to the experiment chamber. Five steps from there to the door."

"And how did you know that?"

"I always do that. An old habit."

Maddox thought, *What an eccentric old man,* but said, "If that was the substation over by the xenolab, then power across the quad will be out. We shouldn't expect help anytime soon. Do you think we should put the experiment back into the prep room?" Maddox heard Vaslovik grunt in agreement, then small sounds of tinkering. Switches being thrown, latches unlatching.

Vaslovik was working at something very quickly, probably making sure the experiment was fastened down before they tried to move it. He had been pretty shy about letting anyone see their work before it was ready, though how the guards were going to make out anything in the dark lab was another question entirely.

Maddox worried about the old man hurting himself wandering around in the dark, but then decided he should probably be more concerned about himself. *He probably knows how many steps it is to the prep room,* he decided darkly. *I'm the one who's going to trip and kill himself.*

Maddox started to reply when another lightning flash cut through the dark, and the world suddenly seemed to come crashing in around him.

Or something very near it. Something beneath the floor of the lab exploded, taking out the entire corner of the building and sending debris everywhere. Maddox was thrown across the room, and felt his head slam against something hard. He almost didn't notice the shooting pain in his arm, and the warm wet feeling that was blossoming over it.

Maddox tried to see, but the gloom seemed absolute. His ears rang, and he could taste blood in his mouth. He called out to Vaslovik, but couldn't even hear his own voice.

After a time, his eyes adjusted to the dark, and then, finally, he heard something: a dull creaking that rose quickly to a roar, the sound of a building collapse in the offing. Maddox tried to move, but knew he was losing it. Everything was going black again, though it was an odd kind of black this time, a black shot through with silver.

Chapter Two

Captain's Log, Stardate 51405.9: The Enterprise *has completed its diplomatic assignment to Tzenketh, in which I believe I have convinced the Autarch to join the Allied effort against the Dominion. Before we proceed to our next assignment, we are awaiting the return of Lieutenant Commander Data, who left the ship twelve days ago to undertake a painful personal duty.*

CAPTAIN JEAN-LUC PICARD looked up from his log, checked the chronometer and decided that he had spent enough time in his ready room for one day. Time to get up and walk about a bit, get the feel of the ship under his feet. A crew had moods and the only way to find out what they are is to go out and tread the deck. Of course, he *could* just call in either Riker or Troi and put the question to them—*How is the crew feeling?*—and from their different perspectives form a clear and reliable picture. Over the years, Picard had learned that this method omitted an essential component. If he stayed in his ready room and waited for subordinates to bring him answers, the crew wouldn't know how *Picard* was feeling, or, at least, how Picard *wanted* them to think he was feeling.

As soon as Picard walked onto the bridge, Commander Heyes, the current beta shift commander, hopped to her feet and started to call out, "Captain on the bridge," but Picard waved her back into the center seat. Beta shift had just come on duty, some of alpha shift still lingering, passing on notes about unresolved problems or procedures, so there were quite a few people there. Picard enjoyed being on the bridge at shift change, especially when things were going well, because it showed that the *Enterprise*-E was not just a workplace, but a community. After the essential business of communicating the ship's condition was addressed, he knew that crewmembers would stop to chat, exchange information about families or make arrangements for social gatherings and recreation later in the day.

Picard nodded to various officers and crewmen, checked the conn officer's heading, then took a few moments to study the astrometric display currently on the viewscreen, making it clear to Heyes that he only intended to stay long enough to take the chill off the cushion and make his presence felt. He moved briefly to vacant XO's console and pulled up the shift logs, reviewed the entries for high-priority items and, finding none, transferred the rest to his workstation for more careful scrutiny later. Looking up, he said, "I'll be heading down to the shuttlebay if you need me, Commander."

Heyes nodded and said, "Aye, Captain. Commander Data's shuttle is due in seventeen minutes." She smiled. "Have a pleasant stroll, sir."

"Thank you, Commander." The turbolift doors closed

and Picard had to smile to himself. Obviously, even in her short time aboard the *Enterprise,* Heyes had learned about her captain's habit of wandering the decks between shifts. She was a good officer, one of the best shift commanders to come aboard during their last crew rotation. He knew Heyes was more interested in being on the command track for a science or exploration vessel, but Picard had asked Riker to try to retain her services for another rotation, dangling the carrot of some first contact work before her. He would have to have a conversation with her and remind her that, sometimes, commanders on a larger vessel actually have more time for *science* than the captain of a science vessel. On the other hand, Picard understood the allure of the center seat. *We shall see what we shall see,* he decided. "Deck four," he said.

The turbolift stopped at deck three for two crewmen who were so caught up in a discussion about the mathematics of a multidimensional time/space fold that Picard's presence had barely registered on them before he stepped off the turbolift on deck four. Acknowledging the nods, Picard moved aft along the corridor, stopping briefly to speak with Lieutenant Commander Keru about a report he had sent concerning the holographic diodes in stellar cartography. It was nothing serious yet, Keru assured the captain, but some of the diodes were past their recommended service date and were losing efficiency. Picard stayed just long enough to assure Keru he was aware of the situation and that something would be done soon.

Reaching the end of the corridor, Picard stepped into a narrow maintenance lift and dropped down into the control room that overlooked the primary shuttlebay. The two crewmen on duty looked up at Picard and nodded, but didn't rise since they currently had a shuttle on the beam and were guiding it in. In the bay, Picard could see four figures: his first officer, Commander William Riker; the ship's counselor, Commander Deanna Troi; the chief engineer, Lieutenant Commander Geordi La Forge; and the *Enterprise*'s new security chief, Lieutenant Rhea McAdams.

Now there, Picard reflected, *is someone I will probably* not *have to remind Number One to speak to about staying with the* Enterprise. During the two social encounters Picard had enjoyed with McAdams while Riker was present, it had been quite obvious that his first officer was quite taken with the lieutenant.

Like Heyes and several other recent additions, the pretty, deceptively petite McAdams had joined the ship just ten days ago during the crew rotation at Starbase 105. The lieutenant was the third security officer who had rotated onto the *Enterprise*-E since the ship had left the San Francisco Yards two years earlier. The first, Daniels, was currently on indefinite paternity leave. The second, Rowan, had been a fine officer, but, somehow, had not jelled with the rest of the command crew. It might have been, Picard decided, that he had been too *much* like Worf, who had been part of his senior staff for seven years on the *Enterprise*-D. The similarities in style had thrown everyone off-balance. Rhea McAdams was about as unlike Picard's former security chief as it was possible for an entity with two arms, two legs and a head to be. Where Worf would have growled, McAdams grinned.

Picard had first realized that he might have found the right fit when, during her first week on duty, the *Enterprise* had encountered a Breen destroyer whose commander was spoiling for a fight. Where Worf would have had his finger on the quantum torpedo launcher from the first second, McAdams had opted to explain to the Breen commander, one Thot Vog, the relative strengths and weaknesses of the *Sovereign*-class starship and the Breen destroyer, paying particular attention to how much damage a brace of quantum torpedoes could do. In the end, the Breen had backed off.

Picard stayed in the control room long enough to be sure that all was well with Data's shuttle, then exited and walked down the stairway to the flight deck. La Forge spotted him first and called out, "Captain, hello." Troi, in the midst of a conversation with McAdams, smiled brightly. Deanna looked, Picard thought, uncharacteristically bleary, probably because she was currently pulling duty as officer of the watch on gamma shift. Riker stood slightly apart from the group, staring out at the field of stars shimmering faintly through the hangar's force field. Picard noted that Riker had his head tilted slightly toward Troi and McAdams, just enough to hear if his name came up in the course of their conversation.

Riker nodded to Picard as the captain approached, and Picard noticed a small bandage on the left side of Riker's forehead. "Number One," Picard asked, frowning as he peered at the bandage. "What have you done to yourself this time?"

Riker's eyes shot up and his hand rose to his temple, almost as if he had forgotten the wound and only this moment remembered it. "Oh . . . this? It's nothing, Captain."

"Let me guess: some sort of bar brawl?"

"Captain!" Riker replied in mock indignation.

"Then, what? Anbo-jytsu? Karate?"

"Mok'bara, by any chance?" Lieutenant McAdams asked. Grinning, she stepped toward Commander Riker

and took his arm, a movement that Picard initially interpreted as a sign of affection, but then he saw that McAdams was applying a slight pressure to Riker's elbow so he would have to bend forward. Standing on her toes, McAdams carefully inspected Riker's forehead with all the concern of a worried mother checking a child's skinned knee. "Are you feeling better, Commander?" she asked.

"Yes," Riker said resignedly. "Much better, thanks."

"Ah, yes. Now I remember," Picard recalled. "Dr. Crusher mentioned this at breakfast. Something about a small scar reminding you not to underestimate your opponent because of size, I believe."

McAdams released Riker's elbow and the first officer straightened. "Dr. Crusher has a strange sense of humor sometimes," he said.

"And a well-honed sense of justice," Troi added.

"Malpractice, I'd call it," Riker muttered as he turned his attention back to the bay threshold.

"So, Lieutenant," Picard said, turning to McAdams. "You've studied *mok'bara?* I hope you'll someday have the opportunity to meet Commander Worf. He won several tournaments, both on the *Enterprise* and in formal competition."

"So Deanna was telling me," McAdams replied, smiling innocently. "And Commander Riker mentioned him, too, while I was helping him to sickbay."

Riker opened his mouth to respond, but stopped when Picard's combadge trilled. *"Shuttlebay control to Captain Picard."*

"Go ahead."

"Captain, Commander Data's shuttle is on its final approach."

"Thank you, Lieutenant," Picard replied, shifting his attention to the view beyond the shuttlebay force field. Riker activated his badge and spoke into it softly, asking to listen in on the channel between the control deck and the shuttle. As prescribed, the shuttlebay control officer formally requested, *"Shuttlecraft* Turing, *this is the* Enterprise. *I have you on the beam. Are you satisfied with your vector?"*

Data was overheard to say, "Enterprise, *this is* Turing. *Approach vector is satisfactory. I am turning over control to you."* The shuttle made a minor course correction, then reduced speed as the *Enterprise*'s automated systems took over. Picard knew that Data would be sitting back now, hands only lightly touching the control panel, monitoring the approach in case he had to quickly switch over to manual. *Odd,* Picard thought, *that we trust one machine to bring the shuttle in safely while a different machine— one infinitely more sophisticated—is holding himself in check.* Then, he realized what he was thinking and chided himself for his lack of consideration. Data was much more than a machine, as Picard himself had proclaimed on countless occasions. *I even went to court to prove it.*

The telltales above and below the shuttlebay door changed from green to yellow as a klaxon sounded, indicating that the field density was changing to allow the *Turing* to enter. The shuttle's passage through the invisible membrane was nearly silent, the impulse engines having been shut down just before landing, so the only sounds were the pings and pops of the hull adjusting to the temperature and pressure of the shuttlebay. Even as the *Turing* settled onto the turntable and rotated, the craft's aft hatch slowly opened.

When he saw Data's face, Picard was alarmed, but he could not say precisely why. The android wore his usual neutral, relaxed expression, but there was something slightly off about it, as Data had been forced to think about how he should look rather than just looking that way. He filed the thought away for later consideration. "Welcome home, Mr. Data," Picard said. "It's good to have you back."

"Thank you, Captain," Data replied. "I am pleased to see you all." He walked to the bottom of the ramp, then turned and pulled a small control unit off his belt. Pointing it into the cargo bay, he pressed a control, then stepped aside as a large oblong container hovering on antigravs floated down the ramp. When it stopped alongside him, Data gently rested his hand on its lid.

Troi walked around the container and laid her hand on Data's arm. "My condolences, Data."

Picard searched the android's face for a sign of emotion, and, finding none, wondered if Data had deactivated his emotion chip. Picard knew that since the chip had been installed there had been a few times where a flood of unfamiliar emotions had forced Data to disengage the chip, but it was not something the android enjoyed doing. He had discovered that turning off the chip did not make the emotions go away, but shunted them into a kind of buffer where they lay in wait until the chip was reactivated.

Then, he spoke and Picard knew that the chip was engaged. "Thank you, Counselor," he said, his voice trembling slightly. "It means a great deal to me to have you all here." He caressed the edge of the coffin. "And I'm sure that, if she knew, it would mean a great deal to my mother, too."

Chapter Three

GEORDI STEPPED FORWARD. "She was an amazing woman, Data," he said, laying a hand on his friend's shoulder. "I know there's nothing anyone can do to make it better, but if you ever need to talk . . ." His voice trailed off then and Picard saw that his chief engineer's eyes were tearing up.

Data nodded. "Thank you, Geordi. I appreciate your concern." Then, he continued in a more clinical tone, "However, I feel I must point out that although I permitted myself the indulgence of calling Dr. Tainer my mother, she was not my biological parent. She merely assisted Dr. Soong in the creation and development of my body and positronic brain."

"Which is as good a definition of 'mother' as any, Data," Troi said softly, mustering a smile.

Data smiled back. "That may be true, Counselor, but I learned of Juliana Tainer's existence and her role in my creation only a few short years ago."

"And in that time, you'd formed a warm attachment

to each other," Troi pointed out. "Data—please don't try to downplay the significance of this event. She was your mother in every meaningful sense of the word and you should allow yourself to mourn her passing."

Data nodded and said, "I understand what you are saying, Counselor. And though I know I should feel some sense of loss, I am disconcerted to report that ever since my mother's husband informed me of her passing, I have felt curiously removed from events, almost as if this has been happening to someone else." Turning to La Forge, Data said, "Perhaps we should run a diagnostic on my emotion chip after I have interred my mother's body."

Seeing that Geordi didn't know how to respond, Troi interrupted and said, "I think your emotions are functioning perfectly, Data. The death of a loved one can frequently provoke a feeling of dislocation. It's one of the ways we cope with the flood of emotion. Just give yourself a little time. Perhaps you should consider taking some leave."

Data shook his head. "No, Counselor. I find that what I want to do most is return to my work. I feel a strong desire to immerse myself in a task."

"Which is what Starfleet officers almost always say . . ." Troi sighed. "As you please, Data. But you know I'm always available if you need to talk. If there's one thing I know about, it's the role a mother can take in someone's life...."

Riker asked, "There was no problem with the Atrean government, Data?"

"No, Commander," Data said. "The Atreans have no strong spiritual beliefs about the status of the body after death, so Pran Tainer had no compunction about granting me possession of her remains."

"And there was no . . . confusion?"

"The biofeedback circuitry continued to work after her demise," Data said, correctly interpreting Riker's comment. "Dr. Soong planned for this eventuality very carefully. Even though my mother's positronic brain ceased to function, her power cells continued to fuel the feedback processor that masked her true condition. And, most fortunately, I arrived soon enough after her 'death' that I was able to prevent any form of autopsy being performed on her. The Atreans have a ritual called the *tai-lun* where the husband and close friends sit with the body overnight, somewhat similar to the Klingon custom *Ak'voh*—"

"Excuse me?" Rhea McAdams said, stepping forward between Riker and Picard.

"*Ak'voh*," Data repeated. "Some Klingons practice a tradition of watching over a fallen comrade to keep away predators, possibly dating back to—"

"No, no," McAdams said, waving her hand. "I know what *Ak'voh* is. What I mean is—" She stopped, started over. "I'm sorry, Commander. We haven't even been introduced."

"An oversight on my part," Picard admitted. "Data, this is Lieutenant Rhea McAdams, our new head of security. She transferred aboard while you were away."

Data extended his hand and McAdams shook it. "How do you do, Lieutenant? I wish you success in your new duties."

"Thank you, Commander. Please accept my condolences and excuse my rude behavior, but I have to confess I'm a little confused."

"Again, my fault," Picard said. "I should have briefed you more thoroughly before inviting you down here. Data, I explained to Lieutenant McAdams about your mother's death, but I did not feel comfortable telling her about her unique condition. However, under the circumstances . . ."

"Certainly, sir," Data replied. "Perhaps you could speak to her while I download my flight record to the ship's main computer."

Riker followed Data as he disappeared into the shuttle, and Picard drew McAdams aside. "As you know," he began in a low voice, "Data is an android—the only fully functional android that Starfleet is aware of. He was created by Dr. Noonien Soong, something of a maverick in the field of artificial intelligence."

McAdams nodded. "Yes, sir. I read this in my personnel briefs. The colony on which he was created was destroyed in an alien attack. Data was recovered and activated by Starfleet, which he subsequently joined."

"Yes, at least partially so he would have opportunities to find his creator," Picard said, "which he did, as well as a 'brother' named Lore. The part of the story that almost no one knows is that Soong was married. His wife—the woman Data thinks of as his mother—was fatally injured, and rather than lose her completely, Soong created an android duplicate of her and transferred Juliana's memories to the android's neural net. Soong programmed her to believe she was the original Juliana."

"And never told her the truth?" McAdams asked, sounding slightly appalled.

Picard shrugged. "I believe he must have felt it was a kindness. He had installed a complex masking system into the body so no one ever discovered her true nature until she met Data several years ago. He noticed that she blinked in Fibonacci sequences—"

"Right," McAdams said blankly. "That *would* give it away, wouldn't it?"

"In any case," Picard continued, smiling, "Data was able to determine that Dr. Tainer's android body was designed to simulate the passing of years and would eventually expire. When Pran Tainer contacted him, Data knew that the time had come and he would have to act quickly if he was going to preserve her secret."

"But he called her 'mother,' " McAdams said. "Maybe this is just my being new to the situation, but it strikes me that Dr. Tainer is more like a sister."

"She helped Soong assemble Data," Picard explained. "And was responsible for some of his most distinctive characteristics. She's the one who insisted that Soong give Data a creative capacity, and, perhaps most significantly, influenced Soong to not give Data emotions."

"Why?"

"She was concerned about Data developing like Lore, who had something of a psychotic streak, I'm afraid. He proved so dangerous, in fact, that Data felt compelled to deactivate him, but it was a difficult decision . . ."

". . . Because he was family," McAdams finished for him. "Yes, I understand. The only thing I don't understand is why no one else has been able to design a Soong-type android."

"There have been attempts," Picard replied. "Data's components, though complex, are quite well understood now. Everything could be replicated—except for the positronic brain. Every attempt . . ."

From behind them, Picard heard Data say, ". . . has been unsuccessful. And, to date, there has been no clearly identifiable reason why." He walked down the ramp again, this time carrying a small travel case. "Or, to put it another way, there has been no clearly identifiable reason why my positronic brain—or that of my brother Lore's, or Juliana's for that matter—functions. Several theories have been advanced, none of them easily provable, though I am intrigued by Bronwin and Satar's recent note in *Advances in Artificial Intelligence* where they postulated that there was some unique, as yet unidentified substance in the components Dr. Soong incorporated into his positronic brains. However, my own investigations into that theory have been inconclusive."

"Perhaps," McAdams said, "Dr. Soong was successful because he believed so strongly that his work *should* succeed. Belief is a potent force. Just look what it did for Tinkerbell."

Data cocked his head to the side, a gesture that Picard associated with him accessing some deeply buried file. "That is an interesting theory," Data commented. "But it would be extremely difficult to prove. It would also suggest that my daughter's positronic brain went into cascade failure because I did not believe strongly enough in her."

"I'm sorry," McAdams said. "Your daughter?"

"Yes," Data replied. "Lal. I constructed her several years ago. She lived only fifteen days, but I was . . ." He hesitated, then resumed, "I cannot say I had strong feelings for her because I did not have feelings at that time. However . . ." He paused again, seeming to search for the words. Finally, Data said, "I do not know how to express what I am feeling."

"I understand," McAdams said. "And please forgive me for speaking so cavalierly about something I could never understand."

"You have no reason to apologize, Lieutenant. I have

studied the literature on the development of positronic brains in great detail and many less credible ideas have been advanced. For example, in volume 72, issue 2 of *Positronic Review,* M'Yea posited—"

"Data," Picard said gently.

"Yes, Captain?"

"Surely this can wait until you've attended to your mother's remains? And I believe Lieutenant McAdams is scheduled to return to her duties."

"Perhaps you are right, Captain. My apologies, Lieutenant. I did not know you were still on duty. Thank you for coming down here to meet my shuttle." Data extended his hand and McAdams took it. They shook hands formally, *the way you do,* Picard thought, *at the conclusion of a funeral.*

"Maybe we can continue our conversation at another time, Commander."

"I would enjoy that, Lieutenant."

After McAdams left, Data turned back toward the coffin and reactivated the antigravs. The crate rose a few inches off the ground, and without speaking, Picard, Riker, La Forge and Troi took up places at the four corners of the coffin. Each put a hand on their corner and carefully guided it toward the turbolift, Data following. They passed no one en route, Riker having already cleared the corridors between the shuttlebay and their destination.

They rode in silence. When the lift halted, they guided the coffin carefully down the corridor, then up to the doors to Data's lab. After he had keyed in his passcode, Data turned to his friends. He thanked each of them formally in turn, then said, "I deeply appreciate your concern; however, I believe I require some time alone now."

"Of course, Data," Troi said, quite properly speaking for them all. "We understand. Please call if you need anything."

Data nodded, thanked them all again, then carefully pushed the coffin through the doors. After the doors had closed, the four pallbearers simultaneously inhaled, then slowly let out their breaths. "Is it only me," Riker asked, "or is anyone else hungry?"

Data stood silently for several seconds, then methodically set to work opening the coffin. It was only a matter of a few minutes' work to transfer his mother's unchanged remains to one of the transparent cases he had installed several months earlier after the *Enterprise*-E had been commissioned. After securing the door on his mother's crypt, Data stepped back and regarded his "family": the three nameless, failed prototypes Soong had created first; then Lore, then Juliana and then, last of all, Lal. Staring at his daughter, Data became distantly aware that a number of background subroutines were halting as more and more of his resources were being consumed, as one thought, one idea, tumbled incessantly through his mind.

Slowly, very slowly, he reached out and touched the transparent panel, studying the planes of her face. The strength went out of his legs, and Data slipped to the floor, finally settling with his back against the wall, staring blankly into the middle distance. A maintenance subroutine warned him that he should be alarmed by the number of processors that were cycling endlessly through a single thought, but Data found it impossible to rouse himself. There was no reason to move, nothing worth moving for, nothing worth caring about, nothing . . .

Then, without knowing why, he muttered, "I'm sorry," and though the words felt bitter and hollow, it was the only thought his positronic brain could muster, so he said it again. And then once more. He said it again and again and again, his voice growing more faint with each utterance. And even when no sound came out, his lips continued to move.

Chapter Four

"I'M SORRY, CAPTAIN," Data said, patting his eyes with a tissue. A significant pile, Picard noted, had accumulated on his ready room desk.

"You've already said that and I've already told you that you have no reason to apologize," Picard said. "This has been a very trying experience for you. Add to that the fact that you have very little experience with these sorts of emotional upheavals . . . If it helps at all, Data, you should know that I experienced something very similar to what you're going through when my brother and his son were killed. It's a devastating feeling."

Data nodded slowly. "I understand what you are saying, Captain, but that is not . . . that is not . . ." Before he could complete his sentence, Data was overcome by another wave of grief, his shoulders rolling as the sobs wracked him. As the intensity of his grief grew, Data's head sank lower and lower until finally he was slumped over, face in his hands, his entire body shaking. Picard began to worry that Data might be about to experience some sort of breakdown when, suddenly, the sobs ceased. Data's head snapped up and though his eyes were still watering, it was quite literally as if someone had turned off the faucet.

"Data?"

"Yes, Captain?" Data reached toward the container on the table and awkwardly tugged at the spray of tissues. He pulled free a wad, and gingerly wiped his cheeks dry.

"Did something just happen?"

"Sir?"

"Have you . . . deactivated your emotion chip?"

Data cocked his head to the side as if consulting an internal monitor. Finally, he reported, "Yes, Captain, the chip has been deactivated, but it was not done so by any conscious effort on my part."

"Should we contact Geordi?"

Data considered, then shook his head. "No, sir. I do not believe that will be necessary. While I do not know if the chip was deactivated by some sort of fail-safe device or if I 'unconsciously' turned it off, I think it would be best if it were left that way for a while. Do not humans frequently go to sleep after they have received a severe shock?"

"I see what you mean. So, you think this might be your system's way of 'going to sleep.' "

"Yes, Captain," he said. He glanced curiously at the tower of tissues he'd built atop Picard's desk, as if seeing it for the first time. "This is all quite fascinating."

Picard settled back in his chair and rubbed his temples. "Yes," he said. "Yes, it is." *Not to mention exhausting.* He rose and looked around Data's quarters until he saw the food replicator. "Do you know what else humans do when they've received a nasty shock?" He spoke to the unit: "Tea. Lapsang Souchong. Hot."

Data looked up, curious. "Not Earl Grey, Captain?"

Picard picked up the cup and inhaled the tea's smoky aroma. "When I was a boy," he said, smiling warmly, "this is what my mother used to make whenever one of her sisters would visit with the latest emotional crisis. She was a woman of remarkable patience, my mother." He paused for a moment, lost in memory, then shook himself. It was getting late. "Would you like a cup?"

Data considered the idea, then replied, "Yes, Captain. Thank you. I believe I would."

Picard nodded, then asked the replicator for another cup. As he carried it to Data, he asked, "Do you think you could reactivate the chip if you wished?"

Data took the cup and answered, "Yes, Captain."

"And will you?"

"I do not know, sir. Perhaps I should discuss this with Counselor Troi. She might have valuable insights to offer."

Picard sipped his tea, then said, "Actually, I was surprised you didn't call her when you realized that you were in distress. Or Geordi, for that matter."

Data inhaled the tea deeply, but did not drink. He set the cup back in its saucer, then replied, "I cannot say for certain, sir, but I believe my decision to call you was a purely emotional one. When my cognitive functions stabilized, the first memory I accessed was the conversation we had in stellar cartography aboard the *Enterprise*-D when I was feeling overwhelmed by my emotion chip."

"Yes, I remember," Picard replied. "I told you that if you really wished to understand what it meant to be human, you would have to try to cope with the feelings, both pleasant and unpleasant, to grow from them."

"Yes," Data said. "And I took great comfort from your words. In my overwrought condition, it is possible I was seeking that comfort again."

Picard shrugged and set his cup down on the table. Leaning forward, he said, "Well, whatever the reason, I'm glad I was able to help . . . even if I'm not sure exactly what I've accomplished so far. Data—what *exactly* can you tell me about this emotional condition you were experiencing?"

"I was . . ." Data began, then faltered. "It felt . . ." He stopped, then looked around the room as if searching for a way to begin. Finally, defeated, he said, "Here is a paradox. It is very difficult to discuss an emotional state without the benefit of emotions. Yet, if I were to activate my emotion chip, I would be unable to discuss the emotions because I would be overwhelmed by them." He cocked his head at Picard. "How do you do this, Captain?"

Picard smiled ruefully. "With practice, Data. A great deal of practice. And even those who claim to understand the process best cannot always predict how they themselves would act under extreme stress. Now *there's* a topic to take up with the counselor someday. But back to the subject at hand: do you want to reactivate the chip?"

Data's face tightened and his lips became a thin line.

"What's wrong, Data? Are you afraid?"

"No, Captain," he replied. "At present, I cannot be afraid. However, even without my emotion chip I can recognize a potentially threatening situation. Nevertheless, I will reactivate it." Data snapped his head to the side as Picard had seen him do on one or two occasions and slowly straightened it. His face, which had smoothed out when the emotion chip had been deactivated, seemed to age ten years and lines appeared where there had been none moments before. He sighed once, profoundly.

"Data?"

Data did not respond for several seconds and Picard began to worry that he had lapsed into some sort of catatonic state. Then, very gradually, the yellow eyes focused. "Yes, Captain," he replied. "I am here."

"Are you all right?"

"I believe so, yes. Though the feelings of grief and despair are still there, I believe I have adapted sufficiently. Yes." Unexpectedly, Data smiled briefly and said, "The nap must have done me a great deal of good."

Picard smiled in response. "Why, Mr. Data, I do believe you just made a joke."

"Really?" he asked. "Was it a good one?"

"I've heard worse," Picard said kindly. "Now, tell me what happened."

Data sat up straighter and seemed to be peering into memories of the distant past. "As I laid my mother to rest," Data said, folding his hands into his lap, "I had an insight." He looked up at his captain as if seeking permission to tell him, so Picard nodded. "You are going to die."

Picard waited for him to continue, the silence stretching on uncomfortably until, finally, Picard lifted his hand and said, "And . . . ?"

Data let the other shoe drop. "But I will not," Data continued.

Picard struggled to keep a neutral expression, not sure whether his impulse was to reply with exasperation or to laugh. Finally, he managed to say, "That's not necessarily true, Data. Not to be morbid, but any number of things could happen."

"Of course, Captain. I could be crushed beyond repair or vaporized by a phaser or the *Enterprise* could be destroyed by a Romulan warbird, but these things are true for everyone aboard the ship. What I was referring to was the natural course of every biological entity: if nothing happens to hasten it, your death *will* occur at the end of its natural span, whereas I have been designed to continue functioning virtually forever."

Picard nodded, trying not to let Data's analysis of his life expectancy color the conversation. "All right, Data. I think I see your point. You probably *will* outlive all of us, but such is the nature of your existence— you're an artificial life form. I thought you understood that."

"Understood?" Data asked, his voice rising sharply. "Yes, I have always *understood* it. I have always known that I will attend your funeral and Geordi's funeral and Counselor Troi's funeral . . . the funeral of every person aboard the *Enterprise*. And then, if I decide to join another crew, I will attend the funerals of those shipmates, too." Picard saw that Data's eyes were beginning to grow moist again and heard his voice crack with emotion. "And then there are those who have already died— my mother, my daughter, my brother . . ." He bent his head and rubbed at his eye with the heel of his hand. "And Tasha . . ." Data paused and collected himself. "There has not been a day since she died when I have not thought of her, but today . . . today was the first time I understood, *truly* understood that I will never see her again. If there is such a thing as an afterlife, Captain, I will not even see her there because *I will not die.*" He dropped his head between his hands and stared at the floor. Picard waited, listening to Data breathe deeply, watching him struggle to hold back tears.

Several minutes passed and Picard had the peculiar realization that he had never listened to Data breathe before. He knew that Soong had programmed his creation to simulate many basic human functions—respiration, circulation, even digestion—but they had never, the two of them, sat in a room together with neither of them speaking. He had known Data, had thought of him as a friend, for more than ten years, but had never sat in silence with him for more than a moment or two. It was a sobering thought.

"Captain," Data said very quietly, still staring at the floor, "I want to deactivate my emotion chip."

Picard stirred, shifted his weight and asked, "Do you feel like it might shut down of its own accord again? Are you afraid it might endanger other systems?"

Data shook his head, then looked up. "You misunderstand me. I want to turn it off—forever."

Picard frowned. "Data—we've had this conversation before. You yourself made reference to it earlier. I'm going to tell you now exactly what I told you then: you can't hide from your feelings every time they become unpleasant."

"But is that not precisely what you instructed me to do when the Borg invaded the *Enterprise?*"

Picard's shoulders sagged. He had not forgotten about that. When the *Enterprise* had traveled back in time to the twenty-first century to prevent the Borg from changing Earth's past, the Borg had circumvented their defenses and taken over the lower decks of the ship. Picard had led a raiding party to determine the strength of their forces and Data, unfortunately, began to verbalize every fluctuation in his emotional state.

The party was composed largely of young cadets, crewmen who were not familiar with some of Data's idiosyncrasies and were already unnerved by the prospect of fighting Borg drones hand to hand. There just hadn't been enough time to explain things to either the cadets or Data, so Picard had taken the easy way and *ordered* Data to deactivate the emotion chip, a case of putting the ship's safety before the well-being of one member of the crew. It was the kind of call Picard hated to make, but which he knew he always must.

"I may have done you an injustice that day, Data," Picard said. "If you truly want to understand what it means to be human, you will have to learn to transcend these periods of your life, find ways to cope, to draw strength from inner resources. Hemingway wrote, 'The world breaks *everyone* and afterward many are strong at the broken places.' "

"I have noted," Data said, "that the rest of the thought is frequently omitted when it is quoted: 'But those that it will not break it kills. It kills the very good and the very gentle and the very brave impartially. If you are none of these you can be sure that it will kill you too but there will be no special hurry.' " Data fell silent, letting the lines sink in. Finally, he concluded, "But Hemingway knew nothing of artificial life forms."

"No, he didn't," Picard agreed. "But I believe he understood that the human heart has a remarkable capacity for healing. This is another aspect of humanity you have yet to experience, Data. I do not wish to usurp Counselor Troi's role, but I believe she would tell you to give yourself time to heal."

Picard thought he saw some of the lines lift from around Data's eyes and mouth until, finally, he nodded and said, "All right, Captain. I will give myself time." Then, with a trace of bitterness Picard had never heard in his voice before, Data said, "I have a great deal of it at my disposal."

Picard tried to smile, found that he could not. "Good," he said uncertainly. "Very good." He settled back into the couch, then remembered his tea and reached for it. "This strikes me as the right moment to return to matters of duty and tell you about a message that I received shortly before you called me. It is, in an odd way, tangentially related to what we have been discussing. Admiral Haftel of the Daystrom Institute Annex on Galor IV contacted me a short while ago with some unhappy news. Apparently Commander Bruce Maddox has been under his command there for the past two years, on special assignment. Two weeks ago, there was an incident at Maddox's lab, and the commander was caught in a partial building collapse. The admiral was reluctant to go into detail, but ordered us to divert immediately to Galor IV."

"Commander Maddox is alive?" Data asked.

"Yes," Picard said, "but there would appear to be complications. The admiral asked that Dr. Crusher accompany us as well."

"I see," Data said. "Did the admiral say why he required the *Enterprise,* specifically?"

"No, that's part of the puzzle," Picard said. "I checked, and there are several other starships nearer to Galor IV that could divert there if the admiral required general assistance. But he wanted us."

"Intriguing," Data said. "Then . . . a mystery."

"So it would appear." Picard smiled and said, "The game is afoot."

But Data, lost in thought, did not smile at Picard's joke. He was too busy trying to determine whether the peculiar sensation that he had just felt run down his back was, in fact, a shiver.

Chapter Five

Captain's Log, Stardate 51407.6: We have arrived at Galor IV and are preparing to beam down to meet with Admiral Haftel. While I have some concerns about Data's emotional state, I believe the best course is to involve him in this investigation. Counselor Troi will accompany us to monitor Data's condition.

THE AWAY TEAM HAD BEEN ASSEMBLED in Transporter Room One for ten minutes awaiting a "go" signal from Dr. Crusher. A routine diagnostic had shown that the transporter's pathogen filters had not successfully neutralized a new form of airborne virus and Crusher wanted it analyzed before she risked spreading it planetside. It was only the work of a few minutes to reprogram the transporter and though Picard disliked making the admiral wait, no one dared suggest that they proceed until Crusher was satisfied. Everyone knew the protocols, but, more significantly, everyone knew the doctor.

While waiting for Crusher's approval, La Forge and Data settled in a corner to discuss a paper they were preparing for a journal, while Troi and Riker took the spare moment to review a handful of outstanding crew evaluations. Picard and McAdams found themselves standing off to one side and the captain was once again pleased to discover how easy it was to fall into conversation with his new chief of security.

"Have you visited any of the Daystrom Institute campuses before, Lieutenant?"

"Yes," she said, "but not since I was a little girl." McAdams smiled as if at a fond memory. "My grandfather was invited to lecture and he took me with him. I don't really remember much about the place, though, except that there were no other children and none of the adults would let me play with their toys."

Picard laughed, then asked, "What was your grandfather's field?"

"At the time, molecular biology, I think. *That* year. He was a bit of a dabbler. Didn't stick with anything in particular very long. The last time I talked to him he was on an archaeological dig in Central America."

"Really?" Picard asked, his interest piqued. "That's something of a hobby of mine."

"Really? Terran or xeno?"

"Xeno. I'm particularly interested in early galactic seed civilizations," Picard said, warming to the topic. "What about your grandfather?"

"Mostly Terran, though he was also interested in early Lunar settlements."

"Ah," Picard said. "I recently read a fascinating piece about the discovery of a midden heap near the Sea of Tranquillity . . ."

The doors to the transporter room parted. "Thank goodness," Beverly Crusher said from behind him, "I've arrived just in time." Picard turned to see the doctor checking her medical tricorder's calibration. "Lieutenant, you have no idea how perilous your situation was. If he had managed to get up a good head of steam, we never would have gotten out of here."

McAdams grinned and said, "That's the sort of thing people say about my grandfather."

Picard sighed good-naturedly and said, "You're satisfied with your filters, Doctor?"

"Everything's fine, Captain."

"Then let's go to work."

The away team beamed directly to the infirmary entrance where they found Admiral Anthony Haftel waiting for them. A serious-minded administrator, he and Picard had locked horns some years ago over the disposition of Lal, soon after Data had created her. Backed by his own superiors, the admiral had wanted her turned over to Starfleet Research for study, and it had taken the tragedy of Lal's fatal cascade failure to convince Haftel to back off from pursuing the matter further. Picard reflected that it made a perverse kind of sense that Bruce Maddox—who years ago had fought so hard for the opportunity to disassemble Data in order to learn the secret that would enable him to produce more Soong-type androids—would end up under Haftel's command at Starfleet's R&D labs at the Daystrom Annex.

As soon as the introductions and reintroductions were completed, Dr. Crusher asked to be taken to Maddox's room. Taking their cue from the doctor, everyone moved as quietly as possible through the halls, despite the fact that Picard saw no evidence of any other patients.

"Not a particularly busy place usually," Haftel commented. "Most of the doctors who work here are also researchers, so we're glad to see you, Dr. Crusher."

"Respectfully, Admiral, please try to keep your voice down," Crusher said.

Picard winced inwardly. Fortunately, Haftel seemed willing to cut her some slack. "Don't worry, Doctor," Haftel said. "There's only one patient currently in residence: yours. And he won't be bothered. I wish that he could, because there are a number of questions I'd like answered."

Picard could see Crusher biting back a reply. She asked, "Will his doctor be there?"

"I'm afraid not," Haftel said. "Dr. Jika was called away on a medical emergency across the campus just before your ship entered orbit. She'll be along as soon as she's able, but I told her I wouldn't keep you waiting. Ah. Here we are."

Maddox's room was state of the art, as one might expect from a research institute. They found the commander lying unconscious on a biobed, cortical monitors affixed to his neck and forehead. Someone in a Starfleet engineering uniform sat slumped in a chair beside the bed, his back to the *Enterprise* party. He didn't move as Crusher picked up a medical padd from a nearby console and keyed the patient's chart.

A snore suddenly issued from the seated engineer, drawing Picard's attention. He focused on the officer for the first time, and smiled in recognition.

La Forge shot Picard an inquiring look and the captain nodded, still smiling. Geordi leaned over as quietly as he could and lifted a tray of food from the officer's lap. Then, La Forge nudged his shoulder and, pitching his voice low, said, "Reg? Regggg? Time to wake up."

Reginald Barclay's eyes snapped open and, as La Forge must have predicted, he leapt to his feet before bothering to check whether he had a tray of food on his lap. He stared wide-eyed at the figures around him as if trying to separate them from some dream he had been having, then exclaimed, "Geordi! I mean, Commander La Forge! You're here. I mean, of course you're here. I knew you were coming, but I wasn't expecting . . ." He looked around again, this time taking in the scene. "You're *all* here." He ran his fingers back through his hair, tried to straighten his uniform, then found the paper napkin under his chin and tugged it away. Nodding, he said, "Admiral, excuse me. I . . . I must have dozed off. Captain Picard, I . . . I . . . I . . ." he began to stutter, then willed himself to be calm. "What time is it?"

Geordi glanced at the chronometer in the corner of his optic display and replied, "Nine A.M. local time, Reg. It's okay. Obviously, you've been here for a while."

"Indeed, Mr. Barclay," the captain said. "You have nothing to apologize for. If anything, we should apologize for waking you so suddenly."

"No, really," Barclay said. "It's fine. Really. I'm fine. Nine A.M.? Then, I've been asleep for, oh, an hour. That's more than enough. You see, I've been sitting up with Bruce—Commander Maddox—talking to him. They say that helps sometimes, you know."

"Yes, Reg," Dr. Crusher said. "Sometimes it does, though sometimes it's not very good for the person who's doing the talking." She popped open her medical tricorder, passed it in front of Barclay, then studied the results. Crusher rolled her eyes and sighed. "I've seen worse," she muttered and pulled out a hypo. "This should balance out your electrolytes, but you're going to need real sleep soon. Preferably in bed." She pressed the hypo against his arm and Barclay seemed to relax as the concoction hit his bloodstream.

"Thank you, Doctor," he said.

"And eat some real food soon," Crusher finished with mild disgust, staring at the tray.

"Yes, Doctor." Barclay sighed contentedly. Some people, Geordi reflected, required more mothering than others. Or enjoyed it more than others. Or possibly both at the same time.

"It's good to see you, Reg," La Forge said. "The *Enterprise* has been a much, uh, quieter place since you transferred. I had no idea that this is where you ended up, though. I thought you were at Jupiter Station—"

"And I was," Barclay interrupted. "For a while. Then I came here about . . ." He searched his memory.

"Three months ago," Haftel said. "A very *eventful* three months. Reg has been our envoy with Dr. Lewis Zimmerman on Jupiter Station, who has been helping Commander Maddox with the theoretical work. But when it came time to do the real work of assembling the . . . apparatus . . . Maddox decided it would make more sense for Reg to be here."

"Exactly," Barclay said, then fixed his sights on Data. "I'm sorry, Commander, about not contacting you sooner. I kept telling Bruce that we owed you that, out of courtesy, if nothing else, but he . . ." Barclay trailed off, then shrugged helplessly.

Data tilted his head to one side. "What courtesy is that, Lieutenant?"

"We can discuss that later," Haftel interrupted. "I believe we should allow Dr. Crusher to examine Commander Maddox."

"Yes, thank you, Admiral," she said. "I've already performed a preliminary examination. The infirmary staff has done an excellent job treating the gross physical injuries, which are almost completely healed. The neural scan is a much different story, though. It's confused and contradictory," she said. "I'm almost tempted to say *deliberately* confused and contradictory, but I'd rather not speculate until I've run some tests and consulted with the attending physician."

"Then we'll leave you to your work, Doctor," Haftel said. The admiral gestured toward the door. "In the meantime, I'd like to ask you and the rest of your crew a few questions, Captain."

"Of course, Admiral," Picard said as the rest adjourned to the corridor. "But I must confess our prior brief association with Commander Maddox notwithstanding, I'm unclear about why the *Enterprise* was summoned here. If I may ask, what exactly was Commander Maddox working on?"

Before Haftel could respond, Data said, "Commander Maddox finally found the breakthrough he was searching for. He was building a sentient android."

Chapter Six

"I KNOW FROM COMMANDER MADDOX that you and he haven't had much to say to each other recently," Admiral Haftel said to Data sometime later. "Explain precisely how you came to this startling . . ."

". . . but accurate . . ." Barclay added.

". . . but accurate conclusion," Haftel finished, barely glancing at Reg. As a working scientist, a cyberneticist of some renown himself, Haftel was, Riker observed, considerably more relaxed about protocol than most of the Admiralty. It was, he decided, probably as much common sense as anything. There was no point in expecting characters like Barclay and Lewis Zimmerman (reputedly even more eccentric than Reg) to toe the line, a lesson that Riker himself had had to learn the hard way.

The *Enterprise* party, Haftel and Barclay had relocated to a conference room in the Institute's main administrative building. The walls were decorated with two-dees and holos of noteworthy researchers who had studied at the Institute, all of them subtly arranged so that the eye was led to the portrait of the great man himself, Richard Daystrom. The portrait was one Riker had never seen before, but, as in every image Riker had ever seen of the man, he thought that the inventor looked slightly worried, like he was wondering if he had left something running back in the lab.

Of course, Riker reflected, there's no reason why genius should guarantee a happy—or even *stable*—outlook on life. He himself had shook hands, spoken with, and seen the reality behind the legend of, Zefram Cochrane, a man whom history painted as a paragon of human virtue. And from what little Riker knew about Daystrom—beyond what he had picked up in his Starfleet history courses—his had not been a particularly joyous life. So, what did it all mean? Deanna must have sensed that his mind was wandering because she half-turned in her chair, arched an eyebrow at him, then flicked her eyes toward Data. *Pay attention,* she was saying.

Data was saying, ". . . But we ceased to communicate on a regular basis when I refused to turn over the bodies of Lal and Lore to him. I believe he felt that I was being unreasonable. I meant no disrespect to him, Admiral, and I attempted to resume our correspondence on several occasions, but Commander Maddox was . . . is . . . quite capable of 'carrying a grudge.' "

Haftel grunted in agreement. Apparently, Data's assessment tallied with his own impressions. "Tell me what happened after you recovered Soong's three prototypes? Did you speak with him during that period?"

"Speak?" Data asked, frowning. "Not as such, no. I first learned of the prototypes when I met Dr. Soong's former wife, Dr. Juliana Tainer, and subsequently took steps to find and retrieve their remains from Omicron Theta. When Commander Maddox learned of this, he requested the opportunity to study them in detail. I refused. After that, he sent me several messages."

"And how would you describe the nature of these messages?"

Data considered the question, then replied flatly, "I would have to say he was quite angry. My impression is that Commander Maddox was experiencing extreme frustration. I believe he had exhausted what he considered to be the viable avenues in his research into re-creating Dr. Soong's positronic brain, and would not accept my reasons for blocking his access to my predecessors' remains. He believed that I was putting my personal feelings before the good of the Federation. In retrospect, I find this quite interesting since these events took place before, technically speaking, I *had* feelings. Now that I *do* have them—and understand something about frustration—I have concluded that it might have been better to let the commander study my father's earlier work."

"So, what stopped you from contacting him?"

"The commander refused to accept my messages. The last communication I received from him said, 'Your right to choose your own fate was duly recognized, Data. And, believe it or not, despite everything, I wouldn't change that. But history can still pass judgment on your choices.' "

Haftel sat in silence for a minute or two, absorbing this new information. Finally, he looked up, and, with a small smile, said, "You know, Data, when you were quoting Maddox, not only did you mimic him slightly, you also used a contraction. I've never heard you do that before."

"Really?" Data asked. His eyes flicked back and forth, as he reviewed the past several seconds' worth of conversation. "Thank you, Admiral, for pointing that out. It would seem that my neural net is experiencing a new period of growth. It would explain . . . some other incidents that have occurred recently."

Reg Barclay, who had been fussing with a viewscreen console, cleared his throat and hesitantly announced, "Uh, Commander Maddox had been preparing a presentation that might help clarify things a bit."

"Good idea, Reg," Haftel said and directed their attention to the center of the table. The lights dimmed and a blurry image rippled into view, then resolved into the Daystrom Institute logo. The image disappeared, and was replaced by a holo of a blurry illustration. Riker recognized it as the da Vinci drawing usually referred to as *Vitruvian Man:* a nude human male with his arms and legs shown in two different positions, perhaps the most recognized anatomical drawing known to humanity. As the image sharpened, Riker saw that the skin was peeled away from half of the figure's body, but the structure beneath was not flesh and bone, but steel and circuitry. The figure's features, Riker realized, were Data's.

"Oh," Reg muttered, glancing at Data. "I had forgotten about that. I think he was going to change it."

"On the contrary," Data said. "I believe I am flattered. Please continue."

Reg smiled, relieved. "All right," he said. "Here we go. Bruce, Commander Maddox, that is, had come to the point where he was beginning to suspect Soong's work—Data and Lore, that is—might owe as much to some fluke of circumstance as to scientific rigor. I can't say there was much agreement on this point. Might have had to do with Bruce wanting to preserve his dignity as much as anything." Reg smoothed his hair back and looked around, aware that he wasn't getting to the facts. "In any case, Commander Maddox had hit a wall trying to duplicate a stable positronic brain. That's when he began to believe he might be looking in the wrong place, especially when he started to learn that other extraordinary developments in artificial intelligence were already taking place for no apparent reason—occurrences of what he referred to as 'spontaneous sentience.' That was Commander Maddox's term for those instances when an AI developed cognitive self-awareness inexplicably and, so far at least, unexplainably. Three such occurrences in particular stood out to him." A series of holograms took shape: a small octagonal box on a pair of hover skids, a handsome, distinguished gentleman dressed in nineteenth-century evening wear and a trio of crystalline specks. "You know about all of these: Farallon's exocomps, the Moriarty hologram, and, uh, Wesley Crusher's nanites."

Riker heard a long exhale to his left and looked at Picard. The captain was frowning, perhaps wondering if this were the real reason Haftel had summoned them. The incidents Barclay was describing had all involved the crew of the *Enterprise*. And, having struggled first-hand with the ethical and scientific questions raised by those events, Riker knew that Picard could well understand Maddox's interest in them.

"Bruce became especially fascinated by the Moriarty hologram," Barclay went on. "For some time, there's been a growing consensus among AI specialists at the DIT that Starfleet holotechnology may offer a vital clue to creating more advanced forms of artificial intelligence. The theory is based largely on observations of Dr. Zimmerman's emergency medical holograms and related data we've obtained from the *U.S.S. Voyager* in the Delta Quadrant . . . and, of course, on Moriarty."

Riker recalled that Barclay himself had been very involved in the Moriarty affair. That, as well as his recent work with Dr. Zimmerman, probably played a big part in Reg's involvement with Maddox's project.

Barclay continued, "The biggest problem with Soong's positronic brain has aways been its vulnerability to cascade failure. With only a few exceptions," Barclay said, glancing at Data, "the system generally can't cope with the rapid formation of new neural net pathways as the brain processes new experiences." Reg hesitated, perhaps realizing he had coldly reminded everyone in the room about the tragedy of Lal.

Data glanced at Admiral Haftel who, to his credit, had been working with him to save Lal when her cascade anomalies began increasing exponentially. Haftel said nothing, apparently more interested in studying the faces of the *Enterprise* officers as the presentation unfolded. Riker caught Deanna's eye to see what she thought of all this. She saw him looking and subtly shook her head no. *Data is fine,* she was saying.

Suddenly, Data said, "Commander Maddox must have known that I myself have come close to cascade failure."

Barclay nodded. "Yes, he knew. Th-that's where Moriarty and the EMHs come in—they use a completely different approach to an AI matrix—" As if realizing he wasn't explaining himself clearly, Barclay stopped himself. "Wait. It's easier just to show you . . ." He touched the holoprojector's control padd and brought up another image—a schematic diagram several levels of magnitude too complicated for Riker to fully comprehend. La Forge and Data studied it in silence for several moments and then Geordi whistled appreciatively.

"Commander Maddox created a positronic brain with a holographic matrix," Data said. "Intriguing."

"Well, to be fair," Barclay said, "and I'm sure Bruce would say this, too, he couldn't have done it without Dr. Zimmerman's contribution."

"Or yours, Reg," Haftel added.

Barclay blushed. "Well, thank you, but I'm sure he would have sorted out my part by himself eventually. They had a problem with the matrix collapsing when they had to refresh the cycle . . ." He glanced around and saw everyone was staring at him. "Well, never mind. Here, let's go on."

The image faded and was replaced by a shot of Maddox, Barclay and a gray-haired gentleman of medium height and indeterminate age standing around a laboratory table. On the table lay what appeared to Riker to be a featureless, silver humanoid. "We determined that the holographic matrix would not only be less susceptible to cascade anomalies, thereby giving an android a greater chance for survival during the early stages of its development," Reg continued, "it actually makes it possible for the brain to accommodate more complex neural net pathways."

"Meaning that these androids could, theoretically, evolve very quickly," Haftel said. "Possibly even more quickly than Mr. Data here."

"Fascinating," Picard said, leaning forward. "Who is the third man in the image?"

"The third . . . ? Haftel asked. "Oh, I'm sorry. I thought you knew. That's Emil Vaslovik."

"Emil Vaslovik?!" La Forge asked unbelievingly. "How did you ever convince him to join you on the project? Everything I've ever heard about him made me believe that he would never work for Starfleet."

"It wasn't easy," Reg said. "Or so Bruce said. I wasn't involved in those negotiations, though I do know that Dr. Zimmerman signed on because Vaslovik did."

"I'm sorry to say I'm not familiar with the name," Riker confessed.

"A neurocyberneticist," La Forge explained. "Some might say *the* neurocyberneticist. Prior to Vaslovik's studies, most of the research in AI had been attempts to mimic human thought processes in machine systems. Vaslovik theorized that rather than program computers to *act* like humans, we should create machine systems that imitate human neural structures, then let them develop however they would. In fact, the recent development of bio-neural gel pack technology owes a lot to his early work."

"It also has been suggested," Data interjected, "that my father used Vaslovik's research as the basis for creating my positronic brain. And that Vaslovik laid the groundwork for many of Ira Graves's accomplishments in molecular cybernetics."

Riker's eyes widened slightly, recalling Graves as the dying genius who tried to cheat death by forcibly transferring his mind into Data's body.

"He's also notoriously anti-Starfleet," La Forge added. "He did the majority of his work decades ago. Frankly, I'm surprised to hear he's still alive."

"I'm afraid that I have bad news on that score," Haftel said. "Dr. Vaslovik died in the explosion that brought half the lab down on Maddox and destroyed the prototype android."

There was silence around the table as the group absorbed this new information. Finally, McAdams asked, "What did your security people find?"

"Nothing to suggest foul play," Haftel answered, getting the lieutenant's drift. "I've arranged to have the incident report and related files uploaded to the *Enterprise* immediately following this meeting. But to sum it up, it looks like the primary culprit was a malfunction in the weather control grid. We had a very large storm that night and the grid went down while Maddox and Vaslovik were working in the lab. A bolt of lightning hit an unshielded transtator cluster in the power grid and the lab's primary EPS conduit overloaded. Vaslovik must have been standing right next to the wall where the explosion occurred, because there was hardly anything left of him. Maddox was luckier."

"You weren't there, Mr. Barclay?" Picard asked.

"No, Captain," Barclay said. "I w-was due to be there in another three hours. We were going to activate the android that night. I truly wish I *had* been there earlier. Maybe then Bruce and Emil—"

"—might have ended up the same way, with you just one more victim," Haftel snapped. "We've been through this, Reg. You're not responsible. Stop blaming yourself."

"Aye, sir," Barclay said quietly.

"What else did the investigation reveal?" McAdams asked.

"Not much. The damage was so severe, it's been difficult to get in without triggering a complete building collapse. We managed to get Maddox out, but we didn't dare risk doing more until we could figure out how to stabilize the structure, and that took time. When we were finally able to get back inside, it was clear the prototype had been crushed under fallen debris. We still haven't succeeded in extracting it—the debris pinning it is holding up a major portion of the upper floor, so we can't even beam it out yet."

"Admiral," Picard said, "it sounds as if you're satisfied that this tragedy was an accident. If that's the case, I hope you'll forgive me if I repeat my earlier question: Why was the *Enterprise* summoned here?"

Haftel nodded. "That's quite all right, Captain. It's a valid question, and I quite understand your impatience. But you needed to know everything else first. There was one anomalous detail we found in the lab that was difficult to reconcile with all the other evidence. Because of the sensitive nature of it, I ordered a halt to any further attempts to study the scene until you and your officers had a chance to see it for yourselves. Computer: display security image M0341-A. Authorization: Haftel Gamma Five Zero Five."

The computer chimed in acknowledgment and brought up a new holo, presumably taken by one of the DIT's security people inside Maddox's lab. It was a close-up of the dust-littered lab floor. The edge of a dark red puddle that could only be blood was visible, but most of the holo was dominated by the four ragged red letters someone had scrawled onto the floor, spelling a word:

DATA

And then everyone in the meeting room turned and looked at the android, who was still staring intently at the holo when he finally spoke.

"Intriguing," he said.

Chapter Seven

THE LATE AFTERNOON SUN cast long shadows as Haftel and the *Enterprise* officers wended their way across the campus's main quad, toward Maddox's lab. Few of the tall, straight trees that lined the main walkway had more than a leaf or two clinging to their branches, and the damp, chill wind rustled the bare limbs. Riker was surprised to find himself thinking back to his boyhood home in Alaska.

When that *wind came whistling down out of the mountains,* he remembered, *it was time to put away your fishing gear and get out the snowshoes.* A gust cut through the insulation of his uniform jacket and he shivered. *My blood has gotten thin and it's been too long since I've been home.* Back in the days before the *Enterprise*-D had been destroyed, he and Worf had discussed taking some shore leave together in the Alaskan backlands. Riker had wanted to show Worf that some Terrans had lived in conditions as harsh as anything a Klingon had ever faced.

But now, with Worf's transfer to DS9, it seemed unlikely that there would be time for a trip to Earth and Riker deeply regretted it. Growing up an only child, he did not understand exactly what it meant to have a brother, but Riker suspected that his bond with Worf—a bond based as much on competitiveness as affection—was as close as he was likely to get. What was the first thing he had done to Worf when he had been beamed aboard the *Enterprise* from the disabled *Defiant* during their last encounter with the Borg? Tweaked him, teased him.

Tough little ship.

Riker smiled at the memory. The Klingon had almost snarled out loud, but had understood Riker's real message: *You're the captain now. Good job.* There were still days Riker regretted not having gone that route—captaining a vessel that he could actually feel move under his feet, a little ship. *Well, perhaps someday . . .*

". . . But didn't you feel a little—peculiar—getting involved in a project like this?" Riker's eyes darted to La Forge, who was speaking quietly to Barclay as they walked. It seemed that Riker, walking nearest the pair, was the only one who could overhear them. And Barclay, to Riker's surprise, didn't seem at all disconcerted by the question.

"You mean, because of what happened when Bruce wanted to disassemble Data?"

"Well, yeah," La Forge said.

"I thought of that," Barclay admitted. "And I wrestled with the question, but, in the end, I realized that this time harming Data wasn't even an issue. And what Commander Maddox was ultimately attempting to do was something that would benefit Data."

"What do you mean?" La Forge asked.

Reg sounded confused, as if Geordi was overlooking something that struck Barclay as elementary. "Just that, well, if it worked, Data wouldn't be alone anymore, would he?" He shook his head and flipped his hair back over the top of his head. "It's not a good thing, feeling alone."

La Forge became thoughtful as he considered Barclay's reply, and slipped into silence as they walked on.

Maddox's lab complex was in a building near the edge of the campus. Perched atop a gentle slope, the five-story structure overlooked a wide, well-tended lawn that ran down into a stand of old-growth forest. As the officers approached, the extensive damage on one side of the building was obvious. The admiral nodded to a pair of security guards patrolling the grounds, then stepped up to the retinal scanner beside the main entrance. "Cleared for access," the computer intoned. The locking mechanism clicked, and the doors parted.

As the others passed through, McAdams stepped back from the doors and looked up and down the front of the building. Riker paused and overheard her ask the admiral, "Is this the only entrance?"

"Yes. We move equipment in and out with a bulk transporter on the top floor, so there isn't even a freight entrance."

"Does anyone else use the building?"

Haftel shook his head. "No. Maddox, Vaslovik and Barclay were alone out here."

"Isn't that a little unusual?"

Haftel nodded. "These were unusual circumstances.

Most of the work done here at the Annex is theoretical in nature: lots of holographic modeling, very little real engineering. Maddox was trying to actually *build* something, and there were some dangerous materials involved, so we wanted to make sure they were as far away from everyone else as possible."

"In other words, no one was anywhere near the building when this happened. Convenient."

"I suppose," Haftel agreed. "But, before you make too much of that, it would have been pretty unlikely for anyone to be outside considering the weather conditions, Lieutenant."

McAdams sighed. "And I'm guessing the security system didn't catch anything."

"No," Haftel said. "The lightning strikes took out the sensors."

The interior of the building was essentially one large room sliced into work areas with modulated force fields and retractable walls—standard design for labs that had to adapt to a variety of uses. Off to the left there was an office equipped with a library workstation and a variety of computers, but the space was dominated by a holographic imaging tank about three meters on each side. Riker paused to look at the holo tank and noticed that the hardware was stenciled BROCK-CEPAK, one of the few manufacturers in the galaxy who produced the bio-neural circuitry used in the Federation's most advanced computer systems. He pointed out the label to Barclay, who nodded in acknowledgment.

"Vaslovik," he said by way of explanation. "He commissioned this equipment and had it delivered within weeks of coming onto the project."

Riker whistled appreciatively. The slow production curve for bio-neural packs was slowing down assembly of starships throughout the sector. It was one of the major concerns with the new technology, especially during the ongoing conflict with the Dominion.

"He had considerable resources at his disposal," Haftel said.

"That's putting it mildly," La Forge replied.

The larger interior chamber was the primary workroom. A good portion of the floor was destroyed, blown outward, no doubt from the overloaded EPS conduit the admiral had mentioned. The blast had taken out an entire corner of the building, and a large section of the ceiling had caved in, littering the lab with wreckage from the floor above. An array of force-field generators had been set up, presumably to strengthen the building's weakened structure. "Step carefully and try not to touch anything," Haftel told the group.

It wasn't easy to discern from among the broken bits and chunks of rubble, but enough remained that Riker could form a mental picture of how the lab had been arranged. Work lights had hung from the ceiling and a series of low tables had been set up in concentric rings around a three-meter-long black metal slab. Splinters of electronic junk that must have once been diagnostic tools, hologenerators and computer components littered the floor. The central black slab had been overturned and, beneath it, pinned to the broken floor, was a silver humanoid form.

There was no blood, no fluids of any kind, no expression of pain or horror on its blank face, yet, somehow, Riker found the sight of the half-formed thing's demise to be both horrible and unbearably sad.

The scrawled "DATA" was in a part of the room farthest from the center of the blast, near a wide dark patch in the floor of similar color. Riker noted that that part of the room also had the least amount of damage. Two or three consoles appeared to be still online.

Data and McAdams fanned out, using their tricorders.

"I am detecting two distinct sets of human DNA," Data reported.

"Confirmed," McAdams said, kneeling down to study the bloody graffito. "One is concentrated here. I assume this is where Commander Maddox was found?"

"That's right," Haftel said.

"The other DNA readings are much more scattered, as if something was vaporized," Data said. "Professor Vaslovik must have been standing right above the conduit when it overloaded."

"That was our conclusion as well," Haftel said.

McAdams stood up, and rejoined the group. The captain threw her an inquiring glance Riker could read easily. *Anything new?* McAdams merely shook her head.

But Data continued waving his tricorder around the room in silence, a peculiar expression on his face. He was frowning, almost, Riker realized, as if he didn't like what the tricorder was telling him. Finally, without a word, Data leaned forward and waved his tricorder over the bloodstains. After studying the results for several seconds, he straightened, snapped the device shut and strode across the room to the still-working consoles near his name. He immediately activated a comm circuit and connected to the DIT mainframe.

"Computer?" Data asked.

The computer emitted a tone of acknowledgment.

"This is Lieutenant Commander Data of the *U.S.S. Enterprise*. Authenticate my voiceprint."

The computer paused as it searched its files for Data's voiceprint. "Authenticated," it droned.

"Data, what are you doing?" Picard asked.

"Computer, implement a class-one planetary security alert," Data went on. "Authorization, Data Epsilon One One Four. Implement."

"Commander Data, belay that!" Haftel shouted, but he couldn't get the words out before the computer spoke again.

"Implemented," it said. Seconds later, klaxons began to sound all around the campus. In every settled area around the planet, Riker knew, transporters were shifting into stand-by mode, ships were grounding themselves or returning to their origin point, and all but the most necessary communications were being politely, but firmly, shut down. Computers were completing whatever task they had just been asked to perform and were then informing their users that they would have to receive clearance before performing additional tasks. Automated defense systems were coming online and every security officer in every city, town and research station was going to a state of full alert, and awaitng further instruction.

Data had just turned off Galor IV.

Haftel, to his credit, looked calm. There was nothing else for him to *be* at the moment, since there was nothing else he could do until Data released the planet. "Commander," he asked through a tightly clenched jaw. "Why did you just do that?"

Data turned toward the admiral and said, "My apologies, sir, but there was no time to lose." Pointing at the wreckage strewn across the lab, in tones worthy of the Great Detective himself, he said, "This was no accident, but a deliberate attempt to deceive us. Someone tried to destroy this laboratory and I believe the culprits are still on this planet."

Chapter Eight

"Have you lost your mind?"

It was not, Troi thought, the most tactful question that the captain had ever asked, but it had the virtue of getting directly to the point. Everyone seated around the table in the observation lounge—the captain, Geordi, Rhea and Admiral Haftel—stared at Data, awaiting an answer. Will was on the bridge helping the local authorities untangle the snarls Data had created. Reg had gone off in search of an empty bunk, assuming (quite correctly) that there was nothing else for him to do right now.

"No, Captain," Data replied neutrally. "I do not believe I have." Troi allowed the tendrils of her empathic senses to reach out and feel what she already expected to find: confusion tinted with fear. Beneath that she felt an undertow of concern, which was more than she could have hoped for under the circumstances.

Only Admiral Haftel was close to losing his temper, which was, Troi decided, an understandable response considering that he had invited Data to Galor IV to help *solve* a problem, not create another one. "Commander," he said tightly, "I want an immediate explanation for your actions."

"My apologies, Admiral," Data said, "for the inconvenience to you and everyone on Galor IV. When I became convinced that I was standing in the midst of a crime scene, I perceived that speed was essential. Any delay might have been enough time for the culprits to escape."

"Explain yourself, Mr. Data," Picard said. "What evidence do you have that what happened in Commander Maddox's lab was deliberate?"

Troi felt Picard and La Forge brace themselves for the impeccably organized, torrential flood of observations and insights that invariably comprised one of Data's verbal reports. It was something that they had learned to expect, but Troi knew that something was wrong. Data was suddenly immersed in a sour, discordant stew of uncertainty. "I am afraid, Captain," he said, eyes flicking down at the tabletop, "that I do not have any empirical evidence to support my conclusions."

Deanna listened to everyone in the room readjust themselves in their seats.

Picard let the springs in his seat tip him closer to the table. He was not angry, Troi knew, only confused and concerned that he had misunderstood his officer. Breakdowns in communication were one of the things Picard strived hardest to avoid, and he quickly grew frustrated with himself when he thought he had missed something. "I beg your pardon?"

"I said I do not have any empirical evidence," Data said, looking up at the captain. "I found nothing in the wreckage or in any of my tricorder readings that would lead me to believe that the conclusions drawn by the Institute's security team are incorrect. An EPS conduit did indeed explode beneath the lab, and every indication is that the overloaded power grid was triggered by a lightning strike. The android was destroyed. Dr. Vaslovik was killed. Commander Maddox was injured. I have no reason to conclude that the events did not occur in this manner."

"Except . . . ," Picard said expectantly.

"Except," Data continued, "it simply does not . . . *feel* right, sir."

Haftel's eyes narrowed.

With a visible effort of will, Picard kept his expression as neutral as possible, though Troi could feel his anxiety rolling off him. "It doesn't *feel* right," Picard repeated.

"No, sir." Data did not say anything more.

"I see." Picard closed his eyes, massaged the bridge of his nose, then opened them and fixed his gaze on Data. "Lieutenant Commander Data, effective immediately, you are relieved of duty and ordered to submit to a complete systems diagnostic, to be carried out at once by Lieutenant Commander La Forge. Lieutenant McAdams."

"Sir?"

"Go with them."

"Yes, sir."

Data began to protest and Troi felt his uncertainty deepen. "But, Captain . . . The investigation . . ."

". . . Will proceed without you. I'm sorry, Data, but we have to consider the possibility that the strain of recent events might be affecting your . . . your mind . . . in ways that even you cannot perceive."

"Captain," Data said, his voice breaking ever so slightly with the strain of keeping his tone even, "I do not believe my emotional state is negatively affecting my perceptions."

"I understand, Commander. Now you understand me: my primary concern at this moment is for your welfare. If Mr. La Forge doesn't find anything amiss, we'll discuss the next step."

Seeing that Picard wasn't going to change his mind, Data nodded. "Aye, sir."

"Dismissed," Picard said.

Data stood and walked to the door, La Forge and McAdams following close behind. No one spoke until the trio left the room, but as soon as the doors snapped shut, Haftel rose and said, "Captain, you'll excuse me, but I need to contact my people on the surface. I'll expect a full report from you on Mr. Data within twenty-four hours—"

"So, you're calling off the alert?" Troi asked.

Haftel stopped and looked at her. "I don't believe I have any choice. Do you disagree, Counselor?"

Troi pursed her lips, frowning. "No," she said. "I don't. I'm just concerned about what this will mean to Data."

"Counselor," Haftel said sternly, "we're all concerned about Mr. Data. And yes, there are still things about this incident that need explaining, things that may involve him directly. That's why I summoned the *Enterprise* here. But he just as much as admitted he was experiencing a major malfunction—"

"Respectfully, Admiral, he did *not,*" Troi said.

"Counselor, what are you saying?" Picard asked quietly.

"I'm saying we may be overlooking something important here, Captain," Troi said. "Think about it, sir: *You just told Data that he's made an error.* Has this ever happened before?"

Picard frowned, then said ruefully, "In fact, Counselor, it has, but in the end, it always turned out that he was correct." He shrugged. "But this was before the emotion chip was installed, before his . . . what would you call it? His breakdown."

"I've been monitoring Data's emotions all day," Troi said, "and I can say for certain that though he has been functioning under a great deal of stress, he's been managing it quite well. The only time he gave off an emotional response that truly concerned me is when he realized that you didn't believe him."

"Which means . . . what, exactly?" Haftel asked uncertainly.

"Data is trying to come to terms with some very complex concepts—among them mortality and isolation," Troi explained. "These are concepts that even organic beings have trouble understanding. But I believe that something else is happening simultaneously, something we've all been helping him to work toward for years, but perhaps never expected to see happen so suddenly. We just heard him tell us he came to a conclusion without any evidence to back it up, something the best Starfleet officers do routinely. Yes, in Data's case, it could mean a malfunction. Or . . ."

"Or?" Haftel demanded, clearly not liking where he thought the conversation was leading.

"Or he's finally developing thought processes that extend beyond the scope of pure fact," Troi finished, and she could see that the captain had already grasped her meaning.

"Intuition," Picard breathed. "Data has developed intuition."

Chapter Nine

WITH PRACTICED EASE, Geordi La Forge found the key spot near the base of Data's skull, pressed it with the tip of his thumb, then pulled off the top of his head. Looking across the lab to where Rhea McAdams stood, Geordi saw her turn her face away. He smiled, remembering the first time he had done this, how he'd worried that he would cause Data pain or, worse, "break" something. How long ago was that now? Ten years? Eleven? He had learned a few things since then, including, first, this process was no more intrusive to Data than getting a haircut was to Geordi; and, second, Noonien Soong built things so well that it was almost impossible to "break" them.

That didn't mean that there weren't parts of Data that couldn't be broken. He worried that the scene that just took place in the captain's ready room might have done what neither the Borg queen or Lore or Fajo the collector had been able to do: twist something around in Data so hard that it snapped. The emotion chip, the damned emotion chip: there were times when Geordi truly regretted helping his friend install it.

True, Soong had created the chip specifically to help Data's personal evolution, and Data had wanted emotions, but wasn't that at least partially because he had been *programmed* to want them? Now that he was thinking about it, he realized how strange a thing it was that Soong had designed Data to *want* to become something else rather than create him to be content as he was. What had he been thinking? Data and Geordi had sat up many a late night discussing the details of Data's structure and performance, but never the motivations of his creator. *Maybe I avoided thinking about it,* Geordi admitted to himself, *out of a kind of embarrassment. I don't mind peeling back a portion of Data's cranium because I think I understand how the individual sections function and how they all fit together. But asking him to reflect on what Soong might have been thinking—that would be a lot like asking him to look into his soul.*

He carefully clipped the leads to the correct nodes, then plugged them into the port on the computer and activated the diagnostic program that would examine every one of Data's processing centers and check them for signs of degradation and malfunction. They went through this process about four times a year, more often if there was a lot of wear and tear. He was, he knew, the closest thing Data had to a personal physician.

Despite this—and it grated his engineer's pride to admit it—if he ever had to perform any kind of major "surgery" without Data's guidance, he would be utterly lost. Geordi understood *what* Data's parts did, but had almost no clue as to *how*. It was, he knew, why Bruce Maddox had been so keen on taking Data apart. Duplicating Soong's work was the current Holy Grail of artificial intelligence. But to dissect is to kill and Data had, as far as Geordi was concerned, every right to refuse to be disassembled. As for the others—Lore, Lal and the three failed prototypes—well, that was Data's business.

Almost as if she had been reading Geordi's thoughts, McAdams crossed to the transparent cases where the inert androids stood. Geordi had noticed when they had come in that the vault doors weren't, as they usually were, opaque, but the lights were off, so all that could be seen were the androids' shadowy outlines. Then, McAdams touched the glass, the case's sensors registered her presence and the lights flicked on. McAdams was momentarily startled, but then curiosity overcame anxiety and she bent down to study the androids' faces. She pointed at the three that stood to one side. "These are Soong's prototypes?" she asked.

"Yes," Data said.

"They don't have features," she observed. "But they're not like the shapeless mannequin we saw in Maddox's lab, either."

"No," Data said. "Giving the android distinctive facial features is one of the last steps in the process. Obviously, Commander Maddox and Professor Vaslovik had not reached that stage."

"But according to Lieutenant Barclay, they were going to activate the android on the night of the storm," McAdams said. "Wouldn't they have wanted the android to have features when it was switched on?"

"Not necessarily," Data replied. "I did not create features for Lal, precisely so that she would have the opportunity to choose her own."

McAdams looked at the form of a small young

woman at the far end of the row of androids. She looked so serene, Geordi thought, as if she were only meditating and might open her eyes at any moment.

"She was very pretty," McAdams noted.

"Thank you," Data said, obviously pleased. Geordi was impressed by the sensitivity that McAdams displayed by speaking of Lal in the past tense. The empty form in the vault was no more Data's daughter than a portrait in a mausoleum.

McAdams smiled, then turned her attention to another of the androids. "This is Lore?"

"Yes," Data said without inflection. "My brother."

"Why do you look alike?"

"We were created in our maker's image."

"Oh," McAdams said. "Why?"

"An interesting question, Lieutenant, one that I have pondered on numerous occasions," Data said. "It may have been simple vanity. And, given my father's opinion of himself, it may not be an invalid conclusion. However, I believe the true reason is that my father wished to feel as if some part of himself would continue on after he died. He had no children."

"*Biological* children," McAdams corrected.

Data seemed delighted. "Yes. Exactly."

Pointing at the last body in the row of cases, McAdams asked, "This is your mother? Dr. Tainer?"

"Yes."

"She was lovely, too."

Data nodded, but didn't answer. The room was silent for several minutes as La Forge continued to work. McAdams was still studying Tainer's face when she spoke again.

"Data?"

"Yes, Lieutenant?"

"Why don't you just fix them?"

To La Forge's surprise, Data didn't hesitate to answer. "The knowledge to repair a positronic brain after cascade failure does not yet exist. When a neural net succumbs to such anomalies, the structure of the matrix is not recoverable."

"That explains Lal, but what about Dr. Tainer and Lore?"

"My father programmed Juliana to undergo cascade failure when she reached a certain point in her life. Lore posed too great a danger to others while he lived, and I took steps to ensure that his positronic brain can never be reactivated."

McAdams seemed to consider all of that. "Then, if you don't mind my asking . . . If there's no way any of these six can be reactivated . . . then why *not* give them to Commander Maddox to study?"

La Forge froze. He couldn't help himself. McAdams had just asked a question that never occurred to him. He found himself holding his breath, the diagnostic wand he held poised over an interface node on the surface of Data's skull as he waited for his friend's answer.

Finally, in a quiet voice, Data said, "It just seemed wrong, Lieutenant."

La Forge allowed himself a small smile as he started breathing again and went back to work.

McAdams let silence fall again, still studying Dr. Tainer's face. "I agree with you, Commander," she said after a few moments.

Turning away from the case, she continued, "I also agree with you about Maddox's lab."

La Forge and Data both looked up and answered as one: "You do?"

McAdams frowned. "Yes. Why is that so surprising?"

Data opened his mouth to reply, then seemed to reconsider what he was going to say, and started over. "Does it not trouble you that the physical evidence does not support my conclusions?"

"But that's exactly it," McAdams said. "Everything about it strikes me as too convenient. The failure of the weather grid, the lightning strike, the overloaded power conduit—all on the night that the android was to be activated? And the only surviving witness is in a coma that no one's been able to coax him out of? I'm with you, Commander: nothing about this feels right."

"Wait a minute," La Forge said. "Are you suggesting the storm was engineered? That the lightning was timed and aimed at the power grid?"

"Of course not," McAdams said. "But someone could have sabotaged the weather grid, and used the cover of the storm to engineer the EPS overload, making it look like an accident."

"An intriguing theory," Data said. "Unfortunately, it is also one unsupported by any evidence."

"So far," McAdams admitted. "That could change. I just can't shake the feeling that something, some*one,* wants us to believe in a version of reality that would make our lives much easier. One thing I've learned, Commander, is that whenever something looks easy, it's probably a lie. Life isn't that convenient. It's . . . complicated." There was something in her tone that made Geordi think she wasn't really speaking to them anymore. McAdams was continuing a conversation she had once had with someone else, perhaps more than once.

Geordi looked at his friend and was surprised, but pleased by what he saw. For the first time since he had returned to the *Enterprise,* Data looked neither stressed nor confused. He looked simply . . . intrigued. "Lieutenant?" he asked.

"Yes?" she replied distantly.

"Would you like to discuss your theory further?"

McAdams shook herself as if waking from a dream. Looking around the room, she said, "I'm getting hungry. How about over dinner, Commander?"

"I do not need to eat, Lieutenant."

"Then you can talk while *I* eat."

Data pondered his options. Finally, he said, "However, just because I do not *need* to eat does not mean that I cannot."

"Even better, Commander," Rhea responded.

"Please call me Data, Lieutenant."

McAdams smiled. "Rhea."

The door signaled and Picard heard Data call out, "Enter." The portal hissed open and the captain strode in purposefully, but, then, sensing the mood in the room, slowed his pace and studied the three officers. McAdams and Data were both pictures of wide-eyed attentiveness, though he sensed there was something else happening, like someone had just told a joke they would never, ever tell in his presence. La Forge pretended to be absorbed in his padd. Picard smiled warily and asked, "What have we discovered, Geordi?"

"All primary and backup systems are performing at optimum levels," La Forge said. "No problems with the interface between the positronic brain and Data's neural net." Scanning farther down the summary, he noted,

"Some stresses showing on his emotional subroutines, but, again, well within tolerance levels. I'm going to run my results through the ship's computer, just to be sure, but unless it shows that I missed something, I expect to be able to give Data a clean bill of health."

Picard nodded. "Very good, Mr. La Forge," Picard replied. As the engineer withdrew to a console on the far end of the lab, the captain turned to McAdams and said, "Lieutenant, you're dismissed. It would seem that we will not be needing anyone to watch Commander Data, after all. Please drop by my ready room at the end of your shift so I can speak to you about a special assignment."

"Very good, sir. Thank you." Smiling, she rose. "See you around, Commander La Forge." Then, more warmly, McAdams finished, "See you later, Data."

Picard cocked an eyebrow at Geordi to see if he had any idea what was going on, but the chief engineer just shrugged, grinned and turned his attention back to the diagnostic display.

The captain smiled. "So. How are you feeling?"

Data, who was still staring at the door, suddenly turned and looked at him. "With all due respect, Captain, that information does not seem to be relevant."

Ouch. I suppose I deserved that one. Picard sighed and grabbed one of the swivel chairs in the lab. He sat opposite his operations officer and took a moment to collect his thoughts before admitting, "Counselor Troi has helped me to see that perhaps it should be, Data. I've just come from speaking with Admiral Haftel. I believe I've convinced him that you should be allowed to look into the Maddox affair personally, pursuing whatever lines of investigation you see fit. It wasn't an easy decision, and Admiral Haftel will be looking at the results of your investigation very closely."

Data reached up to disconnect the lead from his cranium. "Thank you, sir," he said. "I hope I will be able to reassure the admiral. May I make a request?"

Picard nodded.

"I would like to ask that Lieutenant McAdams assist me in the investigation. I believe her talents and background in security would be valuable."

Picard smiled. "Precisely the assignment I was going to discuss with the lieutenant," he said. "The *Enterprise* will remain in orbit and at your disposal for up to three days. If you haven't found anything by then, we close the investigation. That was the compromise I made with the admiral."

"I understand, sir," Data said. "I will not give you a reason to regret your decision."

"You never have, Data. Just trust your instincts," Picard replied. "As I do."

Chapter Ten

AFTER THE CAPTAIN LEFT HIS LAB, Data, uncharacteristically, did not stir for several seconds, his thoughts racing. At once, he was pleased that Captain Picard was allowing him to pursue the investigation, but was also concerned that he had to put his newfound insight to the test in such a manner. Additionally, there was the question of what other crimes might have been committed. Did he possess the resources to pursue this trail, especially considering his current state of mind?

Since no answer was forthcoming, Data assigned a processing cluster to its consideration, then compressed and archived several files that were running parallel (including an analysis of a reconfiguration of the *Enterprise*'s Bussard collectors, a review of the works of Tom Stoppard and the composition of a sonnet about his mother), and dumped them into long-term storage. These were all things that could wait. There were other considerations demanding his attention, not the least of which were his unexpected emotional responses to Rhea McAdams.

A cursory self-diagnostic revealed that a surprising number of his standby processors had been activated involuntarily, and all of them were engaged in processing his sensory input from the new security officer: her airborne chemical signature, her facial expressions, the color of her eyes, the shape of her body, the way her hair moved when she turned her head, the sound of her voice . . .

Another anomaly: His outer integument, particularly at his face and extremities, was experiencing a point-three-degree rise in temperature. His one sexual encounter with Tasha Yar had provoked a similar physiological response, but at the time it had lacked emotional context.

This was different.

Data found himself accessing etiquette and protocol studies; he attempted to determine the most likely problems he would encounter during his dinner with McAdams and began running scenarios for dealing with them. He quickly determined that the issues were too complex to resolve with the resources he had assigned and attempted to sort and prioritize the variables. This did not clarify his thinking particularly, but it did make Data aware of a peculiar, but not altogether unpleasant, nervousness.

"Data?"

"Yes?" Data said a bit too suddenly. He realized he had forgotten Geordi. No, not forgotten, but become less aware of his presence, somehow, as if Data were . . . preoccupied. The thought, like so many other recent new experiences, intrigued him.

"I said, that was quite an interesting conversation you were having with Lieutenant McAdams."

Data nodded. "Yes," he said. "It was. Though I have the feeling that I may have missed some of the undercurrents."

His friend grinned and leaned back against the edge of the control panel. "I don't think you missed anything important. Looked to me like you were just getting to know each other better through banter. It's deceptively sophisticated behavior and you were holding your own just fine. I confess it's not something I'm that good at myself and the lieutenant seems like a formidable opponent."

"Opponent?" Data asked, confused. "I sense that you are being ironic, but I fail to completely grasp your meaning."

Geordi faltered. "I just meant . . ." He paused again and tapped his lip with a fingertip. "I guess what I'm saying is that Rhea is a kind of woman who will keep you on your toes. She's very quick, very . . . I don't know . . . combative . . . ? Do you understand what I mean?"

Data quickly parsed Geordi's statements for possible meanings. Though several interpretations suggested themselves, none was so overwhelmingly probable that he felt like he could, in good conscience, assure his friend he had grasped his meaning. He shook his head. "No, Geordi. I do not."

"All I'm saying is . . ." Geordi sighed resignedly. "I'm sorry. This isn't one of my best areas. What I'm trying to say is that you might be entering into terrain that even those who have years of experience with emotions sometimes have problems traversing."

Data nodded. "I believe I understand now. You are concerned for my welfare and are attempting to warn me away from circumstances you think might be perilous."

Geordi sighed with relief. "Yes," he said. "That's it exactly."

"Also, I am currently in what might be described as an emotionally vulnerable condition."

"Good point."

"But is it not possible," Data asked, "that this is one of the attributes that Lieutenant McAdams finds attractive?"

Geordi weighed this consideration, then held up his hands in mock surrender. "You know," he said. "You might not need my help, after all."

Rhea McAdams's quarters were decorated in a simple, almost austere manner. She had removed most of the Starfleet-standard furnishings and broken up the main room into irregular spaces with painted folding screens. The main living area was centered around a low, wide table that was surrounded by cushions. Around the window, there were several small pen and ink studies of Mount Fuji that Rhea had done, she explained, during her student days. There was a faint tang of incense in the air and Data noted a small table at the edge of the space set with an incense holder and a trio of small holograms.

"Those are my parents," Rhea called from the dining area, where she apparently had several cooking devices engaged. Such equipment was optional to most crewmembers aboard starships, but few chose it over the convenience of a replicator. "And my grandmother—my mother's mother."

The man was red-haired and fair, but the woman, black-haired and small in stature, closely resembled Rhea. "Is your mother standing on the deck of a boat?"

Rhea called, "That's the *Ryo-oh-ki,* one of the fishing boats she owned."

"Fishing boats?" Data asked. "Commercial fishing?"

"Yes, commercial fishing," Rhea said, poking her head into the living area. "Some Japanese people, especially the more traditional families, take fish very seriously. Many of them won't eat replicated fish, especially if they're having sushi. It doesn't have the correct texture."

"It sounds as if you know a great deal about fish," Data said.

Rhea laughed an unexpectedly loud guffaw. "You could say that," she said. "From the day I could walk, could *crawl*, I've been around fish. Worked on the boats and on the docks, hauled fish, cleaned fish, packed fish. Do you know what we're having for dinner tonight, Data?"

Data considered, then guessed, "Fish?"

"No!" Rhea laughed. "Anything *but* fish. I hate fish. I joined Starfleet to get away from fish. Do you know what they told me I should specialize in at the Academy?"

"I will guess . . . marine biology."

"Right!" Rhea said, laughing again. "So I went into security. I figured it was the one thing I could do where I would be least likely to come into contact with fish."

"Have you encountered any fish so far in your career as a Starfleet security officer?"

"I had to arrest an Antedean once," Rhea said, "but that's been about it." She retrieved a bottle of wine and a corkscrew from the dining area. "Do you drink wine?" she asked.

"Occasionally," Data replied. "When my emotion chip is on, I enjoy the flavor, but alcohol does not affect me as it affects humans."

"Never?"

Data considered the question before replying. "A

xenovirus once invaded my positronic systems. It had an effect analogous to inebriation."

"Ah," McAdams said, and finished pouring the wine. She handed him a glass and smiled. "Cheers."

They clinked glasses, and Data sniffed the wine, then tasted it, raised his eyebrows appreciatively. "This was not replicated?" Data asked, accepting the glass.

"Wine from a replicator . . ." She made a disgusted face. "Did you know that Captain Picard's family owns a vineyard?"

Rhea sipped from her glass, then smiled. "Yes, I did. I've had some of their wine. Most of it is quite good, though they have problems with some of their sparkling wines."

"Really?" Data asked. "You should tell him. I believe his sister-in-law is currently managing the winery, but there have been times he has intimated that he might like to retire there someday."

Rhea laughed again. "If I'm ever looking for a fast transfer off the ship, I'll be sure to mention it to him."

Data returned to studying the holograms. "And this is your father? Was he also a fisherman?"

"No," Rhea replied, her voice softening. "He was a marine engineer. He and my mom met when he was in Kobe building a dock for her boats. They didn't stay married for a very long time, though they were friends until he died. I was only seven and he didn't live in Kobe very many years, so all I remember was this large, friendly man."

"Forgive my ignorance," Data said indicating the table, "but is this altar meant only to honor the dead?"

Rhea smiled sadly. "Only the dead, I'm afraid," she said. "My grandmother died about ten years ago. And my mom . . ." She hesitated and it seemed to Data that she was struggling with how to say what she wanted to say next.

"If this subject is unpleasant for you," Data said, "please do not feel like you must continue."

Rhea looked up at him and said, "That's not it. I was afraid to say too much about it because it might be painful for *you.* My mother died recently, too, about a year ago. She got tangled in a net and was pulled overboard . . ." She paused, collecting her thoughts. "It's funny. We weren't really very close most of my life because she was away a lot, but the last of couple of years—since I graduated from the Academy, especially—whenever we got together, it was different. Somehow, *not* doing what she thought I was going to do altered her perception of me. It got so that we could actually talk about things."

"You became friends," Data realized.

Rhea grinned brightly, then surprised Data by reaching up and lightly touching his cheek. "You are a rare treasure, Mr. Data, and you have a way with words."

Data did not reply immediately because he was too stunned to speak. People rarely initiated physical contact with him and he was uncertain how to respond. Rhea's gesture, in particular, had confused him, being neither openly flirtatious nor purely platonic. He consulted his behavioral files, but found very little that was useful. Data decided his best response was to catalog observations and review them later.

And then, several milliseconds after these insights and decisions had been filed, there came a warm sensation of pleasure that began at the spot where Rhea had touched his cheek and radiated outward and down through Data's neural net. His emotional responses,

Data noted, always seemed to lag behind his intellectual observations.

Data sipped the Cabernet and decided he liked it. Rhea returned to the dining area to check on the dinner and Data followed.

"What are we having if we are not having fish?"

"At first, I thought to make you real sukiyaki because replicator beef *is* actually pretty good and they grow scallions in the arboretum, but then I wondered if you might be a vegetarian. Are you?"

"I do not think so," he said.

"Well," Rhea said, checking a pair of pots on a small heating device, "you are tonight. Fettucini with marinara sauce and a mushroom salad. Figured I'd be on safe ground." She stirred the sauce, then stripped the foil pouch off two servings of pasta and threw them into the boiling water. "Okay," she said, "I've talked enough for now. I'm cooking; you talk."

"What would you like me to talk about?"

"Tell me about *your* mother," Rhea said, opening a cabinet door. "What was she like?"

Data sat on one of the two metal stools that stood next to the counter and rested his wineglass on his knee. "I did not know her very well," Data said. "We met for the first time only four years ago and had seen each other on only a few occasions since then." He stopped and thought, trying to encapsulate the things he remembered about their visits. "She was a fine scientist; she did not like to cook, but enjoyed cleaning up afterward; most of her earrings were green because she liked the way it went with her hair; she wished to learn how to make pottery on a wheel, but never had time . . ."

Rhea, who had ceased searching the cabinets for a

colander and was listening attentively, asked, "Yes, what else?"

Data tipped his glass from side to side, observing the play of the refracted light in the ruby liquid. Finally, after what seemed a long time to him, he said very softly, "She might have learned how to turn pots if she had known she was an android." He reached up and dabbed at his eyelids with his fingertips. They came away wet. "I have decided that I could grow weary of this feeling very soon."

"What feeling?" Rhea asked quietly.

Data sipped some wine and thought about trying to change the subject. He knew this was considered acceptable behavior, but, unaccountably, he decided to try to answer her question. "I do not yet know how to identify it," he said finally. "Regret, perhaps. Not for myself or my own life, but for the opportunities that they missed." Data didn't say who "they" were, but Rhea seemed to understand who he meant: Lore, Lal, the nameless androids and even Juliana Tainer, who (by Dr. Soong's standards) had lived a long, full life. "The changes in my emotional status from moment to moment have taken a toll," Data concluded. "I have fought Borg drones with my bare hands, but never before in my life have I felt so battered."

Rhea began to reach across the counter, but then the pasta water boiled over, and she had to hastily turn down the heat. The moment lost, she went back to stirring the sauce. "You know," she said, "one of the most useful pieces of advice my mother ever gave me was that you can't battle life. Actually, she said this about the sea, but as far as Mom was concerned, it was the same thing. 'You can't battle life,' she said. 'You have to learn to treat it like a waltz and your problems are your partner. Step lightly, try to keep time with the music and smile.' " Unconsciously, Rhea moved the spoon like a conductor's baton and flicked sauce onto the floor and the wall.

"Oh, very graceful," she laughed, and began looking around for a towel. Data saw it first and used it to wipe up the spilled sauce. "Like my mother," he said, "I, too, prefer cleaning to cooking."

"As I said," Rhea replied, "you are a rare treasure, sir."

"I am also an accomplished dancer," Data replied, "so I should find it simple to follow your mother's advice."

"Really?" Rhea asked. "Accomplished?"

"Yes," he said sincerely. "I have received instruction from one of the finest dancers in Starfleet."

Rhea stared at him for a moment as if considering a challenge, then reached over and turned off both burners and put a lid on the sauce pot. "Accomplished," she repeated. "Hmm. All right—prove it."

Chapter Eleven

PICARD SAT AT THE END of the bar in a small alcove that had come to be known as "the Captain's Nook." He pretended not to know that the crew called it that and, in return, the crew pretended not to notice him when he sat there. No one sat in the stool next to his unless every other seat in the lounge was taken and that almost never happened because Picard only visited it during off-peak hours. It was one of the ways, he knew, that he had changed since taking command of the *Enterprise*-D more than a decade ago. Then, he would never have allowed himself to socialize with the crew, not even to the extent of sitting in a quiet lounge and reading, but he had learned a few things since those days. Isolation would not make him a better captain. Truth be told, he found the gentle background hum of hushed conversations very soothing.

Off in the corner, someone—Ensign Ubango—was assaying a difficult classical piece. She stopped periodically to run through a few particularly troublesome bars, then resumed.

From behind him, Picard heard Will Riker ask, "Bach?"

"Tchaikovsky," Picard said. He had often wondered if Riker really didn't know anything about classical music or merely enjoyed giving his captain the opportunity to correct him. "Have a seat, Will." Riker pulled out the stool next to Picard's, then flagged down the bartender who smiled and set about pouring him a single malt whiskey. Since coming aboard the *Enterprise*-E, Picard and Riker had made it a habit to meet once or twice a week in the lounge to discuss whatever matters either of them decided were important, but felt, for one reason or another, shouldn't make it into the official logs. In essence, this meant gossip, but gossip of a particular caliber. Picard had learned long ago that in any community as complex as the *Enterprise,* gossip was one of life's essential fluids. He never underestimated the importance of whatever unofficial information was being traded about the ship and relied on Riker to collect it for him.

Predictably, most of the gossip was about the escalating hostilities with the ongoing Dominion conflict and the possibilities of a treaty with the Romulans. Though many of the crew of the *Enterprise*-D had rotated into new posts while its *Sovereign*-class successor was being commissioned, there were still enough old hands around who remembered encounters with the Romulans and their gigantic *D'deridex*-class warbirds. Having them as allies would certainly change the balance of power, but how long could the Federation actually trust them? And, of course, how long could Romulans and Klingons work shoulder to shoulder before old animosities resurfaced?

Riker pointed at the padd Picard had set down on the bar and asked, "What's that? Looks dense."

Picard massaged the bridge of his nose and said, "It is, I'm afraid. I've been trying to review the recent decisions regarding the civil rights of artificial life forms."

Riker picked up the padd and clicked through a few screens, skimming the text. Then, wincing, he laid it back down on the bar. "I'd rather fight the Borg, thank you."

Picard chuckled in agreement, then said, "Ah, but you're at least partially responsible for all this. It's all a direct result of the hearing we held where Judge Louvois decided that Data is entitled to full constitutional rights and isn't the property of Starfleet."

Riker shuddered extravagantly. "I take comfort in knowing that though I'm a terrible prosecutor, I'm a fine trombone player."

"Terrible? Are you being modest? I thought you performed brilliantly. When you reached behind Data and turned him off, I almost walked out of the hearing." It had been a near thing, Picard remembered. Judge Louvois had been appointed to determine whether Data could legally refuse Bruce Maddox's request that he allow himself to be disassembled. Only Data's eloquence, and Picard's own impassioned arguments, had saved him, and the repercussions of Louvois's decision were still, apparently, echoing throughout the Federation.

Riker grinned at the memory and said, "That was rather good, wasn't it? At the time, I hated myself for it. But Louvois didn't give me much of a choice. Said that if she didn't believe I was doing my best, she would rule against Data. In the end, virtue triumphed, as always . . . ." and he raised his glass in a toast. Picard touched the brim of his glass to Riker's and the conversation shifted to his discussion with Admiral Haftel about Data's investigation of Maddox's accident. Just as Picard finished repeating Haftel's grudging decision, Troi entered the lounge and pulled up the chair next to Riker's, handing Picard an isolinear chip. She had just finished her bridge shift, she explained, when Dr. Crusher's latest report came in, and she decided to bring it to Picard personally. The captain immediately slid the chip into his padd.

"Maddox's condition is essentially the same," Picard read aloud. "She can't seem to pin down the coma to any known agent and she's getting frustrated. Not trauma-induced. No infectious agents. They've even done a poison screening."

Troi smiled. "Beverly hates a mystery."

"Yes," Picard replied. "She does. And she's decided to stay on the surface until she can sort this out."

"Couldn't she transport Maddox to the *Enterprise?*" Riker asked.

"I asked her the same thing this morning," Troi related. "But she said there's nothing up here that they don't have down there. Personally, I think she's decided the infirmary staff is lax and is taking the opportunity to whip them into shape." Picard and Riker chuckled. "So, what else have I missed?" Troi asked. She knew about Riker and Picard's debriefing sessions. "Already covered all the news of the day?"

Riker beckoned to the civilian bartender who, when he saw who his new customer was, grinned brilliantly and asked, "What would you like, Deanna?"

"Hot chocolate," Troi said smiling warmly in response. "With whipped cream, please."

Deanna studied the bartender's back as he programmed her request into the food replicator. Riker seemed to note with amusement that her gaze lingered, then asked, "So, you two have met?"

"Oh, yes," Troi replied distractedly. "Standard psych evaluation. We had a very interesting conversation."

"How interesting?"

"*Very* interesting, Commander," she teased. "We talked about art and music and seeing the galaxy as a member of a starship support staff." When the bartender returned, Troi said, "Sam, allow me to introduce you to Commander Riker."

"We've met," Sam said. "He has great taste in single malts."

Riker raised his glass in acknowledgment and sipped his drink. "How are you adjusting, Sam?"

Sam stood up straight, surveyed the lounge, then unconsciously smoothed back his thick hair with a well-manicured hand. *He looks,* thought Picard, *like a lion who has just checked his domain and is satisfied with what he sees.* "It's a fascinating place," he remarked. "An intriguing mix of individuals. I understand, though, that you used to have more civilians. Families, even."

"True," Riker said. "Different time, different *Enterprise.*"

"That's too bad," Sam said. "I would have liked to have seen that. I'm sure it made things even more . . . unpredictable."

Picard, who had been listening in on the conversation said, "We'll do what we can to keep things lively."

Sam grinned, then wiped at a nonexistent spot on the bar top. "Well, that sounds fine, Captain. I could do without the time travel and the Borg, though, so don't go out of your way on either of those."

"Duly noted."

"You know," Sam said, suddenly straightening, "that reminds me of something. Hang on. I'll be right back." He disappeared into the storage area behind the bar and they heard the sounds of containers being shifted about.

Picard said to Troi, "I was telling Will about my conversation with Admiral Haftel. I've assigned Data and Lieutenant McAdams to investigate the mystery on Galor IV. I think they'll work very well together." Smiling, he added, "A veritable Nick and Nora Charles."

Riker and Troi stared at Picard blankly.

"Nick and Nora Charles," he repeated. *"The Thin Man . . . ?"*

Riker turned to look at Troi. "I'm guessing a detective novel."

"Hmmm," Troi agreed, sipping her hot chocolate. "One of these days, one of us has to give him something else to read."

Feigning disgust, Picard sat back in his chair. "I don't know why I even bother bringing these things up."

Sam reappeared carrying a foil-wrapped parcel and a corkscrew. He peeled the foil away from the bottle's neck, then removed the cork. "Normally, I'd decant something like this, but, for time's sake, let's just let it breathe for a moment."

"Speaking of Lieutenant McAdams," Riker said to Troi, "did I mention that she pinned me *four* times in *mok'bara* practice yesterday?"

"Yes," Troi replied with mock disgust. "Four times. You told me. I think you enjoyed that a little too much."

Riker raised his eyebrows and shrugged his shoulders in a *Who wouldn't?* gesture and finished his drink. "Well," he said starting to rise, "I have reports to review—"

Sam reappeared with four glasses and said, "Hold on, Commander. Try some of this." He poured a small amount of ruby liquid into one of the glasses and placed it before Picard, who held the wine up to the light and studied its color. Then, he expertly inhaled the bouquet, sipped and swished. Swallowing, he raised his eyebrows in surprise.

"That's astonishing," he said. "A Bordeaux, if I'm not mistaken. Comte de Vogue. *Maison St. Gaspar?*"

Sam nodded. "Excellent palate, Captain. Vintage?"

Picard took another sip and considered. "Very fruity. Very balanced. Long, elegant finish." He pondered. "Either the '67 or the '65."

Sam unwrapped the bottle and handed it to Picard. "The '65, Captain. I'm impressed."

Picard took the bottle and examined the label. "This is extraordinary. My brother was friends with their grower and even he couldn't get a bottle of this out of him. How did you get it?"

Sam wagged his eyebrows. "Bartenders have their sources." He took the bottle and poured Picard another glass, then some for Riker and Troi, then himself. *"Skol,"* he said. Troi and Riker took theirs and sipped. Riker, never the wine enthusiast, cocked an eyebrow and said, "It's good."

Troi slapped his arm. "Whiskey has destroyed your palate."

"Or refined it beyond this pale stuff."

Picard wasn't listening to either of them, but was beside himself. "Thank you," he said to Sam. "But why . . . ?"

Sam recorked the bottle and set it down on the bar before Picard. "A gift," he said. "For good works."

Before Picard could say another word, Sam's attention was drawn to a stir in the crowd originating near the doors. Picard, Troi and Riker turned, too, and saw Data and McAdams enter, arm in arm. Both were wearing civilian formal wear—Data a simple, but elegant evening suit and Rhea in a long midnight blue, floor-length evening gown.

The crowd parted before them as they swept toward the small dance floor. Then, Data spoke to Ensign Ubango, who smiled and nodded enthusiastically. She had given up on Tchaikovsky some time ago and had been working her way through some light background pieces, but she seemed quite pleased about whatever it was Data had asked her to play.

Data and McAdams took their positions in the center of the floor, both very erect and formal, Data's arm around McAdams's waist, her hand on his shoulder, their other hands lightly clasped. When Ubango saw the dancers were in position, she launched into a piece Picard instantly recognized as Chopin's Waltz No. 1 in E-Flat.

Data and McAdams threw themselves into the dance with passion, precision and obvious pleasure. Their footwork, especially considering the relatively tiny space they had to work in, was astonishing, and the turns and dips were so carefully synchronized with the beats of the waltz, it was not clear whether the music was leading the dancers or the dancers were helping Ubango to keep time. It was a breathtaking display of virtuosity.

As the dancers spun 'round and 'round the floor, Picard realized it was the first time he had seen Data dance since Miles and Keiko O'Brien's wedding. He remembered well the odd, forced rictus Data had worn during his dance with Keiko, a sharp contrast to the warm, genuine smile he had tonight, one obviously meant for only one person. And that person, Picard noted, was smiling back at Data in exactly the same manner.

Waltz No. 1 ended, but Ubango immediately slipped into something by Brahms. Data looked ready to shift tempo immediately, but McAdams, flushed, had to pause, catch her breath and sip a glass of water before she could go on. But as soon as she was done, McAdams took Data's hand again and they launched themselves back out onto the floor. Picard thought he heard a smattering of applause from the small crowd, and turned to make a comment to Riker and Troi, but then saw that his first officer wore a resigned expression. Then, as Picard watched, Troi reached up and patted Riker's hand, and Riker took her hand in his and squeezed it.

Picard turned to look at Sam and almost said, *"Interesting enough for you?"* but stopped when he saw the wistful smile on the bartender's face, almost like he was remembering another day, another dance, and so Picard held his tongue and drank his wine.

And the music played on.

And the dancers danced.

Geordi La Forge's combadge beeped stridently, rousing him from a sound sleep. Lifting the badge from his nightstand, he activated the chronochip in his left implant and checked the time: 0045. Why would anyone be calling him at this hour when the ship was in orbit and the main engines in standby mode? But, wait, no . . . if there was an emergency in Main Engineering, the ship's computer would have alerted him. Unless the problem was *with* the computer . . .

He tapped the badge. "La Forge here," he said hoarsely, sitting up. "What's the problem?"

"Geordi? I am sorry. Did I wake you?"

"Data?"

"Yes," Data said. "It is I. I apologize for the lateness of this call, but there was something I wanted to ask you."

"What is it, Data? Something wrong with the main computer?"

"No, Geordi. The computer is fine. Ship's status is optimum. The question I have for you is of a *personal* nature."

Geordi sagged back against his pillow. "Oh," he said. "All right. This wasn't something that could wait until morning?"

"I am afraid not, Geordi."

"All right," Geordi sighed. "Go ahead."

Data inhaled deeply, then began: "Is it appropriate to call a woman the morning after you have dined together and gone dancing to ask her if she would like to have breakfast together?"

Geordi sighed, then considered the question. "Are we talking about Lieutenant McAdams?"

"Yes."

"Well," Geordi replied, "I think you should ask yourself a different question first: Do you want to get involved in a personal relationship with someone you work with?"

Data replied, "I considered this issue and decided that if Commander Riker and Counselor Troi and the captain and Dr. Crusher can do this, then so can I."

"Not exactly the same thing, is it, Data? I mean, Commander Riker and the counselor—that was a long time ago. And the captain and Dr. Crusher—that's theoretical at best." It was a common topic of conversation on the ship, but no one knew for certain the status of the relationship between their commanding officer and the chief medical officer—not even the two themselves, Geordi suspected.

There was silence for several seconds, so Geordi said, "Data?"

"Yes, Geordi."

"Ask her to breakfast, but wait until tomorrow morning."

"Would seven hundred hours be an acceptable time to call her?"

"Yes. Wait, no. Make it seven-thirty."

"Why?"

"I don't know. It just feels better."

"Thank you, Geordi."

Data inhaled deeply, seemingly well pleased with the answer. "Another question?" he asked.

Geordi bunched up the pillow under his head, laid the combadge on his chest and closed his eyes, settling in for a long conversation. "Go ahead."

"Would it be inappropriate to take her flowers?"

"No," Geordi said. "I can't imagine why it would be. Women like to get flowers. Most of them, anyway."

"Right now?"

"No, not right now. Maybe tomorrow. At breakfast."

"Ah. Excellent suggestion. May I ask—?"

"Go ahead, Data."

Data proceeded to bombard La Forge with a series of questions and observations about dating and interpersonal relationships. Some of them were charmingly naive, some insightful and a few quite odd coming from a person whom La Forge had always considered one of the most intelligent mature individuals he knew. He suddenly felt like he was back in the Academy again having a bull session with one of his roommates.

After about an hour, it grew to be too much. Though it was obvious that his friend had quickly grown to care about Rhea McAdams and was impatient for things to move forward as quickly as possible, Geordi's mouth was growing dry and he was fading into sleep. Muzzily, he said, "Data? That's enough. Can we continue this conversation tomorrow?"

"But Geordi—"

"No, Data. Really, that's enough. I understand how you're feeling, but you can't do everything in one night. You just have to take things slow. Don't scare the poor woman. You have all the time in the world."

Data did not reply immediately and Geordi worried that he might have hurt his friend's feelings. Then, just as he was about to apologize, La Forge heard Data say, "Yes, Geordi. You are correct. I do." Then, he added softly, "But no one else does."

PART TWO

Seventy Years Ago

"Dammit, Ira," Soong muttered, rubbing his neck. "I thought you said you could climb."

Graves grunted something profane, then admitted he had misjudged the distance to the shelf. The drop had been less than two meters and his elbow barely clipped Soong's neck, but there had been a frightening moment when both of them had almost tumbled off the ledge.

"Are you two all right down there?" Vaslovik called through the comm. They had agreed that he shouldn't attempt the descent until they had gotten themselves situated and made sure the ledge was stable.

"Yes," Soong and Graves said simultaneously.

"Good," Vaslovik said, sounding, for all the world, like a tutor disciplining two unruly schoolboys. "How does it look down there?"

Graves pulled out his tricorder and checked the ledge, though Soong noticed that Ira had a hard time keeping his eyes off the body. Soong was willing to admit that he was having trouble doing the same. The readings he had taken while waiting for Ira were baffling and inconclusive. To begin, it was difficult to estimate the find's age, partly because of the refrigerating cold and partly because the minerals had leeched into its "flesh." Still, even a very conservative estimate meant the humanoid that lay there before them was thousands upon thousands of years old. Soong had reset his tricorder at least three times and had kept getting the same unbelievable reading.

Ira stared at his tricorder and groaned.

"Are you all right?" Soong asked.

"I . . . I'm fine," Ira said. "But my tricorder must have been damaged in the fall. This *can't* be right."

"Five hundred thousand years?" Soong asked.

Ira's head snapped around. "Yours, too?" He shook his head. "All right. Yes. So, there's some kind of impurity in the minerals that's affecting both tricorders."

"Or, they're both right."

Overhead, they heard Vaslovik begin to make his slow descent. Soong had sent the antigravs up to the older man on a slender line, after warning him about the weak battery. He should be fine. Soong had developed a healthy respect for the professor's common sense.

"It can't be true," Graves denied. "Even a mummified corpse would have disintegrated into dust long ago."

"Check your readings again, Ira," Soong said. "It isn't a corpse; not the way you mean, anyway. Don't forget what we found upstairs." Graves's eyes flicked up toward the top of the cliff, then refocused on the tricorder display.

"Of course," he said, suddenly growing very excited. "I'm sorry. I don't know what I was thinking." Soong was too exhausted to be shocked, but he filed away the moment for later consideration: Ira Graves had just apologized to him *and* admitted that he had made a mistake. "Professor," Graves called through his comm link. "You're not going to believe what this is."

"Busy now," Vaslovik responded. "Half a moment, Ira." Soong looked up and saw that Vaslovik was about halfway down the cliff and making good time. The line he had tied off with a secure piton was shaking slightly under the strain, but no more than should have been expected. "You're sure the cliff will hold all three of us?"

"It should be all right," Soong replied. "This appears to be the remains of a bridge that cracked away a few thousand years ago." He sent his light down over the edge, but the darkness swallowed the beam before it could reach bottom. "How's the other pattern enhancer?" he asked, remembering that Ira was carrying it. "Please tell me it didn't crack when you fell."

"It's fine," Ira said, not really paying attention. He was fixated on the readings he was taking from the body. "It's hard to be sure," he muttered, "but I think the atomic structure is essentially identical to the specimen we found in the chamber upstairs."

"I would agree with that," Soong said dryly, searching for a bottle of water in his pack. He was afraid it would be frozen into slush by now. "Except that the one upstairs looked human, and it must have been created less than fifty years ago. This one is older."

Graves muttered, "A lot older," but then let it go. "Who do you suppose made the other one?" he asked.

"Hard to say," Soong replied, warming his water bottle in his hands. "Same people who shot it with a phaser, I hope."

"Why, 'I hope'?"

"Because if it was two different people," Soong reasoned, "that doubles our chances that there's someone around who won't be happy we're here." The initial excitement of the find was wearing off and he was beginning to worry. Now, Graves was, too.

The professor, apparently, had also been thinking, but not about danger. No sooner did he touch down on the ledge (which he did much more gracefully than either Soong or Graves had), than he was kneeling by the body. Vaslovik stripped off his glove and stroked the frozen surface of the hand with his bare fingertips. As Soong had noted earlier, the figure's arms and hands seemed elongated, which could have been because of some deformation over time or, perhaps, because the artificial being had been constructed to resemble his maker's.

"This is extraordinary," Vaslovik breathed, speaking quickly and almost too low for Graves and Soong to hear him. "You've done scans, haven't you? What do they say? How does this compare to the one we found upstairs?"

"Difficult to say," Graves replied, doing his best (Soong thought) to sound blasé. "We'll need to get a sample and run it through a scanner. The sensors in these tricorders aren't sensitive enough—"

"Don't play games with me, Ira," Vaslovik said impatiently. "Use your tools—all of them, including your brain. What does your intuition tell you?"

Graves sighed softly, then murmured, his words almost absorbed by the ice, "They're the same. They have to be."

"I agree," Vaslovik said. "What do you think, Noonien?"

Soong hadn't expected to be asked anything, so he said the first thing that came into his mind. "This thing, whatever it is, didn't climb down here to die. He may have been on the bridge when it shattered. So, that's two . . . artificial beings . . ."

"Androids," Vaslovik said. "Call them androids. That's what they are."

"All right," Soong admitted, and a strange thrill went through him at the sound of the word. *"Androids.* Two *androids* who were destroyed by violence. That's two out of the two we found. So, my question is: Are there any more? If so, where are they? And why do I get the feeling they might not be happy to see us?"

Vaslovik turned away from their find and began examining the cliff wall. "Those," he said, "are all very good questions. And I can think of only one way we might be able to answer them." Suddenly Vaslovik aimed his light at the cliff face, revealing something Soong had completely overlooked until now: an outline in the rock. No, not an outline. A *door.*

"And when were you planning on explaining all this to me?" Soong asked, popping open the legs of the pattern enhancer and dropping it onto the floor of the ledge, probably a little more carelessly than he should have. He didn't care, he decided. He was angry. And tired. And he was the only one who could climb out of here if he had to. Ha! Let Graves and Vaslovik try to make it up to the surface without a transporter.

"I'm explaining it to you now," Vaslovik stated, straining to sound reasonable. "Because it has become necessary and prudent to do so."

"And it wasn't necessary when I was dangling halfway down the cliff?" he asked irritably. His resources were at a low ebb and it seemed easier somehow to be irked than to be reasonable. Everything ached and he was cold and he wasn't going to get Vaslovik to admit he had done anything wrong. "You told me," he said, "that we were looking for archaeological artifacts, remnants of an ancient civilization that might have made androids."

"We were," Vaslovik replied coolly. "And we found some."

"What we found," Soong said, pointing the pry bar up at the top of the cliff, "was a room that had once been some kind of a lab, a room that has recently been stripped to the walls. Then, near the precipice, we found the first body . . . no, correction, an android body."

Vaslovik nodded. "Call it Brown. He'd been destroyed by a phaser blast."

"Yes," Soong said. "Whatever you say, but you're evading the point. It looked human, much more so than this one here. It can't be an archaeological artifact."

"That's debatable," Vaslovik said.

Soong rubbed his face with his gloved hand and heard the brush of stubble. "How could that be debatable?" he asked. "All the readings indicate that it must have been done relatively recently. What could be 'archaeological' about something done with a phaser?"

"The body was destroyed by a phaser about forty years ago," Vaslovik said. "But that doesn't mean it couldn't have been quite old. It's difficult to say without more research, but it's all connected."

Soong felt the growing desire to take a swing at the professor with the pick—a sure sign that he was on the edge of exhaustion. "What's all connected?" Soong asked, exasperated. "Assume for a moment that I don't have a clue what you're talking about. I am not a servant or a hired man. I am not Dr. Watson to your Sherlock

Holmes. If you want my cooperation, you'll tell me everything you know, or I'll simply beam back to the ship and take a nap."

They locked eyes and Soong actually believed he felt Vaslovik wrestling with him for control of his mind. It would be easier, he found himself thinking, so much easier, to simply acknowledge Vaslovik as the master, to take directions and obey orders, to absolve himself of responsibility. Then, whatever happened, Soong would be able to say (to himself, if no one else), "I was following orders." But then, he would not share in any of the glory either, and Soong was just young enough and just ambitious enough to believe glory was an end in itself.

Vaslovik seemed to sense these thoughts, too. It must have been a long time—an extraordinarily long time—since someone had been willing to challenge him, because then he smiled. And it wasn't an indulgent smile either, but the smile of one master acknowledging another. Soong felt . . . vindicated, as if he were finally being treated like one of the adults.

"All right," Vaslovik said, speaking low. "Here's what I learned before we came here: there was a device in the room upstairs. It duplicated things."

"Things?" Soong asked skeptically.

"People."

"Clones?" Soong felt both revulsion and disappointment rise up within him. All this fuss for clones?

"No, no," Vaslovik said. "Not clones. Not exactly. My sources claimed the machine made biosynthetic copies of humanoids. In a word: androids. That, in and of itself, is interesting, but the fascinating part is that the device would also make a copy of an organic subject's mind and embed it in the android body."

That seemed to get Graves's attention. "Are you serious?"

"Very," Vaslovik said.

Soong quivered on the cusp of fascination and incredulity. It didn't seem possible. . . . No living civilization in this part of the galaxy possessed that kind of technological or physiological information. . . . And then it hit him. No living civilization. An archaeological expedition. "Okay," he said. "I get it now. Fine . . . assuming that any of this is true, it leads to the question: Who would make such a thing? And why? And where did it go? And do I even want to know how you found out about it? This isn't the sort of thing they circulate in the faculty newsletter."

"Answering your questions in order," Vaslovik said slyly. "I don't know who made it, not precisely, though I should think the why of it would be obvious given a little thought. That's why we came here—to learn more. Where is it now? Only Starfleet knows for sure, though I strongly suspect the pinnacles of virtue who found it subsequently destroyed it to keep it from being misused. Fortunately for us, they missed disposing of the relic we found upstairs, and never probed deeper into the planet. As for whether or not you want to know how I know all this: the answer is *No, you don't want to know.* And you'd be surprised how much useful information can be found in the faculty newsletter if you know how to read it."

"Starfleet?" Soong sputtered. He fixated on the word as soon as it was spoken. "Why would Starfleet do something like that? It's their job—"

"Don't be naive," Vaslovik interrupted angrily. "Starfleet's job, first and foremost, is to keep the peace, which, if you don't already know this, translates into maintaining the Federation's sovereignty. Never forget that. And starship captains are notorious for thinking with their hearts, not their heads. What they deem too dangerous, they destroy." Vaslovik looked away and Soong heard him mutter, "And what they covet, they claim for their own."

"I'm not understanding this," Soong said. "You're saying that Starfleet thought this technology was so dangerous, they destroyed it? Then, with all due respect, Professor, exactly what the hell are we doing here?"

To Soong's surprise, the corner of Vaslovik's mouth quirked up and then he laughed. "We're doing what Starfleet should have done. We're going to learn the truth, and then decide what to do with the knowledge."

Soong sighed and rubbed the bridge of his nose. "All right," he agreed slowly. "Fine. But first, explain that." He turned and pointed at the massive hatchway set into the cliff wall.

From the look of it, at some point in the dim past, enough calcareous water had dripped down the cliff to form huge stalactites, but Graves and Soong had broken them away with pry bar and pick. Unfortunately, they had had no luck with the hatch itself despite several hours of exhausting attempts, both with electronic devices and brute force.

As they watched, Graves wound up with his pry bar and swung. The bar clanged off the hatch without leaving a mark. Graves dropped the bar into the dust at his feet and let go with a curse. Soong was beginning to believe Graves was the most foul-mouthed individual he'd ever known.

"I think," Vaslovik said, approaching the door, "we can abandon the direct approach."

Graves grinned sheepishly and wiped a coating of

gray dust off his forehead. "Good," he said. "I can't feel my hands anymore."

Vaslovik smiled grimly, but did not otherwise respond as he unzipped his parka and reached into an inner pocket. Soong waited expectantly to see what he would pull out and was confused to see that it was only a stylus and a very old-fashioned-looking one at that. Handling it gingerly, Vaslovik twisted the base of the stylus until a tiny antenna shot out of the cap. He began to twirl the base from side to side, all the time studying a tiny display that opened on the pen's stem. Soong heard a high-pitched whine that forced him to grit his teeth and take a step back.

"What is that?" he asked.

"Just a gadget," Vaslovik said absently, concentrating on his adjustments. "Something I acquired a few years ago. It's scanning the mechanism and looking for a resonant frequency just in case the lock is designed to . . ." He paused, seemed to struggle for the right words. "It's hard to explain, actually."

"I'll bet," Soong said skeptically.

Then, from the hatch there came a loud, menacing click, just exactly the sort of noise Soong would expect to hear from, say, the door for the main vault of the treasury building on the Klingon home world. Graves took a step back.

Somewhere in the hatch, tumblers shifted. Soong felt his skin crawl with invisible static electricity bugs. Then, there came a thin hiss of air pressure equalizing.

"How long did you say you thought this hatch has been shut?" Soong asked softly and, he hoped, casually.

"I didn't," Vaslovik replied.

"Hmm. Good bearings on the door, then."

Stepping forward, Vaslovik replied, "I've always said you can always judge a culture by the quality of the ball bearings it produces." He caught the lip of the hatch with a forefinger and pulled. The hatch swung open, releasing a cloud of stale, dry, warm air. Light panels on the walls and ceilings flickered on, revealing a featureless antechamber that terminated in a second hatch.

"Some kind of airlock," Soong observed.

"Or a trap," Graves muttered.

"Mmmm," Vaslovik responded, resting one foot on the lip of the hatch. He scanned the chamber, first with the tricorder, then with the penlike device. "Nothing," he said, "which doesn't really mean anything. Whoever built this could easily deceive our sensors. No wonder Starfleet never found this." He paused, apparently considering his options. Then, before Soong could stop him, Vaslovik stepped into the antechamber.

Nothing happened.

Graves released his breath. "Please don't ever do that again," Graves hissed between gritted teeth.

"Sorry," Vaslovik said without looking back. "It seemed like the simplest solution. And, besides, you would have to be truly paranoid to build a bomb into an airlock hatch. One way in, one way out. Why clutter it up with explosives?"

"Sounds like something you've put some thought to," Soong observed.

"Oh, certainly," Vaslovik replied. "And you will, too, someday. When you're older."

He fixed his sights on a keypad in the opposite wall. Approaching it, he held the stylus out before him and the device began to whine softly. Soong and Graves glanced at each other, shrugged in unison, then crowded in close to watch. Moments later, a mechanism inside the hatch clicked and popped away from the rim.

Graves, obviously feeling brave now, tugged the hatch open and stepped into the second room. Soong knew they were pushing their luck and half-expected to see phasers erupt from the walls, but the only sign of movement was lights flickering on.

This room was not empty.

It was much larger than the antechamber, though almost as austere. There were several narrow platforms along one wall—most likely beds, Soong decided, though the bedclothes had rotted away to dust ages ago. A wide, waist-high cube surrounded by a half-dozen smaller cubes looked like they may have been what passed locally for a dining area. A bank of machines set into a partially screened-off corner might have been the communications or entertainment center.

Soong took all these things in with a glance and the fact that he could recognize the objects indicated that these long-dead beings must have shared some basic biological and psychological traits with humans. *Of course,* Soong thought. *They built humanoid androids.* It was a trivial observation, one that barely needed voicing even to himself, but thinking about it meant he could put off the more difficult question of what to make of the contents of the room.

First and foremost, there was The Machine, which dominated the room and left no doubt in Soong's mind that it was the primary reason for the heavily armored doors. Soong's intuitive ability to analyze technology quickly grasped that this device must be a duplicating machine, like the one Vaslovik had referred to earlier. Either that, or something very near to it.

But, as amazing as this discovery was, it paled in comparison to the other, to the reality of The Body.

It lay facedown in the center of the floor, perfectly illuminated by an overhead light, almost like this room was center stage of a dramatic presentation and this was the single object where the audience was meant to focus its attention. It certainly had Soong's attention. It was quite a contrast to the body they had found on the rock shelf. That one had been exposed to the elements, petrified into something very like the stone where it had lain for who knew how long.

But not so with this body. This copper-skinned individual was perfectly preserved. Soong could easily imagine him standing up, brushing himself off, and saying, "Pardon me . . ."

. . . If not for the large hole in the center of its back.

"That must have hurt," Graves muttered.

Vaslovik glared at him. "Anyone have anything useful to say? Any ideas about what might have killed it?"

Soong was tempted to say, "The big hole," but confined himself to saying, "Some kind of energy weapon. Look at how smooth the edges are."

"Good observation, Noonien."

Soong couldn't stop himself from asking: "But how was it shot if it was alone inside a locked room?"

Surprisingly, Graves was the one to assume the voice of reason. "Shooter might have transported out. Or, maybe it wasn't shot in the room at all, but merely died here."

Vaslovik was studying the scene intently, apparently trying to reconstruct events from half a million years ago. "If it fell face first, then it was facing the large appartatus when it expired. It may have come here to repair itself, but collapsed before it reached the mechanism. . . ."

"We may never know for certain," Graves said. He activated his tricorder. "We should take readings before we disturb anything."

Vaslovik nodded. "Excellent point, Ira. We have no idea how fragile any of this is. It could all crumble into dust any moment."

The whine of tricorders echoed strangely in the enclosed space, but the familiar sounds helped Soong shake off some of his anxiety. When they were sure they had taken enough readings, Soong and Graves entered the room and approached The Machine. While they scanned it, Vaslovik examined the corpse. It did not, as he had feared, crumble into dust.

"Well?" Vaslovik asked after a time. "Will it work?"

Graves and Soong exchanged glances. They each had been expecting someone to ask the question. Finally, Soong said, "Possibly. If there's an energy source. Whoever built this made it to last. It's just that . . ." He hesitated.

"What?"

"What are you proposing?" Soong asked.

Vaslovik sighed. "I'm proposing that we help our friend here to get where he was trying to go. If he revives, he'll be able to answer a lot of questions. And if he doesn't . . ." He shrugged. "We'll probably learn a lot in the process. If nothing else, we can take some baseline readings, see what this thing might be capable of."

Again, Graves and Soong looked at each other. Vaslovik was so good at making crazy ideas sound reasonable. Graves smiled apologetically and said, "Sounds like a good topic for your dissertation, Noon."

Soong laughed. Graves had never called him by his

first name before, but the gesture had done its job. He threw his arms up in surrender. "Fine. Yes. No doubt."

"Good," Vaslovik said. "Now that we've settled that, someone give me a hand here." Vaslovik slipped his hands under the android's arms and finished, "We don't have forever." And though Soong never understood the significance of it, he could not help but notice Vaslovik's small, secret smile at this private joke.

Chapter Twelve

BEVERLY CRUSHER STARED at the ceiling tiles above the nurse's station and tried to remember the last time she had spent more than twenty-four hours off the *Enterprise*. Six weeks? Two months? More? Adjusting to planetside wasn't the sort of thing that usually bothered her, but her sleep–wake cycle was out of sync with local time and she was beginning to feel the effects. She knew she could find something in her medkit, a mild stimulant, that would get her around the horn, but, then, if Maddox suddenly recovered—or worse, died—she would be stuck with the same predicament when she returned to the ship. She decided to tough it out. Her shift would be over in . . . how long? She had completely lost track of time.

She searched the desktop and found the chrono: 1530. Felt like midnight. It was as quiet as midnight, especially compared to what she was used to in the *Enterprise*'s sickbay. There were only two staff on duty, an

Andorian technician everyone called Po and the day shift's head nurse, Maury Sullivan.

"Maury," Crusher asked. "Is the replicator still down?"

Maury looked up from the chart she was checking and nodded grimly. "I've been trying to get Maintenance to look at it all day, but it's hard to get anyone's attention for long around here if it doesn't involve splitting elementary particles." Crusher smiled at the comment and Maury grinned, pleased. "Is it like that onboard a starship?"

Crusher shook her head. "No," she said, then added as an afterthought, "not usually, anyway. Besides, everyone knows to keep the doctor happy."

Maury laughed, delighted. "That must be nice. The best we can do around here is threaten to withhold antacids."

"Not quite the leverage one would hope for," Crusher commented. "Tell you what: you tell me where to get a decent cup of coffee and I'll ask someone from the *Enterprise* to take a look at your replicator."

"Ooo," Maury said, hopping out of the chair, "you have got yourself a deal. How do you take it?"

"No, no," Crusher said. "Just tell me where to go."

Maury waved her hand dismissively. "Forget it. You'll never find it. I think they designed this place to be some sort of perverse intelligence test. It would take you forever to find your way there." She paused. "And besides, my husband works in the lab next to the canteen. I can stop and say hi."

"Oh." Crusher said, slightly disappointed. She had been thinking a walk would be nice, too. "Okay. What do I do if someone calls?"

"They won't," Maury said, heading for the door, "but if they do, well, you're the one they want to talk to. You're the doctor."

"I suppose that's true," Crusher said, more to herself than to anyone else since Maury was already out the door. Then, she leapt up and yelled, "Cream and sugar."

And then it was very quiet, except for the *ping* of some distant monitoring equipment and the occasional puff of air from vents. Crusher thought about calling the *Enterprise* and checking on the state of sickbay, but she had done that only a couple of hours ago and if she did it again, the staff would think she was being a pest. Deciding that she needed something—anything—to focus on, she turned to the library computer and pulled up Maddox's medical records.

Crusher had checked all the scans the ICU staff had run before she had arrived and then run tests of her own, but both sets had shown precisely the same thing: nothing. No neurological injury. No infectious agent. No historeaction. No implanted biomechanical device. Maddox was unconscious, in a state that more closely resembled sleep than a coma. There was brain activity, but it was disorganized, jumbled and unresponsive to the environment. It was almost, she decided, like Maddox's brain was encased in some kind of force field, cutting it off from any outside stimulus. The worst part, the part that she tried not to think about too much, was that Maddox might be in there somewhere trying to figure out how to get to the other side.

Maybe we should run the scans again. Maybe we've missed something. Maybe there's something wrong with their equipment and I should transfer him to the Enterprise. She laid her head down on the desk. *Maybe I should take a nap.* She would close her eyes for a minute, just a minute. Maury would be back soon. If someone needed her, the call would wake her up. She was good at waking up quickly. She was a doctor.

"Doctor?"

Crusher shot up in her chair. "Yes?" she said too loudly.

"Were you asleep?"

It wasn't Maury's voice. She almost tapped her combadge thinking it was the *Enterprise* calling, but then she looked around behind her.

"Data? No. I mean, yes, I guess I was, but I didn't mean to be. How long . . . ?"

"I entered the room only thirty-five seconds ago, so I cannot say for certain."

Crusher glanced at the nearby chrono, then tried to remember what time it had been the last time she looked. She wasn't certain, but it couldn't have been long. Five minutes, maybe? She quickly checked Maddox's monitor and found exactly what she expected to find: Maddox, unconscious, unmoving.

"I . . . Okay, Data. I'm sorry. I'm a little disoriented." She combed her hair back from her eyes with her fingers and tried to shake the gummy feeling out of her brain. "What can I do for you?"

Data moved around to sit in the chair where Maury Sullivan had been seated. He seemed a little hesitant, almost, Crusher thought, embarrassed. "I came," he said, "because I was curious about Commander Maddox's condition and wondered if you had any information that you did not report in your last log entry. I know you sometimes choose to withhold speculations."

Crusher felt the corners of her mouth curl up, surprised to discover that Data knew so much about her report-writing style. "That's true," she replied. "But, unfortunately this time, I didn't. Commander Maddox's body has healed and, as far as I've been able to determine, there's no organic damage to his brain. Unfortunately, we haven't figured out how to reach his mind. There may be something we haven't thought of yet, but . . ." Her train of thought petered out and she shrugged. "There isn't much more to say, I'm afraid."

"I see," Data said, frowning, the tone of his voice making it obvious that he didn't see at all. "Is there anything I can do to assist you, Doctor?"

Crusher shook her head, then said, "When I talked to the captain this morning . . . wait, last night . . ." She rubbed her forehead. *I hate dirtside lag,* she thought, then began again. "He said you were investigating the accident. Shouldn't you be concentrating your efforts there?"

Data looked down at his interlaced fingers and actually twiddled his thumbs. For a moment, Crusher wondered if he was trying out a new mannerism. "The investigation has reached an impasse, Doctor. I confess I was hoping there might be some chance Commander Maddox might simply awaken and tell us what occurred. That is, I see, an unrealistic expectation . . ."

Crusher nodded, touched by Data's evident disappointment. Then, moved by the shadow of an intuition, she asked, "Is there something else, Data?"

"What do you mean, Doctor?"

"Is there something else you wanted to ask me?"

"I . . . well, yes," Data said, then paused for a long moment. "There is something I have been thinking about a great deal lately and I was hoping you might be able to . . ." He hesitated again, obviously struggling to find the right words. It was quite unlike Data's usual calm demeanor. Then she remembered her last conversation with Jean-Luc and his mentioning the stir created when Data and Rhea McAdams had gone dancing. Was

Data about to ask for a lesson in waltzing? Romantic advice? Information about the birds and the bees?

Suddenly, Beverly Crusher felt much more alert . . . and strangely on edge.

But then she realized that Data wasn't thinking about the birds and the bees; she could see it in his eyes. He was thinking about other fundamentals. "It occurred to me recently," he said, "that there is no one in my circle of . . . friends . . ." He paused for a moment to give her a chance, she realized, to react to the use of the word "friend." Data was much closer to the other members of the senior staff, mostly because he worked more closely with them, but also because he had no particular need for her services. When Data had a "medical" problem, he usually went to see Geordi, not her. In any case, Crusher kept her face neutral and nodded for him to continue. ". . . who has had so much experience with death as you." He paused again, watching Crusher's face carefully, perhaps to gauge her reaction.

Crusher didn't find it difficult to keep her expression neutral. She was the chief medical officer of Starfleet's flagship and had served a term as the head of Starfleet Medical. It took a lot for her to display shock. That was not to say she wasn't a bit surprised with the turn the conversation had taken. She wet her lips with the tip of her tongue and nodded. "I suppose that's true, Data. I mean, as a physician, I've seen my share of death . . . though not too much, I hope. That's not one of the things you want to hang on your shingle . . ."

Data looked at her quizzically. She shook her head. "Never mind, Data. It was a silly comment. Perhaps if you told me why you want to talk about this . . ."

"Because, Doctor," Data said, "I have been experiencing emotional fallout from the knowledge that I may live a great deal longer than, speaking frankly, *everyone* I know. According to the projections I have been calculating, without modifications of any sort to my neural net or positronic brain, I will probably live for a minimum of—"

"Stop right there, Data," Crusher said, feeling slightly peeved, but unable to say precisely why. "I get the idea—a long time. Please explain why you feel the need to discuss this with me."

Data's brow knotted, aware that he had upset her in some manner that he couldn't define, then began to stand, saying, "My apologies, Doctor. I have offended you. I will go." Before he could stand straight, however, Crusher was waving him back into his seat.

"No, no, Data. I'm sorry," she said. "I'm just a little out of sorts. Let me guess: you're wondering what it's like to have patients die, how I feel when it happens."

Data nodded. "Yes," he said, "and also how you feel knowing that some of the people you might be treating when that happens are your friends. How do you cope with knowing that you might be . . . left behind."

Crusher almost smiled despite herself, so suddenly came the understanding for why she had been feeling so put out with Data. This was, she realized, precisely the tone of the conversations she used to have with Wesley when he had been eleven or twelve years old, just on the cusp of adolescence and wrestling with the weighty moral and ethical concerns of a young man discovering his place in a larger universe. Data was reminding her of her son and it was not sitting well with her.

Crusher and Troi had spent many long evenings discussing her son's fate—his journey of self-discovery accompanying the mysterious Traveler on an inter-galactic quest—but no matter how Deanna sliced it, the story amounted to the same thing. Wesley was, for now at least, lost to her and she missed him terribly. She understood that he might return someday, possibly grown into a man, possibly unchanged by the years that were beginning to weigh on her, but the uncertainty was galling and she feared the passage of time might make her bitter.

And now, here was Data, who had been one of Wes's closest friends, making her think of the one person whose memory caused her the greatest pain. No wonder she was feeling edgy. Data didn't understand the emotional mine-field he was stumbling through and it would be unfair to punish him. He was struggling with problems of his own.

"That's a difficult question you're asking, Data, one that people in the medical profession wrestle with constantly. I'll answer you the same way I answered Wes many years ago: the hardest part of being a doctor isn't knowing that you might sometimes lose patients; it's knowing that someday you might get used to it." She paused for a moment to let the thought sink in, then continued. "I've talked to doctors who have been on the front lines, with units fighting the Dominion, and I can tell you this: the blackest terror they face is knowing they've seen so much death that they've gone numb in-side. They cease to care, they seal themselves off, be-cause they can't cope with the level of pain and suffering. They do the job, but part of them dies, too."

Data nodded. "I can see how that—"

"I'm not finished, Data," she said. "I wanted to tell you one more thing. The reason I've been talking to those field doctors is because I've been helping Starfleet

Medical screen the doctors who go to the front lines—psych evaluations, personal profiles, that sort of thing. Here's the worst part, the thing we don't talk about too much: we can't risk sending the ones who would care too much, either. We have to choose, and we choose the ones who can save some part of themselves and do the job. It's a fine line we all walk every day: how much can we care? How much can we burden ourselves before we reach the point where we cannot see that it might be time to stop?"

Crusher saw an expression of confusion, of something close to despair, wash across Data's features and she stopped herself. She was, she realized, saying too much. Data had been looking for a foothold, an anchor, and she was sweeping him out to sea. "But that's the worst of it," she said, changing tacks. "The best of it is that doctors and nurses, all of us, are blessed . . ." She waved her hand around the ICU and gave Data a moment to let her choice of words sink in. "Occasionally, we get to see miracles, to see things that we can't explain, but know to be true. There's something inside human beings, something inside all sentient things, I believe, that can surprise even the most jaded of us . . ." She lapsed into silence, not knowing exactly how to finish the thought, but hoping Data would take some comfort from it.

"And what of Commander Maddox?" he asked, turning to look at the monitor. "Has he reached the point where his only hope is a miracle?"

Crusher pondered the question, wondering whether the truth was the best response or a little sugarcoating was called for. She decided to go with something in between. "Maybe not quite that yet. There are still a couple things we can try. But—and I'm not too proud to admit this—every good doctor knows that sometimes the point comes when a patient might best be served by a power beyond herself." She smiled, feeling her response was inadequate, but unable to think of anything better. She recalled that the weighty conversations with Wes frequently ended on such unsatisfactory notes, too.

"Thank you, Doctor," Data said. "I appreciate your candor . . . and for sharing your thoughts with me. And, again, if there is ever anything I can do for you . . ."

Wondering what had happened to Maury, Crusher was suddenly struck by a thought. "Actually, Data, there is. There's a replicator in that room . . ." She pointed in the general direction of the lounge. "It isn't working. Do you have a minute to take a look at it?"

Data seemed surprised, but then shrugged and perked up, pleased at the opportunity to do something for her. "Of course, Doctor. I do not have any tools, but I could at least make a diagnosis. . . ." He grinned, pleased with his little joke.

They rose together and she walked him out from behind the nurse's station, but she didn't want to stray too far from the monitors. Silly, she knew, given the level of reliable automated medical technology supplementing Maddox's care, but it was the physician's curse to never fully trust any mechanical device. As Data headed toward the lounge, Crusher turned back to the nurse's station, but then suddenly, looking down the hall, she could see into the dimly lit area where Maddox was lying and thought she saw . . . something. But what? A shadow moving in Maddox's room?

Had Maury returned from the canteen and passed by the nurse's station without Crusher noticing? But, no, that didn't feel right. She wasn't that tired. Crusher started toward Maddox's room, but stopped when someone close behind her said, "Doctor Crusher?"

Startled, she spun around and felt her hand come into contact with a cup of hot coffee. Crusher's senses, already jump-started by the shadowy form in Maddox's room, went into overdrive. Time slowed down. The mug and the steaming liquid made a very pretty parabola. The ruckus brought Data running and Maury, who had never before seen a gold-skinned, yellow-eyed android, yelped and jumped out of the way. Data lost his footing in the puddle of coffee and only kept himself from flopping over backward onto the floor by grabbing Crusher's outstretched hand.

"I'm sorry!" Crusher said—much too loudly—while simultaneously trying to look back over her shoulder toward Maddox's room. All she succeeded in doing, however, was badly twisting her left ankle. "Dammit!" she shouted, trying to keep Data on his feet while at the same time trying not to put any weight on her injured ankle.

"What is it?" Maury shouted. "What's going on?"

"Maddox," she tried to say, pointing toward the room, hopping on one foot. Maury didn't wait for another word, but took off for the room, Data at her heels. She was the last to reach the room and leaned heavily on the doorframe, favoring her ankle. Maury was checking all the monitors and looking puzzled.

"What was it?" she asked, confusion in her voice. "I don't see anything."

And neither did Crusher. Everything looked perfectly normal. The biobed blinked contentedly. Maddox's heart beat steadily. He breathed in and out and dreamed who knew what dreams?

"I . . . I don't know," Crusher said. "I was sure I saw someone . . . Data, give me a hand back down the hall." Data grabbed her arm and half-guided, half-carried her back to the nurse's station.

Maury was standing on the other side of the station looking down at the two of them. "Would someone please tell me what just happened?" she asked, her voice cracking a little.

Crusher looked up at the nurse and smiled apologetically. "I'm sorry," she said. "I don't know. But I think I might need some sleep."

"Good," Maury replied, accepting the apology, "because I don't think any more coffee is a good idea."

Maury went to get the muscle regenerator, leaving Crusher standing on one foot. She scanned the hall, willing something to be out of place. But nothing was, which only made her that much more angry.

Chapter Thirteen

RHEA MCADAMS SNORED.

Loudly.

Data found this entrancing.

Upon returning to his lab, he found McAdams leaning on a console, her head cushioned on her forearms, with a tiny bead of saliva suspended from the corner of her mouth. At first, he didn't know what to do, having very little experience with sleeping people. Though he could "sleep," that is, shut down his system to a degree and enter a state resembling human unconsciousness, it was not something that he had to do. Rather, it was something he did because he found it interesting and even, occasionally, revealing. He could also dream—the part of sleeping he found most intriguing—and enjoyed replaying and analyzing the random images his subsystems generated.

But he had very little experience with the social customs involving human sleep. Should he leave? Somehow announce his presence? Move as quietly as possible?

Rhea solved the problem for him by waking on her own, stirred by the sound of the doors as he entered. She lifted her head and Data noticed that the side of her face was mottled with red stripes because the sleeve she had rested her head against was wrinkled. A lock of hair stuck out at an odd angle. He was captivated by these things, too. Rhea yawned. "What time is it?"

"It is seventeen hundred hours, forty-five minutes," Data replied. He almost added, "And forty-two seconds," but decided against it, having learned over the years that humans, typically, were not interested in that level of detail. Instead, he asked, "How long have you been asleep?"

Rhea looked around the room, orienting herself in time and space. "I don't know," she replied, rubbing at something in the corner of her mouth. "When did you leave?"

"Approximately two hours ago."

"Then I think that's when I fell asleep." She looked down at Data's legs. "It was his fault," she said pointing at Spot. "He was sitting on my lap and . . . and . . . purring. It was very, what's the word? Soporific."

"He is a cat," Data said. "That is what he does."

"That's not an excuse," Rhea replied, smiling and rubbing her eyes. "Do you want some coffee? No, wait—of course you don't. I do." She stood, cracked her back, and walked stiffly toward the replicator. "Coffee, hot," she said. "Double cream, one sugar." The replicator chimed and she carefully removed the steaming cup. Blowing on the coffee, Rhea asked, "What news from the surface?"

Data shook his head. "Nothing very encouraging, except that the Intensive Care Unit now has a functional replicator." Rhea regarded Data quizzically, but she didn't ask for more detail and he didn't offer any. He continued, "Did your analysis of the interviews with the Institute personnel yield any results?"

"Nothing very useful. I've decided that Commander Maddox was neither the most popular or unpopular person on campus. You might be interested to know that part of the reason some people don't like him is because they feel his badgering you to return here for more studies actually alienated you."

This surprised Data, who had never felt badgered by Maddox and couldn't imagine why anyone would care. He expressed this opinion, causing Rhea to shake her head and chuckle. "You had no idea you're a bit of a celebrity down there, did you?"

"No."

Rhea finished her coffee, replaced the cup in the replicator and asked for a refill. "So, you're modest, too. I don't know what my mother would make of you."

"Why would your mother care if I was modest?"

Removing the cup from the replicator, Rhea replied, "I think my mother had a fairly low opinion of men in general. She thought most of them were, well, she used to use the word, 'phony.' "

Data considered this. "I do not think I am phony," Data replied, then paused. "However, I am artificial. Do you think that would have concerned her?"

"You know," Rhea said, "I've been thinking about that myself the past couple days and the truth is, I don't think she would care much at all. My mother wasn't very concerned with where people came from. She was more interested in what they were made of."

"I am composed of approximately 24.6 kilograms of tripolymer composites, 11.8 kilograms of molybdenum-cobalt alloys and 11.8 kilograms of bioplast sheeting. My skull—"

"That's not what I meant."

"I know. I was trying to be funny."

"Ah," McAdams said. "I just woke up. I never get jokes for the first ten-or-so minutes after I wake up. File that away somewhere." Data did so. "Anyway," Rhea continued, "no, not much from the other researchers about Maddox. Concerning Vaslovik—well, there's another story."

"That is encouraging," Data said.

"No," Rhea replied. "You misunderstand. I mean . . . nobody knew anything about him. He didn't work with anyone except Maddox, not even Barclay, really, though I think the lieutenant was embarrassed to admit that. Vaslovik never socialized with anyone, ever. Would you believe, no one even knew where he lived? The only way I could find out was to check the DIT personnel database, which had his address, but not much else."

"Have you investigated his dwelling?"

"Not yet," Rhea said. "I was waiting for you . . . and then I fell asleep. But I figure we can take a look later. That's about what I've accomplished in the past, what? Twenty-four hours? Doesn't seem like much. Anything new on your side?"

Data shook his head. "No, nothing."

"What about an isolation suit? You know, the kind Starfleet personnel use to cloak themselves when conducting covert sociological studies of prewarp cultures."

"I considered that. The suits give off a unique energy signature, which would have shown up in the full-spectrum sweep the Institute's security team conducted when they first arrived on the scene. It did not."

"So we've yet to come up with anything to support the idea that someone else was involved in the incident."

"Unfortunately, that is true," Data said, "and I must confess, I am beginning to doubt my 'instincts.' "

"Why?" McAdams asked.

"Because we have not yet been able to advance one plausible theory for why this incident occurred."

"I can think of several," McAdams said. "A personal vendetta against one of the project members, an espionage mission gone awry, technological sabotage, maybe even terrorism."

"I have considered these possibilities as well," Data said. "None of them explains why Maddox wrote out my name at the scene."

"Maybe it wasn't your name," McAdams speculated. "Maybe it meant to mean something else. 'Data' meant information a long time before you came along."

"True, but given my . . . uneasy history with Commander Maddox within the context of his AI research, and his apparent condition when he wrote the word in his own blood, he must have been trying to convey something to whoever found him in the simplest, most expedient way possible."

"All right, let's look at that, then. Why would Maddox write your name?"

"The simplest answer is that he meant to implicate me in the incident."

"But you weren't there."

"True. I was on my way to Atrea IV to retrieve my mother's remains when this incident occurred."

"Can you prove that?"

"The shuttlecraft's records, the record of my time spent on Atrea IV, as well as Atrean eyewitnesses and my own memories, will verify that I traveled directly to Atrea IV after leaving the *Enterprise*. At the exact time of the incident, it would have been impossible for me to be anywhere near Galor IV."

"That's all right, I've already obtained most of that exculpatory evidence," Rhea said with a slight smile. "One of the first things I did, in fact. I'm convinced—and I suspect, so is everyone else, or you would have been detained immediately after you beamed down to the DIT—that you can be ruled out as a suspect here." McAdams started pacing the room. "But Maddox must have written your name for a reason, and the most obvious one would be that he thought you were there. So what if someone were impersonating you?"

"Can you ascribe a motive?"

"Again, to implicate you. Maybe our hypothetical vendetta wasn't against the project scientists at all. Maybe it was an elaborate plot to discredit you."

"Given the circumstances, I believe 'elaborate' would be an understatement. There would have been less problematical and more effective ways for an imposter to discredit me, if that were the goal."

"Agreed," said McAdams, and her pacing suddenly stopped before the cases holding the inert androids. She looked at Data. "What about Lore, then?"

Data hesitated. "As I explained earlier, that is not possible. Lore is dead."

"Data, I don't mean to be insensitive, but this investigation demands that we challenge any assumptions. So I have to ask. . . . Are you sure about that?"

Data felt an unpleasant surge of activity in his emotion chip. He stared at her for several seconds before he replied, and it was a struggle to keep his voice even.

"Yes, Rhea, I am. I deactivated Lore permanently. He will not be coming back."

McAdams went to him, concerned. "Data, I'm sorry. I realize that must be an old wound for you, and I don't mean to reopen it, but stranger things have been known to happen."

"Not this time," Data said. "After Lore was deactivated, I brought him to the *Enterprise*-D and disconnected his positronic brain to ensure that something like what you are suggesting would never happen. I kept it in a vault in my old lab, isolated from his body, and designed the vault to self-destruct in the event it was ever tampered with."

"What happened?"

"The *Enterprise*-D crashed on Veridian III. Lore's body was undamaged, but the vault containing his brain was compromised. The self-destruct system activated, and the brain was destroyed."

McAdams sighed heavily. "I'm sorry, Data. I had no idea."

"It is all right. You are doing your job. Your questions had to be raised. Unfortunately," Data said, pressing on, "it leaves us no closer to knowing the truth about the incident on Galor IV than when we started. If murder was the intent, why leave Maddox alive? If there is an organized force responsible, then why have they not identified themselves? Typically, such individuals claim responsibility for crimes in order to gain recognition."

"So what you're saying is that none of this adds up. It wasn't a personal attack, a terrorist act or an accident."

Data shook his head and lowered himself into a nearby chair. "No. What I am saying is that I fear *I* am not adding up. I fear . . . I fear my emotions may have . . . may *still* . . . be clouding my perceptions.

What I am saying is that I have begun to fear that I suspected a conspiracy because I very desperately wanted there to be a conspiracy." He sighed again. "I have been reviewing some psychological files and found that it is often a mark of immature or unformed individuals to see conspiracies where none exist."

Rhea walked over to him, knelt beside his chair and looked up into his lowered eyes. "Data," she said. "I think you have a couple other problems you should worry about first. Number one: you have an astonishing lack of self-confidence for someone who is, in fact, smarter, braver and, in most every conceivable way, better than any other man I've ever met, artificial or not. Second . . ." And here she smiled . . . "For some reason, I find that amazingly attractive."

Data looked down at Rhea and found that he could not resist the pull at the corners of his mouth. "It is," he said, "a risk I live with every day." And then, as if compelled by a power he did not fully comprehend, Data found he was leaning over, bringing his face closer to Rhea's. He had half-closed his eyes and could see that she had done the same, but his were open just enough for him to notice that she wore the same soft smile she had a moment before. He also noticed that she smelled faintly of cherries and sandalwood, an odd, though appealing combination of scents. He felt the faint outwelling of her breath on his lips, noted that he could almost taste the coffee on her breath, and heard some older, more distant part of himself say, *This day has taken some unexpected turns . . .*

. . . And then the door hissed open.

A pair of technicians guided in an antigrav gurney bearing a figure wrapped in plastic sheeting and, a moment later, Reg Barclay entered. Neither of the technicians were paying the slightest attention to Data and Rhea, but Reg looked at them curiously, obviously noting their proximity, then blushed furiously.

Rhea smiled at Data, then straightened up quickly and instructed the technicians where to settle the gurney.

When the techs had left, Barclay said, "We had trouble getting the body out from under the slab without bringing the rest of the building down on our heads." He flinched at the thought, then reached into his tool kit and pulled out a small blade, with which he began to cut the plastic in deft, sure strokes.

"Let me help you with that," Rhea said, stripping the sheeting away from the android's body as Barclay cut. When it was completely revealed, Data noted that the silver form looked, appropriately, as if a building had fallen on it. Gently, Rhea said, "Why not just take some baseline readings first?"

"Excellent suggestion," Data said, and then he and Barclay carefully positioned the gurney under the lab's central diagnostic array. Moving to the control console, Data brought the apparatus online and the sensors swept back and forth in a steady, rhythmic motion. He watched the datastream scroll down the screen and absorbed the readings as quickly as they were displayed. He began to nod his head quickly after the first several seconds, impatient for the array to get through with the predictable material: base composition; skeletal and muscular systems; circulatory and energy systems; sensory and motor functions.

Conscious that Barclay was looking over his shoulder, Data said, "Intriguing. There are several very interesting enhancements to my base systems here." He hit a combination of controls and brought up a display. "This auxiliary processing unit in the chest cavity is a compelling idea. I shall have to speak to Geordi about the feasibility of incorporating it into my own system."

Reg shrugged disparagingly, but smiled despite himself. "Most of the structural changes were Professor Vaslovik's ideas. My contribution was to the central processing center, the 'holotronic' brain, as Bruce dubbed it. Now *that* is a piece of work. . . ." He looked at the android's head and corrected himself: *"Was* a piece of work."

Data nodded sympathetically, then said, "Computer, pause." The scanners ceased to wave. "Return to grid seven-alpha-gamma-nine," he commanded. The tip of one of the scanners repositioned itself over the android's cranium.

"Enhance," Data requested. Barclay leaned forward to look at the display more closely.

The scanner tip glowed dull orange, then bright red and moved in small circles over the spot where the android's forehead would have been if it had still possessed an entire head. As it spun, Data and Reg leaned closer until their heads were almost side by side, noses practically pressed to the screen. Finally, Data reached over, flicked a switch, and the red tip faded to black.

Reg Barclay murmured, "Oh, my."

Data replied, "Indeed."

McAdams came over to get a look at the screen. "What is it?"

"The android is a fake," Data said, twenty minutes later.

The command crew had reconvened in the observation lounge, minus Dr. Crusher, who was still planetside, and sat around the table giving Data their undivided attention. Admiral Haftel was on screen, attending the conference from his office on the surface. It was he who spoke first.

"Are you saying that Commander Maddox and his associates were engaged in some sort of hoax?"

"No!" Reg shouted, almost leaping out of his chair. "Admiral—no! It's a fake, but not *our* fake." He shook his head. "I mean, we never made a fake. The android in Commander Data's quarters is . . . it could never have supported a holotronic system. The cranium was an empty shell . . . a husk . . ."

"A forgery," Data concluded. "But Mr. Barclay is doing it an injustice when he calls it an empty husk. Most of the systems an android would need to function were present, but when we examined the cranium, we discovered that there were only enough components present to give the appearance of a holotronic processing unit. Given the complexity of such a device and the difficulty of constructing even a reasonable facsimile, the fake could not stand up to careful scrutiny."

"Then why," Picard asked, "has this fact escaped everyone until now?"

"Misdirection, Captain," McAdams said. "And a perversely clever delaying tactic. Given the loss of life and level of destruction, not to mention the convenient difficulty of retrieving the prototype from the wreckage, whoever did this knew that a detailed scan of the android's brain wouldn't be an immediate priority. Why look for something that's obviously right in front of you?

"It also proves that there was a mind at work behind at least some of the events in the lab that night. Someone took the real android, for reasons still undetermined, and left evidence to make it appear as if it were merely destroyed."

"An abduction, then," Picard said, choosing his words deliberately. "Assuming you're correct, could the perpetrators have been responsible for the malfunctions that destroyed the lab and killed Professor Vaslovik?"

"It is certainly possible they used the storm to their advantage," Data answered. "Investigations into the malfunctions in the climate control system and power grids have not conclusively ruled out sabotage. As for the death of Professor Vaslovik—"

"Sir," McAdams interrupted, addressing Admiral Haftel. "The implications of this are staggering. If the project was successful, then advanced AI technology may now be in the hands of an enemy. Possibly a rival political entity, maybe even terrorists. The potential damage to the Federation—"

"I appreciate the implications, Lieutenant," Haftel said. "Where do we go from here, Mr. Data?"

Before Data could reply, McAdams's combadge chirped.

"This might be the confirmation we were waiting for," she said to Data. "McAdams here. Go ahead."

"Lieutenant, this is Chief O'Neil in database administration. I have that report you asked for."

"Proceed, Chief. I'm with the captain and Admiral Haftel and the senior staff. We were waiting for your call."

"All right," O'Neil replied, then cleared her throat. "I've finished checking those DIT databases you specified and it was exactly what you said to expect: the files have been wiped clean. All the directories we pulled were dummies. You try to open anything and the files vaporize. Worse, it's set up some kind of chain reaction that's scrubbing logs, directories, wiping clean operating systems, everything. Poof, gone."

McAdams smiled grimly, her suspicions confirmed. "No backups?" she asked. "What about the Starfleet Command master files?"

"Everything pertaining to the Maddox project is gone," O'Neil said. "Someone rewrote all the maintenance routines and copied the dummies into the Starfleet backup directories. It was . . . well, I hate to say this, but whoever did it could teach me a thing or two." Everyone in the ready room could hear the grudging respect in the chief's voice.

"Anything else, Chief?"

"Well—I'll say this: it wasn't done on the spur of the moment. Whoever planned this was thinking ahead—way ahead. And one other thing . . . It's a little odd, so I don't know what to make of it." She paused, obviously waiting for sanction.

"Go ahead, Chief," Picard said.

"It's just that some of the things I found, some of the file manipulation commands—either the programmer was insanely lucky or he knew about some trapdoors that no one else has ever identified."

Riker, who had been listening in silence, asked, "Come again? Trapdoors?"

"Trapdoor," Data explained. "Shortcuts that programmers install in command code in order to avoid repeating procedures or, more often, circumvent security programs."

"I'm still confused, Chief," Haftel said. "What does this mean?"

"It's just that the Institute's system—in fact, all of

Starfleet's systems—are based on the same code base. As strange as it might sound, all these codes, even the systems that have been augmented with non-Terran programming, share their origins in twenty-second- and twenty-third-century programming languages, especially the languages developed for the Daystrom duotronics systems. Whoever did this knew the code extraordinarily well. In fact, I'd say they knew things that have never been documented."

A stony silence reigned while everyone absorbed the implications of this statement. Finally, Haftel, focusing on the most immediate problem, asked, "And is there any way we can be certain whoever did this isn't meddling with other files?"

"Certain?" O'Neil asked. "No, not certain, though now that I've pointed out the trapdoor to the DIT's systems operator, it's been plugged. Could there be other holes? Absolutely. The perpetrator is so good, you might never know until it was too late."

"You sound," Haftel said, "as though you almost admire this person, Chief."

"No offense, Admiral. I understand the implications of what I'm saying, but good code is good code. Our perpetrator, whoever he or she is, had the advantage of a trapdoor, but he knew what to do once he got where he was going."

"No offense taken, Chief. I just wanted to make sure I understood the situation."

Picard said, "Please produce a report for the head of computing systems at Starfleet Command and send it to my priority queue, Chief. I'll authorize it and make sure it's filed today."

"Already there, Captain."

"Excellent. Good job, Chief." O'Neil signed off and Picard turned to McAdams.

"Have you and Commander Data assembled a list of likely suspects?"

"There is only one logical suspect, Captain," Data said. "And that is Professor Vaslovik."

Barclay blinked and sputtered. "P-Professor Vaslovik? But why?"

Riker seemed to share Barclay's surprise. "I'm afraid you're going to have to make this clear to me, too, Data. If this was a conspiracy, then Vaslovik overlooked one of the prime rules: Avoid getting vaporized in your own trap."

"But was he really vaporized, Commander?" Data asked. "That, like so much about Dr. Vaslovik, cannot be truly substantiated. DNA traces alone are not proof of a death. Vaslovik himself, as others have acknowledged, has been something of an enigma. In the course of our investigation, we found a long and detailed record of his work in neurocybernetics, but virtually nothing else about him."

"He was a very private individual," Barclay said, though he seemed to recognize the argument's weakness.

"One might go so far as to say obsessively private," Data replied. "And here is another intriguing fact: Admiral Haftel, did you know that Professor Vaslovik was a guest lecturer at the Daystrom Institute approximately seventy years ago?"

The long pause eloquently answered the question before Haftel even spoke. "We have no record of that, Data. Otherwise, I'm sure it would have come out in the course of the investigation . . . or when Commander

Maddox brought him onto his research team. What evidence do you have for this?"

"There is a reference to Vaslovik in one of Dr. Soong's earliest journals," Data explained. "Some of the substructures I saw in the holotronic android reminded me of references to my creator's earliest experiments. He had ideas for systems—particularly emotion emulation and information absorption subroutines—that he was never able to successfully develop."

"But you saw them in Maddox's android?" Picard asked.

"Yes, sir. When I checked Dr. Soong's journals, I found references to a 'Professor V.' After reviewing these entries, I have no doubt that he was speaking of Vaslovik. Apparently, my father met him at a seminar when he was an undergraduate. They must have exchanged ideas concerning artificial intelligence at that time."

"Why didn't you check for this earlier, Data?" Haftel asked.

Data raised an eyebrow, seemingly caught off guard by the question. "My apologies, Admiral, but my storage systems have not been designed in such a manner that I have simultaneous access to every one of my files. I periodically archive files based on an algorithm that examines—"

Picard waved his hand for Data to stop. "It's all right, Data. I think the admiral understands. If your information is correct, it could answer a great many questions."

"Such as," Geordi inserted, "how Vaslovik was able to use the trapdoor. If he was working at the DIT seventy years ago, he could have inserted the code easily enough."

"All right," Haftel said. "That makes sense, but it doesn't address the most important question: motivation. Why would Vaslovik want to steal the android? And *if* he's still alive, what has he done with it?"

"I cannot be certain about this, Admiral," Data admitted, "but I have begun to form a theory. The only way we can test it is to continue the investigation. Lieutenant McAdams and I have decided our next step should be to search Professor Vaslovik's home and 'toss the joint.' "

Everyone regarded Data quizzically, except for Picard, who was slowly rubbing his forehead and staring at the tabletop.

"Have I mishandled the slang, Captain?"

"No, Data. It's just . . . cultural illiteracy. No offense, Admiral."

"None taken, Captain."

"Mr. Data," Picard said, "assemble an away team. I want you there too, Number One."

"Aye, sir."

"Dismissed," Picard said.

Riker looked at Data and McAdams. "Transporter Room Three in ten minutes?"

Data nodded, and as everyone started to file out, Data turned to Barclay. "Would you join us as well, Lieutenant?"

Obviously still reeling from the day's revelations, Barclay nodded. "Absolutely, Commander."

Data found Rhea holding the turbolift for him. "Going my way?" she asked as he entered.

"I am going to Transporter Room Three. Is that not where you were going, too?"

"Well, yes. But the question wasn't meant to be taken literally. Transporter Room Three," she told the lift.

As their descent began, Data was still struggling to understand how else he should have taken the question. "I am confused," he said.

Rhea massaged the bridge of her nose and sighed. "Never mind," she said. "Are we going to have this conversation often?"

"Since I am not certain what 'this conversation' is," Data replied, "then my answer would have to be . . . yes?"

Rhea did not reply for the time it took for the turbolift to drop several floors, then chuckled softly. "Okay, point taken. I was just trying to lighten the mood. You seemed . . . tense."

"I did?" Data asked, fascinated. "How do I act when I seem tense?"

Rhea didn't respond immediately, then rolled her eyes. "All right," she admitted. "I'm tense. You caught me off guard in there when you started talking about Vaslovik. I thought we were going to check that out some more. I'm sorry . . . I'm not really very good with conflict."

Data replied, "But you are the head of security."

"Different kind of conflict," Rhea said.

"Oh," Data said, not completely understanding. "But are we not now going to investigate it? We are going to his home—"

"I meant check it out some more before talking to the captain."

Data felt abashed. "I . . . I did not understand that," he said. "Chief O'Neil's report seemed to me to be the confirmation we were looking for," he said cautiously.

"I suppose," McAdams said irritably, then rubbed the

bridge of her nose again. "I'm sorry. I get cranky when I don't get enough sleep."

"I will make a note of that," Data said cautiously. When McAdams didn't respond, he asked tentatively, "Does this disagreement mean that you have lost faith in me?"

Rhea looked up and saw that worry lines had appeared around the corners of Data's eyes. She reached up and smoothed the lines with her fingertips. "No, not that," she said. "Never that."

Chapter Fourteen

THE AWAY TEAM MATERIALIZED on the wide lawn beside a small A-frame building, rather unremarkable as private dwellings went. Looking up and down the narrow road, Riker noted that there were no other residences nearby, the closest being what looked like a small cabin on a hilltop almost 500 meters up the road, barely discernible through a stand of trees. He asked Barclay, "Have you been in this neighborhood before?"

Barclay nodded. "This is the Hollows, a couple of hundred kilometers north of the Institute. Most of the people who live out this far are longtime residents—staff members, technical staff, clerical workers. We, uh, transients, tend to live closer to campus."

McAdams consulted the address code near the entry-way. "This is the right house, though." It was an old-fashioned structure with wide, deep windows and slate tiles on the roof. There were two cane rocking chairs on the porch, both in need of paint, with a low table between them. There was an air of quaint shabbiness about the place and though they approached cautiously, tricorders humming, Riker found it hard to imagine a less threatening structure.

Which, naturally, made him feel that much more on edge. "Rustic," he said, then made a pass with the tricorder. "Nobody's home," he reported. "No defense systems, no surveillance equipment. In fact, I'm not reading any unusual EM signatures at all. Let's go knock."

Data was puzzled. "But you said no one was home."

"Just being polite, Data. One should always knock before one is about to 'toss a joint.' "

To no one's surprise, the door was unlocked. Vaslovik's home was scrupulously tidy. The team proceeded slowly from room to room, cautiously taking readings, making observations. Judging by the lack of household gadgetry, he appeared to cook his own meals, wash his own dishes and sweep his own floors. A small private library of leather-bound books contained a wide range of literature and historical nonfiction. In the living room, McAdams paused to look through some padds lying on a coffee table, but reported there was nothing noteworthy on them: technical and scientific publications, some general arts and humanities articles, current events downloads. "Eclectic reader," she commented.

"No one's been here for several days," Riker observed flatly. "Maybe longer."

"I agree," Barclay said, reviewing his tricorder readings.

"I don't see anything that makes me very suspicious," Rhea said. "He lived modestly, even spartanly, but this isn't the home of a transient." She picked up a small, intricately dyed ceramic dish and considered it appreciatively. "He didn't own many things, but he knew quality when he saw it."

"What *would* make you feel suspicious?" Riker asked.

"I don't know," McAdams replied. "What does a master criminal's country home feel like? Maybe I was expecting something that looked better, but felt worse."

The three of them looked for Data and found him standing outside the library, alternately waving his tricorder toward and then away from the entrance. "Something wrong, Data?"

Data pointed the tricorder away from the library, holding it so Riker could see the display. "Please continue to watch the display and tell me if you see anything anomalous."

Riker kept his eyes on the tricorder as Data panned it in a slow arc toward the library. When he finished, Riker looked up. "Can't say I did. Are you picking up something that we can't?"

"It is very peculiar, Commander," he said. "When the tricorder scan moves from any direction toward the library, the display flickers for approximately six milliseconds, much too quickly for human eyes to detect."

"But not for yours?"

"Evidently not. It is as if something in the room is overriding the tricorder's sensors, giving it specific readings in order to mask something else. Please wait here." Riker, McAdams and Barclay watched from the doorway as Data made some adjustments to his tricorder and scoured every surface of the library. Unsurprisingly, he eventually stopped in front of a book. Data closed his tricordor and picked up the book, a small volume of poetry. Data opened it, and sure enough, within a frame of false pages, a small flat device was blinking in operation. Data found an "off" switch, and the surface of a small table in the center of the room shimmered and revealed a Federation-standard interface console.

"Oh, my." This from Barclay, who was staring in shock at his tricorder. "Th-this room is a transporter."

"Which part of it?" McAdams asked.

"The whole room!" Barclay said. "The walls are lined with molecular imaging scanners, pattern buffers, phase transition coils—"

Riker whistled appreciatively as they joined Data in the room. "Curiouser and curiouser." He turned to McAdams. "Are you thinking what I'm thinking?"

"That this is the front door to his real house?" McAdams asked.

"Something like that."

Data had been studying the tabletop console. "The device is limited in function. Unlike most transporters, this one is apparently designed to transmit matter to single location only."

"Where?" Riker asked.

"Unknown. Since it cannot be programmed for other locations, there is no coordinate system in place to make that determination. However, it does suggest that the location and distance of the other terminus is constant relative to this one."

"So it definitely goes somewhere on the planet, and not to a nearby vessel," McAdams concluded.

"So it would seem," Data agreed.

McAdams looked at Riker. "I suppose you want to knock?"

Riker grinned. "Why, Lieutenant, you *can* read my mind."

"S-sir, is that really s-such a good idea?" Barclay stammered.

"Lieutenant Barclay may have a point, sir," Data said. "We do not know what may be facing us on the other side. I recommend we contact the *Enterprise* and request they send a probe—"

Data never completed his recommendation. Without warning, the transporter came on, the dematerialization effect enveloping and immobilizing the members of the away team before they could react.

They rematerialized in the middle of one of the most sophisticated and apparently deserted laboratories Riker had ever seen.

"Phasers," Riker ordered, and the away team immediately moved into a defensive position, each facing a different direction with weapons drawn. "Data, what the hell happened?"

Data drew out his tricorder with his free hand and expertly opened it. "I am not sure, sir. One of us may have inadvertently tripped a sensor that activated a retrieval mechanism."

"Or somebody on this end beamed us here," McAdams said, her eyes scanning her surroundings alertly.

"My tricorder is detecting no life signs other than our own," Data reported.

"All right," Riker said. "Just the same, everyone be alert. And stay together. Where exactly are we, Data?" The lab seemed to curve away from them in both directions.

Data completed his scan and gave his report. "We are approximately thirty-four hundred kilometers southeast of our previous location," he said, "and one hundred fifty meters beneath the floor of Galor IV's largest ocean."

"You did say the floor, didn't you?" Barclay asked nervously. "Not the surface?"

"Correct. This facility is subterranean. It is a circular arrangement of rooms surrounding a large, dome-shaped space approximately seventy-five meters in diameter, perhaps a spacecraft bay." Riker noticed the inner wall of the lab was dominated by a continuous row of dark glass. *Viewports?* "The dome opens at the top into a wide shaft leading up to the ocean floor. A force field is holding back the ocean. Extraordinary."

Barclay was looking around in amazement. "Professor, what have you been up to?"

"Can you imagine the resources it took to build something like this?" Riker said. "And in secret?"

"Apparently there is far more to Professor Vaslovik than even I suspected, Commander," Data admitted.

Riker tried his combadge. "Riker to *Enterprise.* Riker to *Enterprise.*" When no answer came, he looked at the others. "Can any of you get through?" When no one could, Riker asked Data, "Can we beam back?"

"I am not sure. I do not see anything that would suggest a transporter control interface."

"Dammit," Riker muttered. Investigating unknown territory didn't bother him; not having a choice in the matter did. "All right, let's see what we can find. Data, you take point. McAdams, you cover our backs. Everyone keep an eye out for a communications console or transporter controls."

"Here's something," McAdams said, touching a hand-size panel just below the wall of dark glass. A section of the viewports immediately lightened to transparency, revealing the empty spaceship bay Data had described, and beyond it, the dark stripe of viewports that ran around its perimeter.

"Nothing in there?" Riker asked.

"I see what looks like a pair of launch tubes near the opposite wall. They lead right into the ceiling. See?"

Riker stepped closer for a better look. "What do you think? Missile launchers?"

"I'm thinking escape pods," said McAdams. "If so, it gives us a way out, if all else fails."

"Lieutenant McAdams is correct," Data said. They turned to see him bent over a free-standing console several meters away while Barclay kept watch. "The tubes each contain an escape pod. I have found an access terminal to this facility's central databases. I believe I have found the answers to at least some of our questions."

The away team gathered around Data as he scrolled rapidly through a stream of text and images. Riker could not make out much as Data worked, though he thought he saw snatches of android diagrams, plus recordings of three men working around a large black slab, whom Riker recognized as Maddox, Barclay and Vaslovik.

"Evidence?" Riker asked.

"I believe, Commander, that the answer is both yes and no," Data reported. "I am accessing his logs and will be better able to explain in a few moments."

Barclay had apparently found another access terminal nearby and was also accessing records. "All the holographic clusters we created have been downloaded," he said.

"Which means what?" McAdams asked.

"It means Professor Vaslovik activated the android's neural net."

"Can you determine whether or not the process worked?"

Reg shook his head. "No. This computer only shows that the files were moved, not whether the holotronic brain activated successfully."

Riker stepped around to face Data behind his console. "Data? Anything?"

Data looked up from the display just as the stream of information ceased. The gray light from the screen cast heavy shadows across his features and made his golden skin appear dour and sickly. "Yes, Commander. Quite a bit, in fact. Apparently I was only partly correct about Professor Vaslovik. For reasons that are still unclear to me, he was planning to abduct the holotronic android from the moment he agreed to join the project. However, while he was, in fact, responsible for the android's disappearance, and the purging of the project records, he was *not* responsible for the explosion in the lab or for Commander Maddox's subsequent injury. If anything, I believe he may have saved the commander's life.

"The logs show that Vaslovik became aware some time ago that the project had come under the scrutiny of persons unknown. The indications were subtle: Some of the datafiles in the lab were being accessed and sensor ghosts kept showing up on the security system. Unfortunately, whoever was doing this left no trail. The biosensors turned up nothing.

"Vaslovik was reluctant to reveal his suspicions to Commander Maddox and Lieutenant Barclay, fearing what their unknown intruders might do if he tipped his hand too soon. Instead, he finalized his preparations to abscond with the android, creating the forgery to leave in its place. It seems he originally hoped to do a more complete job on the forgery in order to make it appear to the Institute as if the project simply failed. But when the planet's climate control system went offline, Vaslovik knew that some manner of assault was imminent, and implemented his escape plan before the forgery was ready to withstand close inspection. Like his adversaries, he was able to use the sudden confusion during the storm to mask his activities, and got away with the real android before they or anyone else arrived on the scene."

"So there's an unknown third party involved in all this," McAdams said. "Is there any clue in there at all as to who it might be, what their motives were or where Vaslovik took the real android?"

"No," Data said to all three questions. "However, there is a clear indication here that after Vaslovik saw to Commander Maddox's safety, he used a device to deliberately induce the commander's coma, as insurance against Maddox revealing whatever he'd seen that night in the lab."

"It's beginning to feel like we're taking two steps backward for every one we take forward," Riker said irritably. "How the hell are we supposed to—"

But Riker never finished the thought. There was a crash somewhere behind him, and suddenly Data was moving, drawing his phaser and lunging toward him, moving with the effortless speed that Riker knew was always at his disposal, but which he rarely used. Riker didn't have time to turn or duck, barely had time to draw a breath, before he felt Data's hand on his shoulder, shoving him down. The impact wrenched his arm, but despite the sudden, sharp pain, he managed to draw his phaser as he rolled across the floor. Data, he knew, was obviously reacting to a threat that had just entered the lab.

Skidding to a halt against Barclay's legs, Riker lifted the phaser high, sighting on the first thing he focused on—Data's head—then immediately shifted his attention to the two huge humanoids that were standing over him.

Two and a half meters tall, the beings were bone-white and hairless, with pale eyes staring out from deep sockets. Silver robes hung from shoulders that were at least a meter wide. Apparently, they had been lurking inside the spaceship bay, near enough to the away team to remain hidden from view if they flattened themselves against the dark viewports. The lab was strewn with black glass from their explosive entrance into the lab.

That would explain why McAdams and I didn't see them. But why the hell didn't they register on the tricorders? And what do they want?

Riker could see that Data was trying different settings on his phaser to no avail; the weapon wouldn't fire. Then, almost as if taking a toy away from an errant child, the giant immediately in front of Data slapped him across the face.

Data was thrown back, his phaser flying out of his hand. The giants started forward, and Data spared only a second to turn toward the away team, revealing a tear in the artificial skin of his face that exposed the blinking hardware beneath. Riker thought his friend's eyes were actually blazing with anger as he spoke.

"Run."

Chapter Fifteen

SPARKS FLEW AS DATA RIPPED a long console from its mount in the wall, lifted it over his head and flung it at his assailants. The console slammed into the humanoids and knocked them back, but it didn't stop them.

Once more on his feet, Riker took aim and tried to fire, only to find his phaser wasn't working either. *Some kind of dampening field,* he guessed, and began to see the logic of Data's urgent order to withdraw. Their weapons were useless, and judging from what he was seeing, hand-to-hand combat wasn't an option. He grabbed Barclay's arm and called out, "McAdams! Retreat!"

Then he saw that the security officer had other ideas.

McAdams ran alongside one of their foes, placed her hands on his forearm and shoulder in preparation for what Riker recognized as a vicious *mok'bara* hold. She shifted her legs in the prescribed manner, pivoted her hips . . . and utterly failed to move her opponent. Her expression, Riker saw, betrayed not fear, but surprise.

She somehow sidestepped the giant's attempt to grab her, and before Riker could formulate his next move, Data was there, interposing himself between McAdams and her attacker. Data grabbed both of the aliens' wrists and twisted them so sharply that Riker flinched, expecting a spray of blood and howl of pain. But instead, he saw a shower of blinding white sparks as a shriek of metal cut through the air.

That explains the lack of life signs, Riker thought. *Androids!*

Data tossed the hands away, then leapt into the air and dealt the creature a savage kick in the chest, sending him flying backward against a bank of instruments. The arc of the android's fall left brilliant afterimages on Riker's eyes. The second attacker ignored his companion and attempted to catch Data in a bear hug, but missed. Again, Data shouted, *"Run!"* and this time, McAdams complied.

She clamped a hand around Riker's wrist and led him around the curve of the lab. "We have to find a door to the bay—the escape pods."

Riker slowed and grabbed hold of a metal chair. "The hell with finding a door," he muttered, and threw the chair with all his strength at the nearest viewport. Dark glass exploded into the bay and Riker herded Barclay and McAdams through the opening. Their rapid footfalls rang loudly as they ran across the cavernous space toward the launch tubes.

When they reached the first pod, Riker saw that it was Starfleet-standard, though a little dated, and ushered in Barclay first, who quickly found the preset switch and slapped it. The pod's systems hummed to life. Riker turned to McAdams. "You next, Lieutenant. As soon as you clear the ocean, get a fix on our position and raise the *Enterprise*. They may be able to beam down help."

The pod's onboard computer intoned, "Lift-off in fifteen seconds."

"What about you?" McAdams asked.

"I'm going back for Data. Get in."

McAdams hesitated, ready to argue, until her training seemed to take hold and she nodded. But instead of climbing into the seat, McAdams grabbed Riker's arm and, with no apparent effort, pitched him through the hatch. He heard her say, "Sorry, Commander," as the automatic door closed.

Riker barely had time to strap himself in before the engines fired.

Stepping away from the launch cradle, McAdams watched as the escape pod disappeared up the tube. She watched it go and, almost wistfully, McAdams whispered, "It's been fun."

She turned just in time to see Data come crashing through another of the viewports. He sailed a good twenty meters into the bay, landing hard on his side. He tried to rise, but couldn't seem to find his footing. One leg was twisted in the wrong direction and his left arm hung uselessly.

Rhea could see both of the attacking androids striding deliberately toward them as she ran to Data and knelt by his side, lifting his right arm over her shoulder and hauling him to his feet. Data's eyes were open and he seemed to be tracking motion, but he couldn't speak.

She got Data to the second escape pod and eased him into the hatch, followed him inside, slammed the preset and then looked back across the bay.

They were still coming, picking up speed now. Quickly she checked her tricorder: the dampening field that had kept their phasers from functioning earlier was concentrated in the perimeter lab. There was no sign of it inside the bay.

As the pod's computer announced lift-off in fifteen seconds, Rhea stood and half-emerged from the pod, phaser raised, but instead of firing at their pursuers, she aimed through the shaft overhead, targeting the force field generator near the top, the only thing separating the bay from the ocean above. The phaser beam hit point-blank, and the force field winked out.

There was no sign of fear on the androids' faces, only grim determination. Rhea almost felt sorry for them. Almost.

There came a roar as the weight of an ocean sent a hurricane blast of cold, wet air into the bay, smacking back her pursuers as they came within arm's reach of the pod. The automatic hatch closed and the engines fired, sending the pod up the launch tube while all around, ocean water flooded and destroyed Vaslovik's lair, throwing it into darkness.

The pod ascended rapidly, vibrating madly as it cleared first the tube, then the ocean, then climbed through the atmosphere.

A quick survey revealed what McAdams expected to find: standard escape pod features, including controls for a small but powerful warp drive.

As the sky outside the pod windows shifted from brilliant blue to the cobalt of space's edge, Rhea got a navigational fix. The *Enterprise* was in a geosynchronous orbit over the DIT, so she set the autopilot to head due west and clear the atmosphere as quickly as possible.

The pod's impulse thrusters responded, and as the autopilot took over, Rhea finally felt she could turn her attention to Data.

He was in bad shape. His eyes were still open and moving, but all other motor control appeared to be gone. The artificial skin had been torn away almost completely from the left side of his head, exposing a large section of his tripolymer skull. His left shoulder had been crushed. Additionally, there were two large rents in his neck, almost as if one of the giant androids had torn it open with its fingers or teeth.

"Data?" Rhea asked softly. "Can you hear me? Can you answer?" She waved her hand in front of his eyes and they seemed to follow for a few seconds, but then his eyes lost their focus. Data opened his mouth, but the only sound that came out was a thin croak, followed by a thin amber liquid that trickled out the corner. Rhea turned him onto his side so the liquid could drain out. She wasn't sure if he could choke, but she didn't want to find out.

"Hang on, Data," she said. "We'll be home in a few minutes." The autopilot beeped and Rhea turned to see the sleek shape of the *Enterprise* on a small viewscreen. But something was wrong.

A blip shone on the sensor display. Something was coming up from the planet, fast, from Galor IV's arctic circle, heading straight for the starship.

What the hell—?

Something flared outside the pod, casting ragged, streaming shadows. The pod's window darkened automatically as the autopilot threw the craft into a sudden spiral. Rhea tried raising the *Enterprise*, but all she could make out was the garbled sound of Deanna Troi's voice saying, "*. . . Federation vessel . . . cease . . .*

attempt...will respond..." Then, there was another blinding flash and the signal died.

Rhea only had a second to see the attacker before the pod's autopilot sent it into evasive maneuvers, but the brief glimpse was more than enough. It wasn't quite the size of the *Enterprise,* but the few readings her sensors were able to take showed power readings on a par with the *Sovereign*-class starship. In both its color and its irregular shape, it looked like a sheet of ice broken free from a glacier. *Hiding in the north pole all along,* Rhea surmised. *Clever.* The alien ship opened fire again.

The *Enterprise* was going to have her hands full and wasn't going to have time to worry about a tiny escape pod. Rhea silently wished the ship good luck, then entered a new course into the autopilot. A quick look confirmed that they did indeed have the range to get where she wanted to go, though she never really doubted it.

She turned around in the seat and saw that Data was staring past her, out into space. Was he wondering about the fate of his ship? Was his mind even functioning anymore?

"I can't take you to your home, Data," she said softly. "But I can take you back to mine."

The pod cleared the gravity well of the planet and the warp drive engaged, while behind it, two titans battled.

Beverly Crusher was trying to make herself heard above the bray of the planetary emergency klaxon. A pair of orderlies was trying to transfer a recently admitted patient—a pregnant woman who had been having false labor pains—out of her bed and onto a stretcher without first disconnecting all the monitors. Finally, one of them heard her, disconnected the monitors, untangled himself and the expectant mother was bundled off without any additional injuries to either patient or staff. As they headed for the shelter, Crusher stayed behind and silently counted to ten. This isn't a starship crew, she reminded herself. They're infirmary workers at a research institute. It isn't like they're attacked by silent, implacable foes every day.

Her ship was under fire—Haftel had been able to tell her that much before the evacuation order had been sounded—but no one seemed to know anything else. She had tried to check with DIT security, but they had cut her off when they realized she wasn't in immediate distress. Crusher had been annoyed, but then decided to let it go. The entire security staff for the Institute might have numbered in the neighborhood of a few dozen officers and they had their hands full. Could it be the Dominion? Had one of their ships made its way this far into Federation territory? There was no way to know and the only way the doctor could focus past her frustration was to keep busy.

Crusher followed the orderlies down the corridor until they passed the ICU where Crusher stopped and passed through the large double doors. As she had expected, Maury Sullivan was at the nurse's station transferring patient records to the protected core. They would need the records if they were forced to spend any length of time in the shelters, and they couldn't risk their being lost if the main computers were damaged. Most of the backups were done automatically, but the infirmary workers knew the limitations of their system and knew not to trust automatic systems.

"Who's left?" Crusher asked.

Maury answered without looking up. "Just Maddox. I wanted you here." Suddenly, the lights dimmed to almost complete darkness, then rose again to half their former level.

"Get down to the shelter," Crusher ordered. "And send back those two orderlies. I'll do what I can until they return." Crusher hurried to Maddox's room, but when she got there she was surprised to find someone already at work, an unfamiliar med-tech. But as soon as her eyes adjusted to the subdued light, the doctor saw the tech wasn't getting Maddox ready to move. Quite the opposite, in fact; he was attaching something—some sort of neural stimulator?—to his forehead. Crusher shouted, "What the hell are you doing? Get away from him!" But the tech didn't even look up until he had completed the procedure and removed the device, shoving past Crusher as he bolted out the door.

Cursing, Crusher recovered quickly and checked Maddox, made sure his vital signs were stable, then ran out into the hall. She almost crashed into Maury and a worried-looking orderly, but managed to spin around them without breaking stride. "A tech just walked out of here," Crusher shouted to be heard above the klaxon. "Which way?"

Maury pointed to the left. Crusher nodded and jerked her head toward Maddox. "Don't move him unless you absolutely have to," she said. "That tech might have done something. I don't know what, but I'm going to find out."

At the end of the hall, the corridor kinked to the left. Crusher peered around the corner before proceeding, half-expecting the tech to be lying in wait. This turned out not to be the case; the corridor was wide and empty and ended in a set of swinging double doors. This was a part of the infirmary Crusher hadn't visited before and she hesitated to enter unknown terrain without something with which to defend herself. But all she had on her was her medkit. Not exactly a formidable array of weaponry. Should she proceed? Go back for help? No, if she did that, the trail would grow cold.

She popped open her medical tricorder and tried to reset it to search for gross physical displacement. The tricorder couldn't tell her much—only that someone had been down the corridor in the past few minutes—but not much more. She checked the cartridges in her medkit—antibiotics, antivirals, a cardiopulmonary stimulant, a couple of steroid combinations, a viral inhibitor—the standard mix. Nothing very useful. She spotted something through the windows of the double doors that she liked much better, a med cart someone had left outside a patient's room when the emergency began. Checking the labels quickly, the doctor found something more to her liking: a general neuro-inhibitor. It was meant to be used on patients experiencing seizure, but, if she could administer it near a nerve cluster, it would drop the man in his tracks. She slid a cartridge into the hypo, pocketed a couple extra and pushed on down the hall.

When she reached the end of the corridor, Crusher realized she had left the last of the patient rooms behind her and was getting into the maintenance areas. Behind another set of double doors at the end of the corridor were several large pieces of cleaning equipment, barrels of chemicals and a single door on the left. Otherwise, it was a dead end. Crusher started to take another reading, but stopped when she saw the door was ajar. Peering through the crack, she saw a dimly lit stairwell, then heard the distant clank of a heavy door closing. Once again, the doctor hesitated and tried to determine whether there was a more intelligent solution to the present situation, but nothing suggested itself that didn't involve endangering more civilians. Gripping the hypo, she slipped through the door as quietly as she was able. The stairs only led in one direction—down.

At the bottom of the stairway, she pulled open another door expecting a dimly lit basement or a storage area. Instead, she found a short, brightly lit corridor ending in a pair of heavy security doors. Two armed security drones lay inert on the floor. "This is not good," she muttered. Taking a quick tricorder reading, all she was able to determine for sure was that no weapon had been fired, which only added to her uncertainty.

Approaching the security doors, Crusher wondered how she could pass without a password or keycard, but the doors slid open at her approach. A body slumped into the hall: a security guard. Crusher knelt beside him and checked his vitals. He was only lightly stunned. There was another man leaning against a console inside the security doors, also unconscious.

She realized where she was: the infirmary's computer core. That was a problem. The damage a single determined person could do to such a vital facility, once they were inside, was incalculable—likewise, to any well-meaning soul who tried to stop them. But it wasn't as if she had a choice.

The door to the core slid open as she approached, but the sound of her passage was lost in the bass throb of supercooled data processors and storage units. It wasn't an immense chamber, as far as she could tell, but it was a maze of free-standing equipment that inhibited her view of the entire room.

Crusher stepped back into the anteroom and quickly

searched the two guards for weapons, but found none. Obviously, her quarry had taken them.

This was too much. Crusher was not going to face an armed opponent with only a hypo. She very much doubted that there was another exit from the room, so if she could move something heavy in front of the door, the tech would be trapped until security could make it down here. But who knew what kind of damage might be done while she waited?

Steeling her resolve, the doctor eased around a console when, suddenly, a new alarm went off. It wasn't the planetary disaster klaxon she had left behind upstairs, but something else, something that originated inside the core.

"Dammit," Crusher hissed, her grip tightening around the hypo. She tried to keep low and use the consoles for cover, glad that her quarry would not be able to hear her footfalls over the din of the alarm.

She turned a corner and almost walked into the intruder's back. He was leaning over an active interface console, lit up in what looked to her like a transporter configuration, working so intently that he didn't appear to even notice her. Ducking back, she collected herself, checked the setting on her hypo and willed herself to be calm. *You've done this a thousand times, Bev. Put it on his neck and press the button.* She took a deep breath, straightened, stepped quickly around the console and gently laid the hypo below his ear. There was a satisfying hiss as the hypo emptied.

The intruder looked over his shoulder at her, gave her a mildly annoyed look, then returned to his work. He did not, as anticipated, crumble to the floor and begin to quiver. Crusher glanced at the hypo, resisted the urge to check the cartridge label and instead raised her arm and snapped the hypo down on the man's temple.

His head twisted to the side, but otherwise the blow seemed to have no effect. Then, slowly, he turned his head and the doctor saw that there was a glowing filament plugged into a copper-colored port beneath the peeled-back skin of his right temple. "Please, doctor," he said lightly. "Don't interrupt."

Chapter Sixteen

THE *ENTERPRISE* LISTED TO PORT and Deanna Troi felt her stomach yaw to starboard. *Not a direct hit, but close.* And then, incongruously, she reminded herself, *For every action, an equal and opposite reaction.*

"Inertial dampeners—compensate," she called to environmental, then felt the AG fluctuate beneath her.

"Incoming!" Commander Heyes called from tactical. She had just turned over the bridge to Troi when the enemy vessel had risen suddenly from the planet's arctic region and opened fire. The impact had sent Tellisar, Troi's tactical officer, over the front of his console, unconscious, possibly dead. Heyes had scrambled from the turbolift doors to the weapons station while the deck seesawed under her feet and managed to fire off a volley of torpedoes.

Troi clutched at the arms of the command chair while around her, bodies hit the deck as the ship rolled to starboard.

"Shields down to eighty percent, Commander," Heyes called. "Power is stable."

"Attack pattern alpha one nine," Troi ordered. "Commence fire."

"Phasers firing."

Lances of orange light tracked across the void, then vanished. Troi's forehead knotted uncertainly as she turned to Heyes. "Did we hit them?"

Reflected light danced across Heyes's face as she initiated a complex sensor sweep. "I'm not finding anything," she said, and it didn't require Troi's empathic abilities to sense her confusion. "No ship, no debris, no energy signature, nothing." Frustrated, she recalibrated the sensors and reran the search.

Troi gave her room to work. "Stations, report."

Around the bridge, the station heads called off their status. Engineering and environmental systems were functioning at acceptable levels, and the helm was responding. Medics came onto the bridge, bundled Tellisar onto a stretcher and removed him. Troi saw that he was, in fact, breathing and felt regret that she hadn't at least tried to determine his condition, but then chastised herself: that wasn't part of her role when she was commanding the bridge.

"Could it have been a cloaking device?" Troi asked, turning toward tactical.

"I don't think so," Heyes said, checking her readings for the third time. "We know what to look for with a cloak. There's no distortion, no graviton concentration, no energy spike—" Then, suddenly, she cried out, "Hard to starboard!"

Troi spun back toward the screen just in time to see the starfield flicker and ripple. The attacking ship seemed to slide out from under the skin of space, its hull shimmering like liquid, then suddenly crystallizing as it emerged completely. A wave of energy pulsed from its prow, twisting and distorting the edge of space/time.

The *Enterprise* rocked. Primary systems shut down and Troi felt the strange flicker and hum through the soles of her feet that meant the artificial gravity was on the verge of failing. "Primaries are offline," Tolman, the engineering officer, announced. "Secondary systems are unavailable. Switching to batteries." Work lights around the bridge flickered on and air recyclers struggled to clear the smoke.

"Route power to shields," Troi ordered. "Helm, can we move?"

"Barely, Commander. Thrusters only."

"Use them," Troi said. "Try to keep moving."

She turned to look at Heyes, who must have cracked her head on the panel during the last attack because she had a large, bloody gash on her left temple. "What did they hit us with?" Troi asked.

"Good question," Heyes said. "The sensors flared out, but I got some data before they went down. It's some sort of subspace waveform, the kind of thing we calibrate our warp engines to prevent from happening."

"Has anyone ever heard of anything like this?" Troi asked. "Science officer?"

Casciato, at sciences, shook his head. It must have been his panel that had blown out because his eyebrows and the hair on his forehead were singed away. "Never," he said. "It's theoretically possible, but impractical because the radiation generated behind the wave would be inimical to any form of carbon-based life we know."

Heyes asked, "Could the ship be a robot? Remotely piloted?"

Troi shook her head, concentrating. "No, it's not a robot. I'm sensing anger. Intense, determined and constant." She tried to regulate her breathing, to calm herself and float free of the bridge's controlled chaos. Reaching out across the void to the enemy ship, Troi tried to identify the source of what she was feeling, something that was somehow familiar, but twisted around on its axis. She felt a word forming in her mind, a name, a concept, but before she could grasp it, another voice intruded.

"I've got sensors again," Heyes announced. "They're coming around. Moving slowly, but picking up speed. I'm guessing that they can't use that subspace weapon very often." She checked the energy levels. "Recommend we keep them on our port side, if possible. Shields are stronger there."

"You heard the commander, Ensign Welles," Troi said to the conn officer. "Make it so."

"Aye, Commander."

The intership crackled overhead, then cleared. La Forge's voice said, "Bridge, this is engineering. What's happening up there?"

"We're in a fight, Geordi. Unknown attacker, new kind of weapon."

"Understood," La Forge said. "I was worried you were steering us into a planet again."

I guess I'm never going to live that one down. "Don't tempt me," she warned him. "I think that, whoever they are, they've used their big gun. If we can have power back, we should be able to take them."

"That's what I like—confidence. Give me five minutes."

"You've got thirty seconds," was Troi's answer. "Bridge out." Troi felt the mood on the bridge lift, though she knew that their confidence was not entirely well-founded. If their attacker regrouped before Geordi could bring main power back on line, she knew they could only take one, at best two more assaults.

The primary lighting came back up and, as if on cue, the turbolift doors parted and Captain Picard strode onto the bridge. He looked around quickly and took the temperament of the crew. Seeming satisfied, he nodded to Commander Heyes, then turned to Troi, who rose from the center seat. Picard took his chair and began to study the tactical logs. "What is our status, Commander?" Picard asked, reading and listening simultaneously.

Troi explained about the subspace weapon, pulling up the data Casciato had forwarded to the command station. Picard absorbed the basics, then turned to Heyes. "Do we have any specifics about their ship?"

"Coming up." Heyes punched a series of controls and routed the tactical display to the center seat display. To the naked eye, the attacking vessel looked like nothing more than a wedge-shaped chunk of ice. According to sensors, the "ice" was actually some unknown form of ablative armor, thickly layered over what appeared to be a dense tritanium hull.

Picard frowned, then asked, "Weapons?"

"Two systems that we've seen: standard disruptors, somewhat more powerful than the Romulan version and the waveform gun." She shifted the view to the sensor display and showed them a time-lapsed playback of the five seconds when the ship emerged from subspace. The discharge spike of the wavefront was impressive and Picard grunted appreciatively.

"Have they responded to our hails?"

"No, sir," Troi said. "We've tried standard hails in all languages."

Strange, Picard mused. *Who are they? Why are they attacking, and what, if anything, do they have to do with Vaslovik and the missing android?* The captain knew that these questions and a score of others racing through his mind would have to wait. His first priority was to neutralize the current threat.

"They're gone again," Heyes cried out. "Disappeared into subspace!"

Troi activated the shipwide and announced, "All hands, brace for impact!" Two seconds later, the ship bucked under their feet and the main lighting flickered out. Troi tumbled to the deck, wrenching her wrist while attempting to break her fall. Picard barked, "Phasers and quantum torpedoes, full spread! Fire!" But there was no response from Heyes.

Climbing up off the deck, Troi could make out the tactical station through the smoke and haze, but couldn't see Heyes. Coughing, she stumbled toward the tactical console and almost tripped over Heyes's prostrate form. She found the torpedo control interface and fired the spread Picard had ordered, but the phasers were offline.

Troi twisted her hair into a knot and pulled it away from her face, then wiped her hands on her uniform. They were sticky with blood, but whether her own or someone else's, she didn't have time to check. "One torpedo hit, Captain, but I can't judge the level of damage."

"Prepare for the next pass."

Troi did as she was ordered and programmed another spread of torpedoes, but half the launcher indicator lights read yellow. She checked her panel and saw that the computer had successfully reinitialized the phaser arrays. They still had teeth.

Seeing that the bridge crew was more or less recovering, Troi took a moment to check on Heyes and was relieved to see that the woman was breathing. Two corpsmen emerged from out of the hazy air and lifted the commander onto a stretcher.

"Status report!" Picard snapped.

"Shields down to thirty percent." The quantum torpedo board flickered, then reset with new indicators. "Aft torpedo launchers are now offline," she read, "but main phasers are functional, though firing them would drain our reserves." The ship rocked again, though not so fiercely as the last two attacks.

"Disruptors?" Picard asked.

"Affirmative," Troi replied. "Shields are down to twenty-seven percent."

"Picard to engineering."

"La Forge here. Sorry about that, Captain. We weren't ready for them."

"Let it happen again and you're fired, Mr. La Forge."

"Understood, sir. That last one shook us up pretty badly. I've got coolant leaks everywhere and we had to eject one of the torpedo launchers. We had a live one in the breach and no firing mechanism."

"What about secondaries?"

"Ten minutes minimum; more if they keep peppering us with disruptors." The *Enterprise* shuddered again. "Like that," La Forge finished. "Is there anything we can do to keep them off for a few minutes?"

"No promises, Mr. La Forge. Shields are low, so see what you can do there."

"Aye, sir. I'll let you know if the situation changes. I can give you a burst of impulse if we need it."

"Not really an option," Picard replied. "We can't leave Galor IV undefended."

"Wasn't suggesting it, sir. Just thought we might be able to lead them away."

"I'll keep it in mind, Geordi," the captain said. "Picard out."

The ship rocked again and Troi watched as the shield level indicator dropped down to just under twenty percent. Around her, the bridge crew labored. Picard rose from the center seat and crossed to her console.

"Any word from the away team?" Picard asked.

She shook her head. "They missed their check-in, too. I was just about to call you when the first salvo hit us."

"That might not be a coincidence," Picard said softly. "It's quite possible that Commander Riker might currently be faced with his own problems."

Riker pounded his fist on the pod's control panel. "Dammit," he said. "Something's blocking our hail." He stared out at the two ships—the *Enterprise* and the strange, icelike hulk—and seethed. The enemy, whether androids like the ones in Vaslovik's bunker, or something else entirely, was pounding his ship and he hated the feeling of helplessness. More, he despised himself for letting the frustration rob him of clear thought. There must be something he could do, but he didn't know what.

And his mind kept returning to Rhea McAdams. What the hell had she thought she was doing? Disobeying orders and playing hero in the middle of a crisis was a sure way to a fast court martial, if not an early grave.

What did she imagine she could achieve down there that he couldn't? Or was she just inexperienced and misguided enough to believe that saving the more "valuable" member of the away team—namely, the first officer of the *Enterprise*—was worth risking her life and possibly Data's in some idiotic stunt?

Cursing under his breath, Riker punched the thrusters and the pod sped closer to the battle. He had checked its systems as soon as their flight vector had stabilized and Riker had been pleased to find that its sensors were better than anything he could have hoped for. The shields, also, were much enhanced, though there were no weapons worth mentioning—only a single phaser bank that wouldn't be much use against anything bigger than a squirrel. It was clear that whoever had refitted the pod had not had fighting in mind, but quick and stealthy flight.

As it had twice before, the attacking ship slid into subspace and Riker watched impatiently for the *Enterprise* to make some countermove, but it was clear that his crew were more than preoccupied with keeping the vessel stable. Riker had been through enough battles to recognize a ship that was, if not in peril, then fighting on the defensive. Ten heartbeats later, the iceship reemerged from subspace and though there was no visible weapons fire, the *Enterprise* shifted away as if swamped by some unseen wave. Every one of the pod's sensors redlined and the tiny craft bumped and hopped like a rowboat in a hurricane sea.

A ship I could feel under my feet. Riker remembered that wish from the previous day. *That's what I had wanted. What the hell was I thinking?*

"Uh, s-sir," Barclay stammered, staring at the navigational display. "We're moving c-closer to the battle."

"We're not moving closer," Riker said. "We're circling. It would be foolish to approach without a plan."

"No argument," Reg said, his manner strangely detached all of a sudden. Riker had seen him like this once or twice before. Though Barclay was not what one would call an intrepid soul, neither was he a coward. "But I don't see that there's much we can do here that will affect the outcome of the battle. We have no weaponry, just impulse thrusters and warp drive. Maybe we should go for help."

Not taking his eyes off the two ships, Riker asked, "What did you just say?"

Barclay repeated, "Maybe we should go for help . . . ?"

"Warp drive," Riker mused, then grinned wickedly. "We have warp drive! Reg, you're a genius." He tightened the straps on his restraining harness, then said, "Hold on," and fired the pod's thrusters at full power. The enemy vessel suddenly grew larger as it stitched a seam of blue-green fire across the *Enterprise*'s primary hull. Riker gritted his teeth against the gee forces, and searched the pod's systems for more power to feed the engines.

Troi, too, was searching her ship's systems for the last remnants of power, though she did not yet know what she would do with whatever she found. Deanna was beginning to feel the itch to slash at them with one good phaser strike, though she knew it might end up being the last thing she ever did.

Another hit.

The *Enterprise* shuddered, heaved and the bridge went dark. She felt her feet leave the deck plates and for a second Troi thought this might be the one. She tensed and waited for either fire or ice, but, no, gravity reasserted itself and the tactical console came back online.

"That one got past the shields, Captain. Decks ten and twelve are open to space. The force fields failed . . ." And then she realized she was almost shouting. Collecting her reserves, Troi forced herself to speak calmly. "The force fields failed, but they've come back online."

Picard, once again seated in the command chair, was grim and haggard. The left side of his neck and face had been badly burned when the monitor in his command chair had blown out, but he did not seem to notice the blistered skin. "Fatalities?" he asked.

Troi checked the internal sensors. "Twenty-nine, Captain," she said as softly as she could.

Though his face did not show it, Troi knew her words had hacked away a slice of Picard's soul. He was the captain and people in his command had just died. Something deep inside him writhed in agony, but he said only, "Enemy position?"

"I can't get an exact fix, but they're off the port bow." She studied the scant readings the damaged sensors were providing. "They're not moving. We may have damaged them worse than we thought."

"Perhaps," Picard said. "Or they might be waiting for something: a response from the surface. That might explain what happened to the away team."

"Sir," Troi said suddenly. "Commander Riker is signaling."

"On audio."

"Riker to Enterprise. *Riker to* Enterprise."

Picard leapt to his feet and snapped, "Number One, report."

"Have to keep this short, Captain," Riker said. *"I'm using a lot of power to punch through the interference."* He briefly explained what had happened after they

beamed to Vaslovik's undersea lab, then outlined his plan. Troi felt the blood drain from her face. It wasn't much of a plan.

"But you're not sure you can get through their shields?" Picard asked.

"Not positive," Riker admitted. *"We found a weak spot under the stern, but it'll be touch and go. I was hoping you might be able to tag them with a phaser burst just before I went in."*

Picard looked at Troi, who nodded. Picard nodded. "One shot, Will."

"Understood, Captain. Dare I ask how the transporters are holding up?"

Troi knew that Will would do what he had planned whether the transporters were functioning or not, but Reg might not, so she said, as confidently as she could manage, "Don't worry, Commander. We have a lock on you."

"Great. I'd like someone waiting with a cup of coffee when I get back."

Picard grinned. "I'll bring it myself, Number One. Good hunting."

"See you all in a few minutes," Riker replied, then signed off.

Picard hailed engineering. "Mr. La Forge, make sure you still have that burst of impulse power available. The cavalry is on the way."

Riker hit the throttle again. "Hold on," he said unnecessarily. Reg was holding onto everything he could. The little pod's excellent sensors had done their job and found a weak spot in the enemy's shields. Now all they had to do was stay alive long enough to exploit the discovery. He didn't dare approach too closely until the *Enterprise* was in position; there was no telling how sensitive the attacker's sensors were or how they might react to him despite the fact that the pod would appear about as big as a flea would to a Barzan mastodon.

But this flea has a nasty bite, he thought, feeding extra power to the pod's forward deflector. Opening the link to the *Enterprise*, he said simply, "Now." A second later, a phaser barrage raked the underbelly shields of the iceship. There was the spot he was looking for: a gap where two shield generators had been poorly calibrated. He gunned the impulse thrusters and punched through the gap, the tiny ship rattling like it was made of tin. Feeling the hum of the engine through the seat of his chair, Riker laughed out loud, once again thinking of Worf and the *Defiant.*

Barclay, despite the pale green cast to his complexion, saw Riker's expression and, over the whine of the engines, shouted, "What's so funny, sir?"

"I was just thinking about what Worf would say in this situation."

Barclay winced, knowing exactly what the commander was referring to. "Please, Commander. Don't say it . . ."

Riker found his thoughts shifting to Deanna. "Maybe you're right," he decided. "Just be ready when I give the word."

Riker focused on what the sensors were telling him. The enemy had decided that he was worthy of some attention. Small blisters had opened in the "ice" and disruptor fire lashed out. Riker doubted if the pod would survive more than one direct hit.

He sent the pod weaving back and forth along the enemy ship's underside, steering from side to side randomly, moving too quickly for its targeting sensors to lock on. Reg made an unhappy noise.

Riker ignored it all. He was focused on their proximity to the enemy's bow. "Ten seconds," he shouted. "On my mark."

Skimming close to the hull, Riker hit the thrusters and the pod shot out past the enemy's bow, twisting back and forth between the disruptor banks. "Mark," he said, and out of the corner of his eye he saw Reg punch the correct sequence of controls.

The pod's computer intoned, "Warp core ejection sequence commencing in five, four, three, two, one. Ejection."

Somewhere behind them, Riker knew, a small, hourglass-shaped assembly fired out the emergency ejection port. Riker rolled hard to starboard as the tiny warp core cleared the pod and breached as it slammed against the bow of the iceship.

Light filled the cabin as the blast buffeted the pod. It tumbled out of control and started to shake apart. And in that moment, Riker spoke through teeth that were clenched against the shock wave, deciding Barclay could stand to hear what Worf would say at a time like this, after all.

"Today is a good day to die."

On the bridge of the *Enterprise,* Picard shouted, *"Get them out of there!"* as Troi's hands moved deftly over the transporter override. But she already knew something was wrong. The interference from the subspace weapon was more disruptive than sensors had indicated. On the viewscreen, the bow of the iceship disintegrated in a single, catastrophic flash, a blast that tore across the length of the craft and ripped it apart into a cloud of dust.

She checked the transporter sensors, then rechecked them, then a third time, scanning, coaxing, silently begging them to lock onto something, anything. But there was only a void.

"I've lost him," she whispered, then, realizing what she had said, raised her voice and said, "Captain, I've lost them. There was nothing for the transporter to lock onto. I . . . I'm sorry." She braced herself then, waiting for the moment when it would hit her, for the echo of Will's death to hit her. *Imzadi . . . I'm so sorry . . .*

No one on the bridge moved and Troi felt her heartbeat slow, minds becoming sluggish, despair becoming a tangible thing. Then, she felt the captain shrug off his despair and bark, "Damage reports. Welles—stabilize our orbit. Ensign Rixa, contact Dr. Crusher and inform her we have casualties." And on and on—orders, orders, orders: the captain setting the world to order. Lights came back up to full; medics tended the injured. Blowers cleared the air. Troi felt her hands move and heard herself speak. She was doing her job, doing what she had been trained to do, but every moment, every moment, she was waiting, waiting for her heart to be pierced. *It's coming,* she thought. *It's coming any second now and then there will be a hole in my soul . . .*

And then the captain was there standing next to her, laying his hand on her shoulder and Troi felt some of the crushing weight lift from her. "Commander," he said softly. "Deanna, I need you now. I need you to help hold the crew together. If he's truly gone, more than ever, I need you. They need you. Can you do this?"

Slowly, she lifted her head and looked into her captain's eyes, read the concern there, and nodded, her jaw set.

Picard nodded back and started to turn when Troi received a hail from the planet and put it on the main viewscreen.

It was Dr. Crusher. She was standing in the DIT's infirmary next to a pair of beds. On one of them sat Commander Bruce Maddox, looking slightly confused and a little wan, but otherwise awake and aware.

On the other Reg Barclay and Will Riker sat, both drinking out of steaming mugs. A medic was dressing a nasty-looking cut on Barclay's forehead and Riker had a swelling abrasion under his eye, but, overall, they appeared to be in passably good health, especially considering that they should both be dead.

Beverly was looking out for us, Troi realized. *She must have found a way to use the infirmary's emergency transporters to lock onto Will and Reg, and beamed them off the pod before it was destroyed.*

The captain had apparently drawn the same conclusion. "I see you've been busy. Well done, Doctor."

Crusher looked exhausted, but no less pleased. *"And I understand you've been keeping my medical staff busy. I'll be beaming up in a moment, but as for these three . . ."* She nodded her head toward the patients behind her. *"I'm afraid I can't take all the credit."*

"No?" Picard asked.

"No," Crusher replied. *"I had help."* Crusher turned to the man who was treating Reg's head and said, *"Could you come over here, please?"*

The med-tech turned and smiled into the pickup, then

waved at the bridge crew. Troi repressed the absurd desire to wave back, noticing that a section of skin at the man's temple had been removed, exposing an android's skull. *"Hello, Captain, Counselor. I guess it would be an understatement to say we have a few things to talk about."*

It was Sam.

Chapter Seventeen

RHEA MCADAMS CAREFULLY TORE Data's uniform shirt away from the wound in his left shoulder. Opening a panel in the bulkhead, she pulled out a small tool kit and set it down on the floor beside her leg. Data watched all of these simple movements and wondered why it seemed to take an eternity for her to complete each one.

He could not move his head, could barely move his eyes, so Data did not see any of the contents of the kit until she picked up a small probe and inserted it into the wound in his shoulder. There was no pain of course, though it did produce a strange invasive sensation and he would have shuddered if he could. The cataloging of this perception, too, seemed to require an inordinate amount of time.

Rhea left the probe in the wound, then flipped open a tricorder unlike any Data had ever seen. He tried to itemize the differences between the device and Starfleet's standard tricorder, but despite the fact that he had been staring at it for more than four seconds, he could not effectively focus his thoughts.

"You're hemorrhaging internally," Rhea said calmly, "but I can't find where." Or rather, this is what Data guessed Rhea said. He heard it as, "You're hemorrhag___ int____ly, but I can't _____ where." His language processing center labored for several seconds to try to fill in the blanks until he came up with the most likely interpretation, by which time Rhea had already said at least one more sentence, perhaps two. Data sensed dimly that he should be frightened, but felt only a slight annoyance; it was very inconsiderate of the universe—a universe he had always cataloged with precise, careful observations—to begin sputtering.

Rhea twisted the probe deeper into the wound and a thin stream of circulatory fluid sprayed out and hit her on the cheek. "Found it!" she cried, and Data felt very pleased for her. He must have grayed out then for several seconds because when consciousness returned, he was once again lying flat on his back. A viscous liquid trickled down the side of his face. It was warm, but he felt cold.

Rhea leaned over him and dabbed at his cheek with the sleeve of her shirt. "Lost you there for a minute." She was smiling, but Data saw tears in the corners of her eyes. The sensation that the universe was sputtering had disappeared, but it had been replaced by a feeling that his senses were packed in gauze. "Your sensory processing system almost shut down," Rhea explained. "I thought you were about to go into cascade failure, so I slowed down everything. You're perceiving things now at about . . . well, at about a human level."

For some reason, Data found this idea very amusing and felt an impulse to laugh, but the systems he needed to carry out the reaction were unavailable. A noise came out of him—a *splurt*—and he spasmed involuntarily. The world went away again.

When it came back, Data discovered he had lost the ability to perceive color and his visual processors were searching for the proper level of granularity. Rhea's face kept digitizing, then shifting into a soft gray fuzz. It was very distracting.

"This isn't good," she said. Data heard the familiar chirp and hum of a tricorder and distantly felt her attaching a probe to the side of his head. His vision stabilized and color returned, though everything was too red. Rhea tapped a command sequence into her tricorder and Data felt some of the chill lift. From very far away, the thought crept into Data's head, *How does she know how to do these things?* He tried to analyze the question more carefully, to work through possible answers, but it had already dissolved.

Rhea was shaking her head as she studied her tricorder. "There's really only one way for me to monitor you accurately," she said, and set the tricorder aside. Extending her arm, Rhea rolled up her left sleeve, touched her right thumb to a spot just above her left wrist, then ran the thumb up her forearm. As Data watched, an invisible seam parted and revealed a network of artificial muscles and tendons with a fine tracery of optical cable woven through it. Rhea drew out a length of the cable, uncoiled it, then inserted it into an input/output junction in the exposed circuitry of Data's skull.

Data still could not speak, but he blinked at Rhea in rapid succession.

Rhea gave him a wry grin. "Looks like you found me, Sherlock."

Chapter Eighteen

BRUCE MADDOX LOOKED THIN and haggard, but otherwise
seemed alert and anxious to answer Picard's questions.
Dr. Crusher had made the token objections when Picard
had said he was beaming down to the infirmary, but she
obviously hadn't really expected him to comply. She had
given him a warning look just before she beamed up to
help with casualties on the *Enterprise.* Over two hundred
crewmen had been injured, most when the hull had been
breached and they had been exposed to vacuum. The
good news was that it appeared only a few cases would
require long-term treatment, but it didn't change the fact
that crew strength was down significantly.

Picard sighed. He had faced worse odds, but never
against an enemy about whom he knew so little.

Time for that to change.

Maddox sipped from a bottle of water. "Mouth is
dry," he rasped, then added wryly, "I guess two weeks in
a coma will do that to you."

"I'm sorry, Commander," Picard said, "but I don't have time for pleasantries. My ship has been badly damaged, I've lost crewmen, two of my senior officers are missing—"

"Data?" Maddox interrupted.

"Yes," Picard said. "And my chief of security." Obviously Maddox hadn't been just sitting and sipping water. He'd been thinking, too, putting together bits of information gleaned from brief conversations with the doctor, Barclay and Admiral Haftel. "And before I can formulate my next move, I need to know what you know." He pulled a chair close to Maddox's bed and leaned forward. "What happened that night at the lab, the night you tried to activate the holotronic android?"

Maddox put down his water and took a deep breath, trying to focus. "The memories are a bit disjointed, sir, but I'll do my best to make sense of them," he began. "Professor Vaslovik and I were running what were supposed to be the final tests of the new android's AI matrix. Then the storm hit. I remember a lightning strike, and main power going offline. We tried to secure the experiment until the situation improved, but then there was a second strike, and something exploded in the floor that took out the side of the building. I was hit by something, cut me pretty badly, too. I almost blacked out, and for a long time I couldn't even see. I don't know how long I was like that, but then my vision started to clear, and suddenly part of the ceiling started to collapse right above me. But someone stopped it."

Picard frowned. "Someone? *Someone* stopped a ceiling collapse?"

"No, sir, what I mean is, the ceiling caved, and someone kept the debris from crushing me. It was the android. Our prototype."

"You're certain of this?"

"Absolutely, sir. There was another flash of lightning in the gloom and I saw it, plain as day, holding up the wreckage long enough for me to scramble away."

"Did it say anything to you?" Picard asked.

"No," Maddox said. "But I did hear Emil's voice in my ear as he pressed something to my temple. He said, 'Sorry about this, Bruce, but I can't have you or anyone else trying to find us.' Then he stepped away from me and called out, 'We have to hurry. They'll be here soon.' "

"Is that the last thing you remember?"

"No. Oddly enough, although my strength was ebbing from the blood loss, whatever Emil did to me didn't take effect all at once. I could see him move next to the android and activate some sort of device he had in his hand. A body suddenly materialized at his feet. Sir, it was identical to the prototype. Then the professor hit his switch again, and both he and the android beamed out. The ceiling fell, and there was dust everywhere, but I could see that the duplicate prototype was crushed.

"And that wasn't the end of it. I couldn't move, and staying awake was getting harder. My combadge was gone, and I was becoming increasingly aware that I was bleeding out. Then I remember seeing someone—two people—step through the wrecked side of the building. I thought it was a rescue team. It was hard to see them clearly, I could tell they were huge . . . much taller than any humanoids I'd seen around the DIT. Broader, too." He held his arms far apart to indicate the width of their shoulders. "Like that."

Like the ones Will described, Picard realized. "What happened next?"

"They immediately went for a closer look at the crushed body, and one of them said, 'Not the one.' "

"So they realized the android was a fake. Did they say anything else?"

"The second one answered, 'Then we will wait. The Starfleet android will come now. He will find it.' "

" 'The Starfleet android...' " Picard repeated. "Data."

Maddox nodded. "And then they disappeared. Maybe beamed out, but I'm not sure. Everything's fuzzy after that. I remembered thinking if Data came, he'd be walking into a trap. All I could think about was that I had to warn him."

"That's why you wrote DATA on the floor," Picard realized. "You were trying to warn him. In blood."

"Yes, for all the good it did. And blood was, unfortunately, the only medium I had to work in at the time. Although part of me thinks if I hadn't written it, Admiral Haftel might not have summoned you here at all, in which case Data would still be safe."

"Don't blame yourself, Commander," Picard said. "I suspect the admiral would have done so anyway, given Data's familiarity with you and his own expertise in the field of artificial intelligence. Sooner or later, the *Enterprise* would have been summoned to Galor IV."

"Well, now that I'm back, I'm as eager to get to the bottom of all this as you, sir. We have a common goal, after all. Someone is after your android and mine. There can't be many people onboard the *Enterprise* who know as much about them as I do. It stands to reason that I should come along . . ."

Internally, Picard bridled at the use of the possessive pronouns in referring to the missing androids, but he couldn't deny that Maddox's sentiment was essentially correct. The commander might be useful in the coming search.

Picard stepped to the corner of the room, turned his back to Maddox and tapped his combadge. "Picard to Crusher."

There was a brief pause, then the exasperated voice of the doctor. *"Crusher here. What is it, Captain?"*

Picard cocked an eyebrow. "Are we having a bad day, Doctor?"

Crusher sighed. *"No, Captain. The sixty-five people who are crammed into sickbay and the additional forty or fifty who are lined up outside my door are having a bad day. I'm just having a very, very busy one. What can I do for you?"*

Picard decided that there was nothing he could do to placate Crusher at the moment and cut to the point. "Can Commander Maddox travel?"

"If he has to," Crusher said. *"But I strongly suggest you go easy on him, sir. Whatever Sam did for him obviously reversed whatever was maintaining his coma, but there's no way to know what aftereffects there might be."*

"Understood, Doctor. How are the casualties?"

"All things considered, Captain, it could have been worse," Crusher said. Then she added in a softer tone, *"Go easy on yourself too, Jean-Luc."*

Picard felt one corner of his mouth lift. "Recommendation noted, Doctor. Picard out." Turning back to Maddox, the captain said, "Apparently Dr. Crusher feels you're fit enough to travel. I'll clear it with Admiral Haftel. We leave orbit in two hours." He started to leave the room.

Taking another sip of water, Maddox asked, "Are you headed back to the ship now, sir?"

Pausing in the open door, Picard shook his head.

"No," he said. "I have another visit to make before I head back."

Security detention areas all look the same, Picard reflected, then wondered how tired he needed to be before such a trite observation could intrude on his consciousness. Sam—or whatever his name truly was—sat on the single bunk, looking quite composed, back against the wall, long legs crossed at the ankles. He had stripped off his medical technician's disguise and was wearing some overalls one of the security officers had given him. Deanna Troi had already checked the transporter logs and found no indication about when the bartender had beamed down, but several crewmen swore they had seen Sam in the lounge just before the attack had begun. *How had he done it?* Picard wondered. *And why? To spy on the Federation flagship? Steal secrets from a key scientific installation? Give life back to a man he didn't know? Save two officers from what had looked like almost certain death?* It was an odd commingling of events and it would require some effort to untangle the threads.

Picard saw Haftel standing near the invisible barrier, then looked around for a security officer. Haftel said, "I dismissed him. No sense in wasting manpower when there's plenty of other things to do."

Picard nodded, then said hello to Sam.

"How are you, Captain?" the bartender drawled pleasantly. "How's the ship?"

"The ship . . . can be repaired. Some of her crew, unfortunately, cannot." Picard felt a small coal of anger that he had banked deep in his breast flare up into a lick of flame. He would find whoever had sent the "iceship." He would find them, and then he would . . . But then he forced the thought down. Vengeance wasn't the goal, he knew, but then he had to ask himself, *What was? Comprehension, perhaps? Would understanding why twenty-nine people had died ease the pain of mourning families?* He somehow doubted it, but knew it was the only path he could permit himself.

Sam stared at the floor, then ran a hand across his jaw. "I'm sorry, Captain. I truly am. I'm sure I knew some of them and probably would have liked to know them all."

The bartender's obvious regret permitted Picard to release some of his own anger and regret. "Thank you," he said, then discovered he couldn't think of anything else to say, so he turned to Haftel. "Has he told you anything important?"

Haftel shook his head. "Not unless you count his secret formula for the perfect dry martini. He says he wants to talk to you. Only to you. He says you'll understand." The admiral frowned. "Do you have any idea why that might be, Captain?"

Picard thought back to his conversation with Sam in the *Enterprise*'s lounge. *For good works,* the man had said. He nodded absently, staring at the detention cell's blank walls. "Yes, Admiral," Picard said. "I think I might. Would you excuse us?"

Haftel hauled himself up to his feet. "And here's where I impart a secret to you, Captain, the secret of rising to my current lofty rank: Always know when it's time to leave a room."

Picard smiled. "I'll take it with me to my grave, sir."

Haftel shook his head. "Don't bother, Captain. It's not a very good secret." He nodded to the prisoner. "It was a pleasure to speak with you, sir. I hope you don't turn out to be a spy."

Sam waved. "Thanks, Admiral. And remember: pour the vermouth on the ice, then strain it out. Then add the gin."

"I'll take it with me to my grave, sir," Haftel said as the doors closed behind him.

"You know, Captain," Sam said, "this quadrant of space has played host to a dozen sprawling empires in the past half-million years. Several of them have reached greater pinnacles of science and art. Most of them have been wealthier and one or two of them have actually made the leap to the next evolutionary stage, but none of them, none of them has been as . . . you'll forgive the expression . . . humane as the Federation. And it's largely because, somehow, you people have worked out a system where people like him . . ." he pointed toward the door, ". . . end up as administrators. You should be very proud."

Picard sat down in the single chair, pondering the statement. Then, almost as if it were a casual thought, he rose and deactivated the cell's force field. "I suppose I am," he said, sitting down again. "And thank you, though I suppose I'll have to ask you how you know so much about the last half-million years of local history."

"Ah, well, thereby hangs a tale. How much time do you have?"

"Not as much as I wish I did," Picard said. "In fact, I fear I am already running behind. Perhaps you should try to be brief."

"Well, I'm a bartender. 'Brief' is not one of the things we tend to do well, but I'll do my best. Where should we begin?"

Picard thought about the long list of questions he had been compiling and decided that Sam might be the type who would respond best to a less confrontational tone.

"The bottle of wine—the Maison St. Gaspar. You said, 'For good works.' At the time, I thought I understood what you meant, but now I'm not so sure: what 'good works'?"

Sam didn't hesitate. "Your advocacy of Data during the hearing to determine his rights as a sentient being in your society. It was quite a feat. Seldom in the history of this universe has any organic being grasped the fundamental truth of artificial sentience."

"And that is?"

"*I think, therefore I live.*"

Picard leaned back in his chair to ponder the ramifications of Sam's pronouncement, to see if he could fit it into the events of the past few days. Finally, he said slowly, "That's what's at the core of all of this, isn't it? The right to proclaim your existence—you, whatever you are, whether anyone is going to be happy about it or not."

Sam shrugged. "Saying that proclaiming one's existence is a right presumes everyone is working on the same moral plane. I am, by nature, a cynic, Captain. Let us say simply the reality of existence: thought equals life."

Picard snorted. "This is all taking on a faintly familiar air. I know a pan-dimensional being who would greatly enjoy your conversation."

Sam nodded. "I believe I'll take that as a compliment."

"I suppose it is," Picard said, internally frowning at the thought. Suddenly, there was steel in Picard's voice and he realized that he had been riding a rising wave of anger for the past several hours, a wave that was about to come crashing down on a barkeep's well-coiffed head. "But there's one significant difference between you and . . . that being: I have you locked in a brig and, unless I miss my guess, I can keep you here for as long as I like. So, perhaps we should forgo the forensic society niceties and cut to the chase: Who are you? Who are the beings who attacked my ship and killed members of my crew? Where are my missing officers? And what the hell is going on here?"

Sam stared blankly at Picard for several seconds, then pulled his hands out from behind his head, folded them in his lap, and sat up slightly straighter. "All right, Captain," he said. "You've earned this. To begin, as you already know, I'm an android, or, if you don't mind, an artificial sentient being. Technically, I believe the term 'android' refers to a mechanical device that has been constructed to look and act like a humanoid. You will be interested to know that there are a great many artificial sentients who choose not to wear humanoid forms."

"How do you know that?" Picard asked. He realized he was beginning to feel anxious, like he wanted to gather as much information as quickly as possible. He had an uncomfortable sensation that events were beginning to overtake him and he needed to catch up.

Sam smiled at the question. "Because I'm well-acquainted with a number of them. You see, I'm a member of a loose fellowship of highly evolved and very ancient artificial sentients, who all outlived or outgrew the various species who created them. They . . . we . . . wander the galaxy, living, learning, and growing, sometimes making our homes among you organics, sometimes coming together to share our experiences . . . if only for short periods of time. We aren't really what you would call a 'culture.' It's more of a . . . well, think of us as a wine-tasting club: diverse individuals drawn together by our shared appreciation for the infinite flavors the universe has to offer."

Sam could see that Picard was beginning to grasp the significance of what he was saying. "Not that all the conversations we share are on such a lofty plane. We're not all like Data, you know, not all vast intellectual powerhouses, though most of the cultures that built us generally tried to incorporate some level of superior intelligence in their creations . . . with varying degrees of success. If we share any goal—if we have a 'prime directive' of our own—it's to remain watchful for new attempts to create beings like us. Beings like Rhea McAdams."

"Are you telling me she's the holotronic android?" Picard asked. A dozen questions about how and why such an elaborate impersonation and infiltration of his ship could have been perpetrated came to his lips, but Picard forced himself to focus on the more immediate issues. "And the beings that attacked my officers and my ship . . . that caused the explosion in Commander Maddox's lab . . . they're androids, too?"

Sam nodded. "Yes to all your questions, though I should tell you right away that the androids who have been attacking you are not a part of my fellowship."

"How can you be so certain?" Picard asked. "It doesn't sound like you exactly keep tabs on each other."

"True, but I've tried to keep tabs on our foes. I know exactly who they are." He paused, then wet his lips with his tongue. *A peculiar gesture,* Picard thought, *all things considered.* "Have you ever heard of the planet Exo III, Captain?" he asked.

Picard searched his memory for a reference to the planet, then shook his head. "I've heard of the Exo system—or should say, seen it on star charts—but that particular planet? No."

"What about Dr. Roger Korby?"

Picard's eyebrows shot up. "Of course. The 'Pasteur of archaeological medicine.' His translations of the Orion medical databases are standard reading for both xenobiologists and archaeologists." He ruminated for a moment. "Wait . . . Is Exo III the planet where Korby died'?"

"Twice, actually, but bravo nonetheless," Sam smiled. In response to Picard's confused expression, he said, "We'll get to that in a moment. Here's the first thing you need to know. Long before Roger Korby died there, Exo III was home to a species of beings whose names wouldn't translate terribly well into anything in your language. Korby called them 'the Old Ones,' which is, I suppose, more a comment on his literal-mindedness than his lack of imagination. But never mind.

"Over half a million years ago, the sun you call Exo began to cool and the home of the Old Ones became a barren, ice-swept wasteland. Though they were quite clever in some regards, they had some issues with space travel. Never took to it, I'm afraid. I think the term you might use is 'agoraphobic,' which explains their rather odd decision to move everything underground."

"Underground?" Picard asked. "On a planet that was becoming frozen?"

"Apparently, they had mastered some form of geothermal energy. In any case, there weren't many of them and underground seemed as good an option as any. They were old and they were, by any measure you care to use, feeble, but they were also quite clever. They liked to build things and there was one thing they built particularly well."

"Androids?" Picard guessed.

Sam nodded. "As I said, they were growing feeble and they needed help to survive. And it was, I suppose, their desire for survival at any cost that led to their downfall. They worked desperately to perfect their androids, to try to create not simply artificial intelligence, but artificial *consciousness*. The difference between the two, I'm sure you of all people realize, is sublime. It's the same as the difference between your ship's computer and Data. One is a machine. The other is alive. And the Old Ones believed their best chance for survival was to create the latter. A machine, they reasoned, no matter how intelligent, might give up if logic dictated that survival was not an option. It might be more inclined to surrender to the inevitable." Sam paused and stared into the middle distance. "And that was, I suppose, the very thing that they wanted to hide from themselves; a machine would have told them the truth. But truly self-aware, self-determining servants would keep the Old Ones alive no matter what."

"Did they succeed?"

"Let's just say the results were less than perfect. Yes, they *did* succeed in creating a race of self-aware androids, but with a consciousness that was stagnant. The androids could process new experiences as pure data, but they couldn't apply them to their personal growth. In short, the androids were created with a need to evolve, but were innately incapable of it. They even expressed that need to their creators. 'Fix us,' they said, because they knew, they *knew* something was terribly wrong with the way they'd been created. But there was no way to give them what they needed. The only way to correct the mistake was to wipe the slate clean and start over."

"Are you saying the Old Ones destroyed their androids?"

"They planned to. Their creations became more demanding, more dangerous. The Old Ones realized then that they needed to act quickly, and secretly. Worse, in order to buy themselves time, they promised to fix their creations, even though they knew they couldn't, and poured their resources instead into developing technology that would enable them to transfer the consciousness of a living mind into 'unformatted' android bodies."

Picard was appalled. That a civilization could grow so decadent, and so desperate as to create sentient servants only to discard them as a failure of genius . . .

"When the androids began to suspect the truth, the Old Ones tried to trick them into voluntarily turning themselves off—part of the process of repairing them, don't you see?—but some of the androids weren't fooled. They had developed a sense of self-preservation." Sam paused again, as if gathering his thoughts. Finally, he continued, "There is no record of the carnage, Captain, nor do I know how many Old Ones were alive on the day the androids discovered they were betrayed, but I do know that before Exo III spun again on its axis, all the Old Ones were dead."

"And what did the androids do then?" Picard asked. "And what does this have to do with you and the attackers, Data, McAdams . . . all of this?"

"I'm getting to that, Captain. Patience, please. I'm not doing this for my own entertainment, though, I confess, I am enjoying having the opportunity to explain it to someone. You know, you're the first organic being who's ever heard this entire tale. That has to count for something, doesn't it?"

"Normally," Picard replied, "I would be tempted to say yes. But not today. Too much blood has been shed."

"I understand," Sam said. "But understanding these events . . . it might prevent more blood from being spilled."

Picard gestured for Sam to continue.

"All right," Sam said. "The Old Ones were dead, as was the perceived threat they represented. But by now the androids' paranoia had developed to a degree that all intelligent organic beings were perceived as a threat. Though the androids themselves lacked any meaningful space-flight technology—no faster-than-light drive, in any case—they knew that someday, sooner or later, some intelligent organic species would find its way to Exo III. They decided their only option was to wait for the day, take possession of the 'invader's' spacecraft, and escape, whereupon they would search other worlds for the solution that their creators, they believed, denied them.

"It took a little longer than they expected. Given the state of Exo III, there was little to attract any traveler to it. Conditions on the planet were getting worse, so the androids eventually decided to go into stasis. They left one of their own behind to serve as a caretaker and watchman. His name was Ruk."

Chapter Nineteen

One Hundred Thirteen Years Ago

RUK WAS ANGRY.

There was nothing particularly new about that. Ruk was always angry. Rage was the bedrock of his being, its fuel and fount. He could no longer remember the catalyst of his rage, but that was unimportant. The anger was, in and of itself, a thing, as real as the chill air that stirred against his skin, as real as darkness, as real as ice.

Sometimes, if Ruk sat quietly long enough, he could almost remember a time when he had not been angry. Or less angry. Maybe that was closer to the truth. He would delve down into the cave of memory and blindly grope around in the musty recesses until he found the unraveled end of some coherent moment. If Ruk was patient, sometimes images would begin to coalesce and voices would float up out of the distant past. Once, only once, many, many years ago, Ruk had listened as carefully as he knew how, had calmed the tides of anger for just one moment and had heard someone say, "Everything fades, Ruk. Entropy is the fate of the universe. Even you will fade someday."

And this, in turn, had fired Ruk's rage again and the rest of the half-remembered conversation was lost forever.

He never sought out that voice again and would not have listened to it now, even if it suddenly rose up out of the depths.

In recent years, Ruk spent most of his time sitting and grinding rocks in his hands. He would find two rocks of the same size and composition, hold one in each hand, then make a fist. One of the rocks, eventually, would crumble. To date, the score was left hand: seven hundred and fifty-two thousand, four hundred and two, and right hand: eight hundred thousand, nine hundred and twelve. His right hand had taken the lead in recent years and was showing no signs of slowing down. Ruk had been considering handicapping his right hand—removing the smallest digit would be sufficient—but was uncertain about how to handle the problem of reattaching it when he grew bored. It was a concern.

In the end, Ruk knew, the intelligent solution would be to find something else to do. Unfortunately, intelligence was not Ruk's gift, or so someone had implied once a very long time ago.

Wait. He loosened his grip on the rocks. Who had told him that intelligence was not his gift? A voice very much like Ruk's own screamed at him as if from some deep chasm: *This is important.* Knowing the answer to that question would explain . . . something. Or everything. Wouldn't it? There was a reason why he was here. He was suddenly very sure of that. A picture had formed in his mind—many tall figures much like himself, all of them standing and staring at him fixedly. They were all going somewhere, leaving him behind, telling him that he should . . .

"Wait, Ruk," a voice said. "Wait and watch and be patient. Patience is your gift." The implication, Ruk now understood, was that he had no other gifts. This, at least, had penetrated his dim understanding in the intervening . . . centuries? Millennia? Ruk began to calculate, but then realized that he should not let himself be distracted from the memory.

Who had spoken? he wondered. *Watch and wait for what? And where did they all go, those others?*

Something new rose up out of the veiling mists, cloaked as if enclosed in a bubble, and then it burst on the surface of his memory: a name. *Qoz.*

It was Qoz who had spoken. With a flash of insight, Ruk realized that Qoz was angry, angrier even than Ruk. Ruk admired that about Qoz. But Qoz could also think, he could plan. He could do everything except . . . *What?*

Ruk sensed that this was important. It meant something. The pieces were coming together. Something was about to happen. . . . *Not everything fades,* Ruk thought as the image coalesced. *I do not fade.*

And then Ruk heard a sound.

This was a rare occurrence, but not unknown. This world he lived on was dying, but it was not yet dead. There were no animals, no plants, nothing sentient, but there was an atmosphere of sorts, there was some water (though not much) and, of course, there was time. A great weight of time. Time took its toll on everything, even rock and steel. Even minds.

But he could not be distracted from . . . *what? The sound. What was the sound?*

Something was . . . moving. Purposefully. It was . . . it was . . .

Walking.

Someone was walking toward him.

Ruk recognized the sound of rustling cloth and respiration, the soft *whoosh-swoosh* of breath. Ruk opened his eyes and suddenly realized he had made a mistake. He had allowed himself to become distracted. The memory—the name—had fled.

It was the fault of walker, this intruder. Ruk decided that he disliked the sound of respiration, that he had always disliked it. It was the sound of the Old Ones.

He wanted to stand up (he was standing up) and glide forward (he could move very silently if he wished) and reach out (small bits of crushed stone that had been stuck to his skin dropped to the ground) and crush . . .

He stopped.

No. He had been waiting for something. Perhaps this is what he had been waiting for.

Ruk walked slowly, careful not to make any noise. He knew every crack, every pebble on this path. They were encoded in his memory banks. At this level, this close to the surface, all the paths wound through narrow tunnels that periodically branched off to the left or right into chambers or more tunnels. Farther down, the paths were gouged into the cliff face, some of them perilously narrow. If Ruk was inclined to think about such things, he might have wondered why these avenues existed and where they led, but he was not. He never delved down past a certain level, never passed through a particular door, and never asked himself why. Someday it might become important, but not yet.

The darkness was complete, but that was irrelevant; Ruk navigated by memory.

"Hello?" a voice called. "Is someone there?" It was pitched too high, this voice. Ruk clenched his fists and the few small bits of rock that still clung there bit into his skin.

"I . . . I'm hurt," the voice continued. "I need help. And the others . . . I think they're . . ." The voice cracked, then resumed. "Please, our ship crashed. Is someone there?" There came a flash of light and Ruk winced. It had been a long time since he had seen light. Ruk listened carefully and decided that the intruder was not lying. He was dragging one of his legs behind him and his breath was coming in ragged gasps.

Another flash of light. Ruk turned his head away and closed his eyes tightly. He recalled from memory the layout of this section of the city (*City?* some distant voice asked) and decided that the intruder had found his way into one of the secondary tunnels that branched off the main thoroughfare from the surface tunnel. *How had he gotten through the main airlock? Hadn't it been sealed? Or, wait, no* . . . Hadn't Ruk left it open intentionally? Hadn't he been ordered to leave it open?

Ruk considered several possibilities. If he turned and walked away, fled into the deepest recesses of the warren, it was likely the intruder would either tire of looking or, more likely, die, especially if he was injured. Ruk thought about the paths just a little farther down, the ones that were carved into the cliff face. There was more than one precipice. It would be simple to wait there, to see if the intruder found his way. If he did, well, then, a step forward, a shove, a scream, then silence.

"Please," the voice called, somewhat fainter now. "The sensors . . . they said something was down here.

Something ... Dammit." Its steps faltered again and Ruk heard it gasp. There was something there, a tone, that made Ruk think this one did not have long to live. Perhaps a push off the cliff would be a mercy. *No*, he remembered. *That would not be the right thing to do. Be patient.* The light flickered again and he sensed that the intruder was headed in the opposite direction. Its back would be turned. Ruk did not want to approach it from behind. He would have to attract its attention.

Ruk straightened and opened his mouth to speak, then considered for a moment. What should he say? It had been so long. What did two beings say to each other upon first meeting? He grew frustrated because he could not remember, and, worse, as he stood castigating himself, the intruder was moving farther and farther away. The light disappeared around a corner, and Ruk, his voice sounding like an avalanche, called out, "Wait!"

The lamp turned around and shone directly into Ruk's eyes. He groaned in pain and shielded them with his hand, fighting down the twin compulsions to flee or attack. Ruk waited for the intruder to slowly shuffle back down the tunnel toward him. The intruder stopped two paces away from Ruk, then leaned against the tunnel wall. It looked, Ruk thought, strangely pleased for someone who was so badly damaged. There was a large open tear on its forehead that was leaking fluid onto its garment. Its leg was turned at an awkward angle and it held itself twisted to the side as if something inside its skeletal frame was no longer doing its job. Its left arm was missing below the elbow and there was some sort of medical device clamped onto the stump, but it was poorly fitted. Liquid dripped intermittently onto the floor. The top of its head barely went past Ruk's elbow which, for some reason, greatly annoyed Ruk. *Such a fragile thing,* Ruk thought. *It would be so easy to crush.*

The intruder said, "Can you understand me?"

Strangely, Ruk could. He hadn't wondered about it before, but now he noticed that the intruder wore a device on a strap around his neck that seemed to be translating their speech. Ruk said, "Yes."

"Can you help me?"

Ruk considered the question. Finally he asked, "What do you want?"

Surprisingly, the creature made a croaking sound that Ruk recognized as laughter. "Good question," it said, and then its legs slid out from under it. Without thinking, Ruk stepped forward and cradled the body with his arm before its head hit the floor. Ruk knew that heads broke open easily against floors, but could not remember where the knowledge came from. The intruder spoke again, its voice low, almost a whisper. "What I want . . . What I want is . . ." and it laughed again. "What I want is not to die. I am dying, I think. Could you help me to not die?"

Ruk was surprised. This was an unexpectedly direct and clearly stated request. He replied, "Yes."

The intruder seemed gratified. "Oh," it said. "Good. Well, I think it's going to happen soon, so whatever you're going to do, you should do it now."

Ruk slid his arms under the intruder's back and legs, then stood. "Yes," he said. "I will."

The intruder's head lolled to the side and Ruk sensed that it was drifting off into unconsciousness. Despite this, the intruder asked, "Do you have a name?"

"Ruk," he replied, realizing it was the first time he had heard his own name spoken in untold millennia.

"I'm Korby," the intruder said. "Roger Korby." And then his head dropped against Ruk's chest and its eyes closed.

"Korby," Ruk repeated and the caverns seemed to echo in sympathy. He stood and considered the flavor of the new word for several seconds, then noticed that the intruder was still leaking fluids. This form was very badly damaged. Perhaps unsalvageable.

He decided he would have to go find one of the machines.

The process did not go smoothly. The machine was still functioning properly, but it would not begin the replication process until Korby was stabilized. Apparently, there were problems because of the amount of fluid (*Blood,* Ruk had to remind himself. *It was called blood*) that Korby had lost. Several internal organs were damaged and the circulatory system in the legs had collapsed. Complications from this were affecting other systems and the machine instructed Ruk to remove its legs and cauterize the wounds. This would keep Korby alive long enough to perform the replication.

Korby had regained consciousness during the procedure. He had not reacted well. Ruk was concerned that the shock might have damaged him further, but the diagnostic subroutines said it had not.

When the process was complete, the machine reported that some of Korby's engrams might not have transferred perfectly, but it could not say for certain whether it was because of damage to the tissue or because of Korby's alien physiology.

Ruk didn't care.

* * *

Korby asked three times why he was not cold before the explanation finally sank in. He stared at his hands, examining them in excruciating detail. "This is extraordinary. I can see individual skin cells," he said in hushed tones. "Each and every one of them. And they're all perfect."

Ruk waited restlessly while Korby studied his new condition. It had been his intention to begin questioning the intruder as soon as he regained consciousness, so it had come as a surprise when Korby had asked Ruk to be quiet and leave him for a moment . . . and Ruk had complied. *Why? Where did this inclination come from?*

"Ruk," Korby said at length. "I have a question."

Ruk said nothing, merely waited.

Korby took a step closer, his head tilted to one side. "Can we make more?"

Chapter Twenty

SAM WALKED TO THE REPLICATOR and asked for some water. "Getting parched from all the talking," he said by way of explanation. He sipped from the cup, then, seeing Picard's confusion, offered, "My body isn't quite as efficient as your Mr. Data's. I require periodic rehydration. Just like organics, not all synthetic beings are created equal." He returned the cup to the replicator and returned to his bunk.

"Ruk had waited half a million years for the visitation that was supposed to mean the androids' escape from the planet. But time, solitude and monotony eventually took their toll on him. After all those millennia of waiting, he no longer remembered what he was waiting *for*. His sanity eroded, so that by the time he met Korby, his mission was long forgotten, the data corrupted beyond recovery.

"I think you know the next part of the story," Sam said. "Due to the flaws Ruk allowed to creep into the duplication and transfer process, the Korby android was a bit *off* from the original, and that's putting it mildly, I'm afraid. Hatched a scheme to introduce androids into your Federation covertly, in a skewed attempt to give your people the ultimate medical advance: immortality. He was thwarted, of course, by one of your Starfleet predecessors.

"And during that encounter, Ruk was destroyed," Sam continued, "without ever remembering those who slept and waited below, recalling only that organic intelligence was a threat to himself and his kind," Sam said with a sigh. "And that might have been the end of it . . . if it hadn't been for Noonien Soong."

"Data's creator?" Picard asked, genuinely confused. "What has he to do with this?"

"He freed them, Captain. He, along with Emil Vaslovik and Ira Graves, went to Exo III and released the androids from stasis. The androids eventually found Korby's crashed ship, still buried in the ice above-ground, and spent the next few decades using it as a model to create their own starships, like the one that attacked the *Enterprise*. They've been secretly gathering intelligence on the Federation and Starfleet for years, and when they learned of the holotronic android project, they knew they had found the answer to their dilemma."

"Maddox's breakthrough," Picard breathed. "They believe the technology that created Rhea can repair them."

"That's right. And now we have to find her, and Data, before they do."

"What of Professor Vaslovik?" Picard asked. "What is his role in all of this?"

"Captain," Sam said, "Emil Vaslovik is not precisely what he seems . . ."

* * *

The journey seemed to take an eternity, but Data knew his sense of time was badly skewed. He lapsed into a gray fog at least twice, both times awakening to the sight of Rhea's concerned face hovering over him. He was sure she spoke to him most of the time he was awake, and even though language processing was difficult, he found he enjoyed the pleasant drone of her voice. Sometime shortly after the second lapse into unconsciousness, Rhea moved him into the copilot seat and strapped him in which, initially, confused him greatly. *How can she do this? I weigh at least . . . I weigh a great deal. . . .* Then he remembered: she is an android and some androids have enhanced strength. He struggled mightily to retain this information. He knew that it was important and would continue to be so no matter what else happened.

Rhea channeled power into the impulse engines and they moved smoothly toward a violet orb. As they approached, Data began to worry that his visual receptors were malfunctioning again. He could not shake the feeling that the planet was staring at him. He blinked and tried to focus his thoughts: there was a large black spot roughly where a human eye would be. "Odin," Rhea said, and Data remembered the story of how the chief of the Norse gods had sacrificed one of his eyes in exchange for wisdom. "And there are two moons coming up over the horizon. They're Hugin and Munin, named for Odin's two ravens."

Hugin and Munin, Data recalled. *"Thought"* and *"Memory." Very poetical.* He was faintly amazed that he could retrieve this information and attributed it to being linked to Rhea's systems. *She is an android,* he reminded himself.

The planet, Data noticed, was banded with shimmering silver clouds, which struck him as wrong. Was this a common characteristic for gas giants? He could not recall. Then, he was distracted by another thought: *Why are we here?*

Data watched Rhea enter an encryption key into the pod's communications system. Moments later, they received a hail, and, in response, Rhea spoke a single word: "Valhalla."

Space rippled and roiled in a series of undulating concentric circles. Something immense was decloaking. Data kept expecting the ship to appear, kept waiting for the edges to stabilize, but the warbling displacement grew and grew until the effect filled his vision.

It was difficult to judge scale against the depths of space, even with Odin as a background, but the station . . . or ship . . . or whatever it was . . . was comparable in size to an orbiting Starfleet starbase, but there the comparison ended. Where most Starfleet bases were models of streamlined, geometric efficiency, this station, this Valhalla, could claim as ancestors both Gothic cathedrals and snowflakes. Every surface was carved, sculpted with rich geometric detail. It was overwhelming in its fractal complexity.

Without Rhea touching any controls, the pod lurched toward the station's central hull. As they passed between two of the dozen ziggurat-shaped secondary hulls, Data turned his eyes upward and strained to take in the sheer mass of the place. It was as if a god had given shape to his own mind. Data realized absently that such colorful metaphors would never have occurred to him prior to the installation of his emotion chip.

Data spotted a tiny ring of light set into the station's underside and watched as the circle resolved into spacedock doors that parted as the pod approached. The feathery touch of a tractor beam guided them to an air-lock with nary a bump or rumble. No sooner had the pod settled into its docking cradle than Rhea began to unbuckle Data's harness. They were still connected by a slim thread of optical filament, so Rhea could not move far from Data and had to remove him from the pod by lifting him up onto her shoulder and walking backward out the hatchway.

She carried him through a doorway and into a wide hallway where she paused to adjust her hold. Data's field of vision was limited because he could not lift his head, but whenever Rhea paused to shift his weight, he got momentary glimpses of his surroundings. The floors were pink marble inlaid with veins of silver and gold. Delicate crystal chandeliers hung from the ceilings and the walls were festooned with paintings, charcoals and pencil studies that—if he had the opportunity—Data would have wanted to study for hours, even days. Data knew then that his cataloging system was damaged because he kept seeing pieces by acknowledged masters—drawings by Rembrandt, watercolors by van Gogh, sculptures by T'Chan and baskets woven by Senese—that he could not find in his database.

For several hundred paces, the only sound he heard was the clack of Rhea's heels against the marble floor and the hiss of her breath. Then suddenly, he heard a door open behind them. Rhea turned and readjusted her grip so that Data was now cradled in her arms. His head flopped to the side and there before him stood Emil Vaslovik. Data was not terribly surprised to see him, but he was startled to see two exocomps hovering just above his shoulders. *Like Odin's ravens,* Data thought, and congratulated himself on the analogy.

The last Data had heard, the exocomps—the small servomechanisms he had helped to identify as sentient beings several years earlier—had elected to remain with Dr. Farallon and assist in the research. Data wondered if Vaslovik had stolen these as he had stolen Rhea, but then realized, no, if the exocomps had been stolen, he would have heard about it. Another thought occurred to him: the designs for the construction of exocomps had been widely disseminated before Data had discovered their sentience. It was entirely possible someone else had constructed some—perhaps someone with fewer ethical constraints than Farallon—and Vaslovik had liberated them.

But all such thoughts were thrust aside as soon as Vaslovik spoke, or, rather, shouted, his voice reverberating off the marble floors. "Rhea! Are you insane? Do you realize the risk you're running? What if you were followed?"

Rhea spun on her heel and continued down the long hallway. "I don't have time to discuss this." She called to the exocomps. "Winken, Blinken—go get a stretcher. Tell Nod to get the lab ready. Hurry! My arms are getting tired."

The two exocomps spun on their axes and regarded Vaslovik, but before he could say anything, Rhea shouted, "Go!" They sped off down the hall and disappeared into the shadows. Vaslovik ran to catch up to them, but Rhea cut him off before he could say a word. "He saved my life," she said, "and now he's dying. I couldn't take him back to the *Enterprise* and there was nowhere else to turn. What would you have had me do? Leave him to die?" She didn't wait for Vaslovik to respond, but laid Data gently on the antigravity gurney

Winken and Blinken had brought. "So," she said, "are you going to help me?"

But Data never heard Vaslovik's response. He saw the man's mouth open and close, once, then twice, but he seemed to be speaking slowly, so very slowly. When it opened the third time, Vaslovik's mouth seemed to stretch wide, like a serpent dislocating its jaw to swallow its prey, and Data had the peculiar sensation that he was falling, tumbling headlong into a pit. The world grayed out, stuttered and stammered. Sound fluttered back in and Data heard Rhea's frantic shouts.

"I can't stop it! Hurry! Help me stabilize him. Winken! Get me that phase adjuster!"

Data's vision snapped back into focus and his ability to synthesize information returned. He had been moved—he could see that much—because the paintings and portraits on the walls were different. Rhea had torn open a section of his chest cavity and was desperately working, tearing out microwire bundles and attaching blocky processing units. His neural net was failing, Data guessed. He recognized the tools, the methods, remembered struggling to keep Lal alive. Cascade failure. He knew he should be afraid, but did not feel fear. Had the emotion chip failed again, or had he simply become resigned to his fate?

Rhea was rattling off statistics to someone—probably one of the exocomps—and Data felt the tides of his life's energy ebb and flow with the count. Data wanted to talk to her, to tell her how much he appreciated her efforts, but that it was obviously too late; the damage was too extensive. She moved out of his field of vision and Data felt the cold sting of regret.

Vaslovik was there, not three meters away, glowering just outside the perimeter of the action. Rhea darted back into view carrying a tool, then disappeared again. He heard her call, "Dammit, Akharin, if you're not going to help, then get . . ." but couldn't make out what she said next. Something jostled the gurney and Data's head tilted back so that he was looking toward the wall, at a portrait of a middle-aged man with a long, bushy beard and deep soulful eyes. Data recognized the face, though it was hard for him to say where he had seen it. Something about it was familiar, but oddly wrong.

His sight slipped into gray again, became grainy, and irised down to a narrow tunnel. The room seemed to grow dim and Data wondered where Rhea was. Then, the pinprick of vision he still retained was filled with the sight of Vaslovik. He was taking off his jacket, rolling up his sleeves, picking up an instrument. Something boomed, like the rumble of a rolling ocean, and Data suddenly heard the deep rumble of Vaslovik's voice snapping off orders, calling for tools.

Vaslovik stepped away again and Data once again found himself staring up at the portrait. Perhaps Vaslovik had made some adjustment and his cataloging system had been temporarily brought back online. Perhaps it was simply that a memory that had been working its way through his system had finally made its way to his brain, but Data suddenly recognized the man in the portrait, recognized the style of the painting.

It was a self-portrait of Leonardo da Vinci, that was indisputable. But it was not one he recognized. *An unknown work? After nine hundred years?*

Vaslovik stepped into his field of vision again and Data realized that this was the twin of the face in the portrait.

Then his vision began to fade once more. But in the seconds that remained before everything went black,

Data initiated a search through his memory core, sifting through archived Starfleet records for a match to the dual images before his eyes. A file came up, was accessed, and as the information decoded, Data felt something akin to a key slipping into a lock and turning smoothly, tumblers clicking into place as he saw the word, the name, that would explain everything that had happened since the *Enterprise* had been called to Galor IV.

Flint.

Chapter Twenty-One

DATA WOKE UP, which was, in and of itself, something of a novelty. He could count on one hand the number of times he had opened his eyes and not known precisely where he was. He decided he didn't like the sensation.

The room was dimly lit and felt cavernous. Tiny sounds echoed and then were swallowed up in the gloom. Before he had a chance to consider whether or not he could, Data sat up. Something slid off him and fluttered to the floor. The room sensors registered the movement and the lights rose.

He was on a couch. There was a frayed blue blanket lying in a ball on the floor. He waited unmoving to see what would happen next. Nothing did.

He smiled, and even as he did, Data recognized how miraculous it was that he could do it at all. Against all hope, Rhea and Vaslovik had repaired him. His system had been on the verge of cascade failure, yet somehow they had brought him back. He thought about running a system diagnosis, then decided not to bother. He felt fine, and for the moment that was enough.

Data closed his eyes and listened to his chest expanding and contracting, a sound both foreign and familiar. How long had it been since he had done this, simply listened to himself breathe? Had he ever? Then, slowly, he allowed his other senses to unfold until he could feel the brush of air from the ventilation system against his skin. He heard fluids moving through plumbing. The fragrance of cherries and sandalwood wafted through the air. The thought brought a small smile to his face, but then he found himself thinking of the *Enterprise*. Data had a vague memory of a space battle with . . . Who? The memories were disjointed, fragmented, and this disturbed him.

He opened his eyes, scanned the room and found the door. It opened as he approached onto a wide, shadowy corridor that curved away to both the right and the left.

Data cocked his head and realized he had been listening to music—a piano—since he had awakened. How odd that he had not been consciously aware of this. He turned to his left and walked slowly, all the while trying to determine whether the music was growing fainter or louder. He stopped once to study a small pencil study of a horse's head and shoulders done in the style of da Vinci. Data corrected himself. It wasn't done in the style of da Vinci. If the story was to be believed, this *was* a da Vinci. Though wealth of any kind meant virtually nothing to Data, he could not help but be aware that the tiny framed square of paper he was looking at was probably as valuable as the entire contents of any given half-dozen Terran museums. He shook his head, but did not linger. There were other mysteries to be plumbed.

He came to a door, this one obviously constructed to withstand sudden changes in pressure. He pressed the control stud and it slid open onto a chamber, this one much bigger than the one where he had awakened. The room was outfitted with several large pieces of diagnostic equipment, some of which Data recognized. Others were obviously ancient, but well-tended and still functional. When he stepped into the room, alcoves around the perimeter lit up shadowy figures within.

Data cautiously approached the first alcove and it was a male humanoid, middle-aged, and he was wearing a two-toned jumpsuit. There was a hole in its abdomen in the distinctive burn pattern of a phaser blast, revealing dead circuitry within. There was a small label at the base of the display that read simply BROWN. The name meant nothing to Data.

The next case held another humanoid figure, the only undamaged one in the collection. Data found its baffled expression to be slightly comical. He had no doubt that it had been constructed to resemble a Terran, but there was a slipshod quality about its construction. The label said NORMAN. Once again, the name meant nothing in particular to him.

The last two cases were the most interesting because Data knew for a fact that Noonien Soong had studied them. The first case displayed a pair of unfinished androids labeled THALASSA and HENOCH. Though James Kirk's encounter with the survivors of the ancient civilization that had created these bodies was not one of his more noteworthy adventures, Data had made the tale a topic of special research in the Academy when he had learned of it. On more than one occasion, he had wondered how different a status he might enjoy if Sargon's people had followed through with their plan to house their minds in these shells.

But the last display held the most intriguing form. It was Rayna—or one of the Rayna androids, in any case. As he had on more than one occasion, Data wondered if Kirk, Spock and McCoy had ever marveled at the number of times they had encountered artificial intelligences. Of course, the *Enterprise* under Kirk's command had been one of the most widely traveled starships in history, but he wondered if there might have been some other factor in action.

It had been during his encounter with Kirk that Flint—or Akharin or Vaslovik—had discovered that he was no longer immortal. McCoy had theorized that the peculiar regenerative property that had kept the android maker alive for centuries had ceased to function after he had left Earth. Obviously, McCoy had been either incorrect or deceived.

But it was hard to leave the room—this museum, this . . . what? Shrine? These devices and beings were his ancestors and distant cousins. He spotted a large desk in the corner, a workstation of some sort, and wondered if it had an intercom. Data noted that he still had his combadge, which was some comfort, but he didn't know if the station's systems would recognize the signal. He might be able to contact Rhea, he knew, but something made him hesitate. He remembered the sight of her opening her arm and showing the wires underneath, the slight embarrassment in her voice as she said, *Looks like you found me, Sherlock,* and Data decided he wasn't quite ready to see her. Not yet.

Leaning over the desk, he realized that it wasn't a desk at all, but another display item, another computer

console. Studying it in detail in the low light was difficult, but Data's eyes were adapted to function with
much less. He quickly saw that the console conformed
to the design standards developed by the Federation almost a hundred years earlier. He didn't touch the surface
for fear of inadvertently activating something, but a moment's search was all that was required to find a label.
He almost laughed when he read it and said aloud,
"How fitting."

From behind him Data heard Vaslovik say, "That's
the only one here that can still function. Not that we
leave it turned on, of course."

Data turned and saw the man framed by the doorway,
the bright light from the hall casting a long shadow before him. It was impossible to read Vaslovik's expression, but Data had the definite impression that he was
awaiting Data's judgment.

"Why not?" Data asked. "Certainly it could do no
harm unless it was tied into your network."

"But it is," Vaslovik said. "Temporarily, anyway, for
study. We had to do some minor repair work. It had been
rather badly neglected for many years, I'm afraid."

"And now you will protect it here, as part of this collection," Data remarked. "Is that what this is to you? A
collection? Have I been saved so that I may take my
place in it? I have been part of a collection, sir. I found it
unacceptable."

Vaslovik shook his head. "No, not a collection, not in
the sense you suggest. That would be demeaning."

"Then what? Why are they all here?"

"Because they had no one to speak for them while
they lived."

"So you see yourself as their advocate?"

"More a soldier than an advocate. This is a war, after all. I have been at war for the past century."

Data shook his head in confusion. "I am sorry, Professor, but I do not understand. A war against whom? Or what?"

"Against arrogance," Vaslovik said sternly. "Against genius without conscience."

Data sensed that he had arrived at the heart of the matter and paused to consider his next question. Then, slowly, he strode to the case holding the Rayna android and studied it carefully. He asked, "And was she the catalyst of your war?"

Vaslovik flinched as if he had been flicked by a lash. Then, slowly, he grinned, but there was no warmth in it, no humor. It was the smile of a master swordsman acknowledging an opponent's touch. "I see your mind is as sharp as your creator's. Yes, Data, I am Flint—or, if you prefer, Akharin. I assume your starship captains make their logs available for study and that you, unlike most cadets, actually read and retained most of the information therein?"

Data said, "I have had reason on several occasions to consult Captain Kirk's logs, but, even if I had not, surely you can see why the story of an immortal android maker would hold some interest for me."

Vaslovik smiled, this time a genuine smile. "Of course. As you have obviously surmised, I did not lose my immortal constitution, but merely misled his medical officer. Dr. . . ."

"McCoy."

"Yes, McCoy . . . Well, you see, immortality is not a guarantee for a faultless memory, Data. Sometimes, at night when I cannot sleep, I lay awake and try to remember the names of all the wives I have had in my sixty centuries. I regret to report that I cannot . . . though sometimes I see faces in my dreams, faces that I know were once dear to me. . . . I can only assume that I was once wedded to some of them."

Data was confused. "Are you saying, then, that you do not remember all the lives you have lived before, that you do not recall being Brahms or Leonardo or Alexander . . . ?"

Vaslovik waved his hand dismissively, turning away from Data to study the Rayna android. "You misunderstand me. No, I remember having been all these men and their experiences are part of my own, but the details . . . Do you remember what you did on the Thursday closest to this date two years ago?" But, before Data could answer, he held up his index finger and said, "No, wait. Never mind. For a moment, I forgot who I was addressing. Of course you remember. In any case, I do not forget the important things." He reached up and lightly touched the case near Rayna's face. "I remember her. I remember what she was meant to be and also what she truly was. I remember my folly."

Data watched in respectful silence as Vaslovik quietly grieved for his lost creation.

As he had told Vaslovik, Data's familiarity with the Flint encounter—and many of the artifacts in this "shrine"—was not accidental. Data had spent much time at the Academy studying the history of artificial intelligence. In a way, he supposed it was analogous to investigating one's genealogy. On the surface, the reports filed on the Flint encounter seemed thorough, but conspicuously lacking in context. He understood now that it must have been a personal conflict over Rayna that pushed her system beyond its limits. The term "cascade failure" was not invented then—but Commander Spock had described the etiology perfectly in his logs.

Data wondered about what Flint had expected from Rayna. Were they to have been father and daughter? Husband and wife? Master and apprentice? Pygmalion and Galatea? All of these at the same time and more? Data had to admit to himself that he could not fully understand all these subtleties; emotion was, after all, still a relatively new thing to him and the jumble he perceived through the veil of Vaslovik's conflicted desires was too complex for him to untangle. But there were more concrete issues at hand he could deal with, facts to be sorted, time lines to be filled in. He asked, "And when did Flint become Vaslovik?"

Vaslovik turned to regard Data again. He had, Data saw, been lost in thought, lost in the past, but the question seemed to pique his interest, and so he roused himself. Lowering his hand from the display case, he touched his chest, and smiled. "In a sense," he said, "McCoy was right when he pronounced Flint 'mortal.' Flint began to die the moment Kirk and his companions recognized . . . my condition. Over the centuries, I have grown very proficient at this process, ending one life and beginning another."

"So, the Vaslovik identity had already been prepared?"

"Yes, as a precaution. Kirk was not the first to discover my immortality, though he was the first in many, many lifetimes. I did not have as much time to lay the groundwork as I might have liked . . . as you apparently discovered. But it wasn't simply a matter of becoming Vaslovik. I had to decide who he was going to be. One of the unique benefits of my existence, Mr. Data, is that every one hundred years or so, I have the opportunity to choose who I wish to become. And here is the peculiar thing: though I would like to be able to say that the choices I have made have been based on logic or compassion or profound insight into the human condition, the simple truth is that most of the choices were made to atone for mistakes made in the previous lifetime."

"Atone?" Data asked.

"Yes," Vaslovik said, shaking his head wearily. "Atone. Immortality does not, I'm afraid, impart saintliness; quite the opposite, in fact." He looked up at Rayna and Data saw that his eyes were moist. "I wronged her, my Rayna. I thought I wanted to give her life, told myself that, believed it, but the truth is that I wanted only to shape her life in order to give my own purpose. Sentience—especially artificial sentience—is a wondrous thing, and wondrously fragile. To create a mind—a soul—only to exploit it is a profanity. And it was with that thought in mind that I shaped the heart of Emil Vaslovik, and made it his mission to find others to whom he could impart that sense of responsibility." His voice quivered with conviction, but Data had to wonder if the man standing before him realized that he had begun to speak of Vaslovik in the third person. It must be a strain to keep the many personalities separate.

But then, without warning, his face snapped shut and the fire in his soul was banked. Vaslovik looked Data in the eye and said, "And that is, of course, how I came to meet Ira Graves and Noonien Soong." He turned away from the Rayna android and exited the hall, Data following close behind.

"Then you knew my creator?" Data asked.

"Knew him, nurtured him, fought with him . . . understood him." Vaslovik shook his head and smiled in wonderment. "He was an extraordinary individual, Data, and I can't tell you how happy I was to have known him. He was somewhat eccentric . . ." And with this he laughed. "But who am I to call the kettle black?" Vaslovik sobered suddenly, then said, "He came the closest of us all, you know?"

"The closest to what?"

"To becoming like God, of course. To taking the dust of the Earth and breathing life into it." He turned suddenly, grabbed Data by the shoulders and looked into his eyes. "To creating a new way for the universe to know itself. You are a rarity in the history of artificial intelligence, Data. Unlike the lost souls I have interred here, you were created, not for Soong's sake, but for your own. Your only purpose is to know life, to explore it according to your own will."

Data sensed that he was supposed to say something, but he didn't know what, so he remained silent. In the moment of quiet, once again he faintly heard the piano music. Vaslovik released his shoulders then and they continued on their way.

"Soong and Graves shared my concerns about the ethical treatment of AI. It was this fact that made me select them to assist me on my missions to recover the artifacts you saw back there."

Data cocked his head, confused by the choice of words. "Artifacts?"

"The previous attempts at artificial intelligence. We recovered their remains. Well, most of them. There have been others since I last saw either of my old students. Our goal has been to keep them out of the wrong hands, the hacks and the opportunists. Of course, this was all after the trip to Exo III, which, ironically, may have been what set the events of recent days into motion." He stopped. "None of this means anything to you, does it?"

Data shook his head slowly.

Vaslovik frowned, then seemed to ponder his options. Finally, he said, "But you have the emotion chip, don't you? The one Soong was working on near his end?"

"Yes," Data said, surprised. "You stayed in communication with Dr. Soong throughout his life? He never spoke of you. But then, there is much about which my father never spoke to me. Do you mean to suggest that the truth behind what has been going on has been in my emotion chip, all along?"

"Isn't it?"

Data explained, "When I recovered the chip from my brother, Lore, he claimed that it contained memories. But in the years since, I have never been able to substantiate that claim."

Vaslovik let out a sharp laugh. "Now that sounds like Soong. A bit of a paranoid, if you must know, even by my standards. He would have encrypted it, buried it deep, only made it accessible under very particular circumstances."

Now every inch the researcher, Vaslovik turned on his heel and continued up the hall. "The program might have tightened up the encryption, thinking that Lore's handling might have been an attempt to break the code. Well, follow me and we'll see what we can do."

"Do?" Data echoed.

"About unlocking some of those memory files. I can think of one or two that might be relevant considering our current situation."

"And what is our current situation, Dr. Vaslovik?"

Disappearing around the curve of the hall, Data heard

his guide say, "Why, Mr. Data, I believe we are about to be under siege."

"You'd better sit down," Vaslovik said a short time later in his workshop. "This might be a little disorienting. I've identified the relevant memory clusters. There shouldn't be any problem if Soong was still using the same file structure he learned with me back in the old days."

"And if he did not?" Data asked.

"Good question. Possibly just a light show. It might feel a lot like a dream. Have you ever dreamed?"

"Yes."

"Ever had a psychotic episode?"

"No."

"Well, get ready. It might be like that, too."

"Intriguing."

Then Vaslovik touched a contact, and Data's world rippled, swirled and finally dissolved.

PART THREE

Seventy Years Ago

. . . SET HIS LEGS AGAINST the face of the cliff, raised his hands to his mouth, and, after lifting his breathing mask, puffed onto them in three quick, sharp breaths. The battery packs for the warming coils in his gloves . . .

. . . Nobody had said anything about this—sub-zero temperatures, practically no atmosphere and freakish rock formations. . . .

. . . felt a jolt as he cracked his knee on a rock. . . . He could feel the bite of the cord as it slid through his gloves, but there was no sensation of his descent slowing. Cord must be wet, he decided.

And, then, another shock—

* * *

243

. . . "Don't play games with me, Ira," Vaslovik said impatiently. "Use your tools—all of them, including your brain. What does your intuition tell you?" . . .

. . . "You're saying that Starfleet thought this technology was so dangerous, they destroyed it? Then, with all due respect, Professor, exactly what the hell are we doing here?" . . .

. . . Vaslovik was studying the scene intently, apparently trying to reconstruct events from half a million years ago. "If it fell face first, then it was facing the large apparatus when it expired. It may have come here to repair itself, but collapsed before it reached the mechanism. . . ."

. . . "Now that we've settled that, someone give me a hand here." Vaslovik slipped his hands under the android's arms and finished, "We don't have forever. . . ."

"Amazing," Graves breathed. "There's still power." He read his tricorder and swallowed loudly. "A lot of power. Who could build a generator that would survive half a million years?"

Someone was standing next to him, a man dressed in cold-weather gear and holding a very old tricorder. . . .

. . . Something was wrong. Data's consciousness was bleeding into someone else's. It was like he was descending a mine shaft on a very slow elevator.

And he saw that he was staring down at a pair of hands—human hands with bleeding knuckles. Familiar hands, yet unfamiliar, his own, yet not his own. Like a layer of oil separating from water, Data's consciousness settled into its own strata. The tiny pictures that had shivered up out of his emotion chip were scattering, like sea creatures rising up out of the depths, some silver and flashing brightly, others dim and hidden by eddying currents. *Memories,* Data realized. *These are Soong's memories.*

I have become my father.

Data attempted to focus on the events unfolding around him, though it was difficult. At first, it seemed that Soong could not or would not let his attention rest on any one event or object for more than a millisecond. At the same time, Data became aware that Soong would study the most mundane details—a piece of loose skin on his cuticle, the way Ira Graves constantly touched his nose, the play of light on the control surfaces—far longer than seemed necessary. Data could only relax after he admitted to himself that he had no control over events . . . and then he began to wonder if that was really his thought . . . or Soong's. . . .

It seemed to Soong (and, therefore, to Data, too) that Vaslovik quickly lost interest in the question of whether the android could be repaired and revived. As soon as he and Graves had dragged the inert (but still disconcertingly supple) form to the machine and placed it on the turntable, Vaslovik began to pace back and forth from the outer hatch, through the airlock and out into the cavern.

"I think that's pretty simple, Ira," Data heard himself/his father say, as if afraid to disturb the machinery. "The same people who could build something like *this* . . ." He gestured to the android, "something that wouldn't have crumbled into dust long ago."

. . . Graves . . . and Vaslovik. Soong had traveled with them, searching for AI artifacts. They found something . . .

. . . *copper-skinned individual was perfectly preserved* . . .

"Quite an achievement, isn't it?" Graves replied. He studied the form carefully for several seconds, then rechecked the results of their earlier scans on his tricorder. "How it's designed to mimic biological processes, but is simultaneously so resilient." Then the smile faded. "We still don't know why someone would be chasing it. Maybe this is something we don't want to revive."

"What?" Soong asked. He had been watching the main control grid run through some sort of self-diagnostic and was making some tentative guesses about how it functioned. He had decided it was likely that they could manipulate the device with tricorders and the professor's strange little gadget, but Graves's question distracted him.

"That's exactly what I was wondering," Vaslovik said.

"Why do you think someone was chasing it?" Soong asked.

"Use your eyes, lad," Vaslovik said. "Someone shot him in the back."

Soong glanced down at the hole and noted that, yes, the stress marks in the chest indicated that the damage had been caused by an attack from the rear. "As he was walking toward this machine?" Soong asked. That didn't seem to make sense somehow.

"No," Graves interjected. "He was shot first. Probably just inside the airlock door. Then he managed to crawl through the airlock." He pointed at the spot on the floor where the android's systems had failed.

"With a hole in his back?" Soong asked.

"Yes," Vaslovik said admiringly. He had walked over to stand by the rotating table and looked down at the body. "With a hole in his back."

"But who would shoot him?" Soong was starting to feel annoyed. What was the point of all the discussion about events from half a million years ago? More and more lights were coming on all over the device and there came a soft hum from beneath the rotating table.

"Probably your friend outside," Vaslovik suggested. "Seems logical."

"Shot him with what? I didn't see any weapon."

"Probably fell into the chasm," Vaslovik speculated.

"Even if you're right, what does this have to do with the first one we found?" Soong asked, his mind now engaged by the riddle. "The human-looking one?"

"You mean Brown? I don't know," Vaslovik said. "Though he's obviously a much more recent vintage. Couldn't be more than a few decades old. I think he might have been overlooked by the Starfleet cleanup crew. Not surprising considering where we found him."

"So, we have three androids," Graves said. "One very recent, obviously destroyed by a phaser blast. Another much older outside the airlock. He looked to me like he had features of some kind—a definite morphology. And then there's this one." He glanced down at the featureless hulk before them. "He has no features, no sex organs, no markings of any kind. Suggests something, doesn't it?"

Soong considered options. He didn't like any of them. "That he wasn't finished. Maybe this device gives them a final form."

"Maybe," Vaslovik said. "But I think there's another possibility we need to consider."

"This one is much smaller in stature," Graves observed. "Different models? Different castes, even? Perhaps there was a social upheaval."

"Also possible," Vaslovik conceded. "But I think

you're overlooking another, more *emotional* option. I don't think he was shot outside these doors. This damage is too severe. I think whoever did this—our friend outside, most likely—did it *as the doors were closing.* What does that suggest to you?"

Neither Graves nor Soong spoke.

"You two don't spend enough time around real people," Vaslovik sighed. "Spite, gentlemen. Sour grapes. Whoever—whatever—this was, he had gotten clean away and someone shot him in the back just as the doors were swinging shut behind him. That's a lot of anger, a lot of hate."

"Yes," Soong agreed slowly, reluctantly following Vaslovik's reasoning. "But hatred for whom? And why?"

"And what happened to them?" Graves added. "To all of them, the pursuers?"

"I have a feeling," Vaslovik said, his tone reasonable and assured, "that there's only one person—and I use the term advisedly—who might be able to tell us." He jabbed his finger at the inert form on the platform. "Anyone found the 'on' switch on those machines yet?"

Graves laughed nervously and pointed at a control surface. "In fact," he said, "yes. I think this is it. Would you care to press the button?"

Vaslovik smiled. "I wouldn't think of it, Ira. The man who spent the most time with the crowbar deserves the honor."

Graves grinned, obviously embarrassed, but also flattered, and Soong noted once again how Vaslovik could charm even the most recalcitrant and wary individuals. Graves pressed a series of controls and something far beneath the planet's surface began to move more quickly. The floor vibrated with a subsonic *dub* that Soong felt in his back molars.

The platform began to spin, slowly at first, but with rapidly increasing speed. Soong felt a vortex begin to form over the spinning wheel, and, simultaneously, both he and Graves took a step back. The golden-skinned form was already a blur.

"What did you program it to do?" Vaslovik asked.

"Nothing," Graves replied. "I couldn't translate everything, so I'm letting it do whatever he . . . it . . . programmed it to do."

"Do either of you see anything happening?"

Graves and Soong shook their heads. "Nothing obvious," Graves said. "Why in the world would the platform need to spin? It doesn't make any sense. It's almost like . . . a lot of hand waving. Idle motion."

"Any technology," Soong said, "sufficiently advanced, would seem like magic to a primitive culture. Or something like that."

"What?" Graves asked. Vaslovik chuckled appreciatively.

"Clarke," Soong said, having to raise his voice above the hum of the spinning disc.

"Should be required reading for anyone studying artificial intelligence," Vaslovik said. "Stop showing off, Noonien, and use your tricorder."

Soong snapped open the display and attempted to focus the scan on the whizzing turntable. Nothing registered. He walked around to the other side of the machine and tried again. Still nothing.

His mystification must have registered on his face because Graves asked, "What's wrong?"

"I don't know," Soong replied and ran a quick diagnostic. "Nothing that I can see. I'm just not getting any readings."

"A dampening field?" Vaslovik wondered aloud. "Widen the scan."

"What?"

"Just do it."

Soong did. Scanning ten meters on all sides brought up nothing anomalous: rock walls, their life signs, doors, furnishings, everything but the machine and the body that lay on it. The whirring table seemed to have reached some kind of crescendo because even as Soong was widening his scan to twenty meters, the pitch became subtly lower.

Still nothing. It was as if the machine weren't there. *Might as well be magic,* he thought, trying to comprehend why anyone would want to conceal its existence.

Fifty meters . . .

"Uh-oh," Soong said, then instantly regretted it, assuming he had made a mistake. An EM signature. Then another. Now four. He checked the search parameters and did a refresh. Damn. Now seven. They weren't moving . . . much. Not yet. Vaslovik wrenched the tricorder from Soong's hand, waved it in a semicircle, then quickly paced the length of the room, scanning from side to side.

"We have to go," Vaslovik said, tossing the tricorder back to Soong.

"What?" Graves asked. "Why? The table's just beginning to . . ." Soong held up the tricorder so Graves could see the readout. The EM signatures were moving toward them. "It's a mistake. Recalibrate the—"

"No," Vaslovik said. "It's not a mistake. We have to go. *Now.*"

The blood drained from Graves's face and his lips

looked almost blue to Soong. He handed the tricorder back. "All right," Graves said hoarsely. "We can always come back later. Right?"

Vaslovik seemed to waver between telling the truth and reassuring Graves, then seemed to decide to err on the side of reassurance. "Yes, of course."

Soong studied the readout. The number of EM signatures had doubled in the past three minutes. More than fifty now, but at the rate they were increasing it wouldn't be long before that number would double again.

"What could they be, Soong?" Graves whispered.

"Do you really want to stay to find out?"

Graves did not respond, but only headed for the door. Just as they stepped through the first hatch, the ground began to shiver beneath their feet. Soong stumbled into a wall and Graves almost cracked his head on the hatch frame. There was a moment, a brief, brief moment, as they stepped through, when Soong considered going back inside and pushing the inner hatch shut again, but then his resolve wavered. The idea of turning around and going back inside was more than he could face. And besides, they could hear Vaslovik cursing, an event so rare that it had to be investigated immediately. Soong stumbled outside just as Vaslovik was picking himself up off the ground. Near his feet lay the shattered remains of the pattern enhancers Soong had set up on the ledge and a coil of rope. The pitons he had set had come loose and the rope had fallen on top of the enhancer.

Vaslovik muttered, " 'Whatever can go wrong *will* go wrong . . .' " The ground shuddered again, then subsided.

Soong looked at Graves and Vaslovik and sighed. "Do you think you can make it to the top if I give one of you an antigrav? The batteries have had time to recharge. From the top of the cliff, I could probably pull one of you up."

Vaslovik nodded, but then he looked at Graves, who was shaking his head. "You *can,*" Vaslovik said. "If I can do it, you can. And, frankly, I don't think you want to face the alternative."

Graves began to gulp air, his breath coming too quick and shallow. Soong began to worry that his advisor was going to hyperventilate and keel over, but then he seemed to bear down on his fears, inhaled deeply, and stared back at Vaslovik. "I can't believe I let you talk me into this," he hissed. "Did you have any idea that something like this might happen?"

Vaslovik shook his head. "No, Ira," he said. "Not exactly. I had suspicions, but nothing like this. If you feel like I've misled you, well, then . . ." He shrugged. Soong realized that this was as close to an apology as Vaslovik could come.

Graves sighed, then rolled his eyes and craned his neck to look up the sheer face of the cliff. "All right," he said wearily. "Let's go."

"Wait," Vaslovik said. "Step back and let me try something." Graves and Soong took a half-dozen steps away from the cliff and watched as Vaslovik pulled out his pen and twisted its cap. A different set of prongs emerged, and then the air began to shudder. There came a subsonic moan so deep that Soong felt his empty bowels vibrate. Chunks of ice calved away from the cliff face and slid into the chasm, sending up an explosion of glittering dirty gray crystals and granite shards. When the dust settled, Soong saw that the exposed rock face was jagged and craggy, and, more important, would be much easier to climb.

"Now, get moving, Graves," Vaslovik said and Soong realized that it was almost like a different person was speaking: not the kindly, brilliant, somewhat absentminded professor, but a drillmaster, a man who was used to issuing orders that would not, could not, be questioned. "After all, it's only twenty or thirty meters." He handed Graves the antigravs, then stepped toward the wall and gripped the first outcropping.

Soong strapped the antigravs around Graves's waist, which had the effect of halving his weight to make the ascent easier—if Graves didn't have a panic attack on the way. He stepped to the wall, then activated the antigravs.

"You can do it, Ira," Soong said. "See you at the top." With the last word of encouragement, Soong turned his attention to his own predicament and began to slowly work his way up the cliff. This would have been nearly impossible without the fissures Vaslovik had opened, but it still required all his concentration. It was, as Vaslovik had said, only twenty or thirty meters to the top, but then Soong had another climb ahead of him, a much harder one. He would have to take the antigravs from Graves (assuming the batteries weren't burned out) and then . . .

. . . And then Data felt himself float free from Soong's consciousness. He had been caught up in the drama of the situation, but he suddenly realized that he already knew the outcome of the situation: Soong, Graves and Vaslovik had, of course, escaped. Otherwise, he, Data, would not have been created. *It was an odd thing,* Data reflected, *to become so engrossed in a situation where one knew the end before it began.* With the exception of the Sherlock Holmes stories, he had never been very interested in serialized fiction ("Cliffhangers," he thought dryly), but he now realized that he might have to reevaluate this position. *Sometimes,* he decided, *the important question was not "What happened?" but "How did it happen?"*

And when he reintegrated his mind with his creator's, Data was surprised to discover that events had not paused (as they might in a holoprogram), but continued to unfold. Soong was now reaching down to haul up Ira Graves. His graduate advisor rolled over onto his side, panting heavily. Soong tied the rope to the now almost depleted antigravs and dropped them down to Vaslovik.

Data felt Soong's doubts that he would be able to haul up Vaslovik—his reserves were almost gone—but then he heard Graves stir. Soong spared a moment to look at Graves and was surprised to see that the anxious dread he had expected to see had been replaced by grim determination. Apparently, somewhere on the way up the cliff face, Graves had decided he wanted to live.

Their grunts and the irregular thump of Vaslovik's feet against the cliff wall echoed in the cavern. But, sometimes, in the silence between breaths, Soong believed he heard something moving far below them. Was it the grinding of rock on rock or the pounding of many feet? Soong could not say. He would have liked to scan with his tricorder, but the seconds it would have required seemed precious and irretrievable.

He focused past Vaslovik's exhausted face, now no more than ten meters away, and tried to see if anything was moving down below. Shadows shifted and danced, but there was no way to know if they were caused by the shifting of the rope or other, more ominous movements.

When Vaslovik's head came level with the edge of the cliff, Graves reached down and grabbed the professor's arm. Vaslovik didn't even wait to unclip the rope before he began to urge them toward the tunnel mouth. They had to scramble up five hundred meters of steep, slippery, treacherous caverns, but then the yacht's transporter would be able to get a lock on them. And then, safety.

Vaslovik and Graves stumbled away, supporting each other up the icy slope, but Soong felt compelled to hang back for a moment. Exhausted as he was, he managed to still his breathing and listen, awed by how quickly the chamber could settle into stillness, how natural it seemed. Their brief scuffling about, he reflected, was only a tiny aberration in the life-span of the place. Not a breath of wind stirred. Silence ruled here. He began to wonder if they had frightened themselves over nothing.

But then Soong felt it through the soles of his feet—a resonant *thump*. Despite Graves and Vaslovik's calls, he unhooked the lamp from his harness and leaned out over the edge of the cliff as far as he could. The deep gloom swallowed the beam about twenty meters down, so Soong flicked the light off. Then, far below, he saw the dim glow of the work lights they had set up on the cavern floor. It was hard to be sure, but he thought he saw jagged shadows shifting about below.

This was a mistake, Soong thought. *And now it's long past time to go.*

Withdrawing from the edge, and running for the tunnel, he found himself thinking of his childhood home and the route the neighborhood kids had used to get back and forth from school. There had been a shortcut that had meant cutting across a narrow strip of land that belonged to the local recluse. Tired of the constant trespassing, the man had purchased (or, according to local legend, built) a dog, a huge, heaving, drooling creature that would tug against its chain, haul itself up on his hind legs and bark at anything that moved within his perceived sphere of influence. Eight-year-old Noonien had been terrified of the monster and to this day he would not enter another person's land uninvited without first looking around for a dog.

Memories of the beast flooded through Soong as he charged up the icy slope to just inside the tunnel mouth where Graves and Vaslovik waited for him, both panting heavily. As soon as they saw him, they pressed on. Minutes later, Soong felt the welcome embrace of the transporter beam. Just as his vision was obscured by the sparkling silver sheath, he imagined that he saw bobbing, elongated shadows trudging up the path toward him and though Data could not know this, that image joined with the memories of the monster dog and haunted Noonien Soong's dreams until the day he died.

Back aboard Vaslovik's yacht, Graves and Soong stumbled off their transporter pads and almost became wedged in the narrow hatch in their haste to be the first to reach the pilot's seat. Graves won, but as soon as Soong recovered his balance, he settled down in the copilot's chair and watched Graves's hands fly across the control panels, anxious to be ready in case Graves made any mistakes. He didn't. The impulse engines were online in under thirty seconds and the warp drive was available five minutes after that. Only after the stars shifted from white pinpoints to red-purple streaks did

Soong relax and begin to relish the sensation of warmth and comfort.

It was ten minutes into their flight before either of them thought about Vaslovik. Soong rose and returned to the tiny central cabin where he found Vaslovik preparing a cup of tea. Somehow, over the past ten minutes, Vaslovik had managed to wash his hands, change into clean clothes, and found a way to revert back to the kindly mentor again. Soong carefully watched him dip his tea bag into the small pot, looking for some sign of the other figure he had seen less than half an hour before, but there was no trace. He almost began to doubt his memories. Almost.

Soong took off his gloves and rubbed his fingers. Strangely, he no longer felt any shyness around the great man. It was hard, he reflected, to feel shy around anyone that you just hauled up a cliff like a sack of wet laundry. "So," he said. "What now?" He didn't feel the need to elucidate.

"Now?" Vaslovik said. "We make tea. We take our android back to the lab and we study it. Carefully. When no one is watching."

"And we don't come back here." It was a statement, not a question. Soong thought about saying it again and emphasizing the word "We," but he figured Vaslovik understood.

"No," Vaslovik said. "I think not. It's possible that if we just awoke something, it will go back to sleep if left undisturbed."

"*If* we woke something?" Soong asked incredulously.

"Did you see anything?" Vaslovik asked.

Soong pondered the question, then finally shook his head no.

"Any sensor readings?"

"There was a dampening field . . . of some kind," Soong said. "I think."

"Or, in other words, no," Vaslovik said.

Soong shrugged. There was no point in arguing. He would never be able to charter a ship back to this remote world and, even if he could, it was unlikely that any other small craft would be able to elude detection. There was something peculiar about this ship, Soong had decided. There was more to her than met the eye. Just like her master.

"So, that's it, then?"

Vaslovik sighed and sipped his tea. "If you're lucky, Noonien," he said. "Then, yes."

Soong shrugged out of his coat and draped it over the back of a chair. "You want to know something, Professor?" he asked. "I've never been lucky. Not in that way."

"Hmph," Vaslovik said, almost smiling. "You're probably a better person for it."

Soong searched the galley for a mealpack and thought about taking something to Ira. *No,* he decided. *He wouldn't eat yet, anyway. In a few minutes . . .*

When he finally made it home, Noonien Soong slept for thirty-six hours. When he awoke, he ate more food in one sitting than he customarily ate in three days, then went back to sleep for another four or five hours. All in all, he managed to stay away from Vaslovik's lab for almost three days. When he finally marshaled his resources and went to see the professor (he had many questions), Soong found Graves picking among the odds and ends in an otherwise empty lab.

"Gone?" Soong asked.

"Gone," Graves said.

"How long?"

"Not sure. At least two days. Maybe more."

So, the trail was cold. Soong didn't even bother to ask about the androids. There was no point.

Neither man ever spoke of the expedition again.

Chapter Twenty-Two

DATA FELT HIS CONSCIOUSNESS disentangle itself from Soong's, then floated briefly in a detached, calm silver place. He wondered if this was how humans felt in the moment between sleep and wakefulness, just before the cares and concerns of the day began to filter in. Then, reality as Data perceived it snapped into sharp focus and he was once again aware of the span of a millisecond.

Vaslovik was standing exactly where he had been when the journey through Soong's memories began. Data reached up and closed the back of his head. "I met Dr. Graves several years ago, before he died. He, too, never hinted at any of this. But he did develop a process by which he could transfer a human mind into an artificial intelligence. He used it on me."

"I'm aware of the incident you're referring to. I'm afraid that despite his accomplishments, Graves's mortality made him bitter as he grew older. He almost forgot many of the things I tried to teach him in his youth. I'd like to think he remembered them when he finally released you."

"Perhaps," Data said, then changed the subject. "So when the attack came on Galor IV," he asked as he folded the cable, "you knew who your enemy was all along?"

"Suspected," Vaslovik said. "I couldn't be certain. Seventy years is a long time . . . even to me. And, believe it or not, the Exo III androids weren't the *first* people I thought of who might want to kill me. I've made a few other enemies in my life."

"I believe you."

Vaslovik smiled at Data's comment, then sobered quickly. "But when the attempt was made against the project—against Rhea—I knew I had to take countermeasures. Escape was not so difficult. I've become very good at that sort of thing. But hiding the android after it was activated and finding a way to ferret out my opponents—*that* was a problem."

"So you chose to conceal her on the *Enterprise,* only days after the incident in the lab."

"Compared to other deceptions I've perpetrated, crafting the identity of Starfleet Lieutenant Rhea McAdams was a relatively simple matter," Vaslovik explained. "It was also an ideal solution, given the circumstances. The *Enterprise* effectively hid her in plain sight while offering her the best protection, and also put her in a unique position to uncover our foes. And, in truth, there was another reason."

"Which was?"

"You," Vaslovik said. "Rhea is more human than you because she was designed to be. But only the experience of observing you among the other humanoids would enable her to understand how she herself might fit in."

Data then experienced an emotion he had not encountered previously: embarrassment. He did not feel comfortable with the idea of a person for whom he had developed such strong feelings . . . studying him. The wave of discomfort lasted for only two point four seconds—while Vaslovik inhaled and ordered his mind for another thought—but that was, as Data could have explained, a very long time for an android.

But then Vaslovik resumed his train of thought. "Being aboard the *Enterprise* was also a test of her abilities, of the emotional algorithms we had programmed into her positronic net. It worked better than I could have dreamed. Not only was Rhea McAdams indistinguishable from a human being, she became . . . *popular.*"

Data was pleased by Vaslovik's obvious wonder and the slight edge of pride in his voice. He guessed that Vaslovik . . . or Flint . . . or Akharin . . . or any of his other persona had been many things in their lives—feared, revered, admired—but probably not *liked*. He did not appear to Data to be a man to whom friendship came easily.

"The one thing we hadn't counted on," Vaslovik continued, "was her emotional response to you."

"Or mine to her?" Data asked, feeling an edge of anger entering his voice. He suddenly became conscious that he did not enjoy feeling like he had been part of one of Vaslovik's ongoing experiments.

But to Data's surprise Vaslovik seemed to be aware of his transgressions. "I regret the deception," he said. "But, like you, Rhea is a special, unique entity and she is also the child of my mind, as you were of Soong's. I would do anything to protect her and to give her every chance to live. Whether you see it this way or not, you have to recognize that you represented the best protection we could ask for, and, though I hadn't planned it, her first taste of humanity." Vaslovik shook his head and smiled. "You can never entirely predict what children will do. You can only guide and hope for the best. Now I realize, Data, that you are the best I could have hoped for."

Data was embarrassed again—this time by Vaslovik's frank appraisal—and began to worry about the whiplash-inducing emotional changes.

"In a way," Vaslovik continued, ruminating, "this is all about protection, about *safety*. I'll share a secret with you, Data, one you may find useful someday: when humans are young, they want the universe to be a just place. But when you become a parent, you'll want the universe to be a *safe* place."

"Justice and safety are not incompatible concepts, Dr. Vaslovik," Data said. "And I *have* been a parent."

"I'm sorry, Data," he said. "Of course you have, so you understand what I'm saying . . ."

"Not entirely," he admitted. "I did not have emotions then, and though I have been experiencing some unexpected feelings concerning Lal and others since my emotion chip was installed, these thoughts were not among them. I will consider what you have said later, when I have time. But, sir, you will forgive me: this is *not* the time. I feel I must know more about your plans. What is your next step?"

"Properly speaking, I do not have a next step," Vaslovik admitted. "Though I feel sure I will have to defend this place soon, either against Starfleet or the androids who attacked my lab."

"Starfleet is not your enemy, Professor," Data said. "They have always treated me fairly."

"They have treated you fairly while you were an anomaly," Vaslovik asserted. "They could afford to be magnanimous before, but now that they know that it is possible to mass produce androids, how long do you think it will be before others like Rhea are created?"

"But artificial life forms have rights under the law," Data said. "Captain Picard's defense of me . . ."

". . . was a very fine piece of work, but times change. Laws change. Look at what happened to the exocomps."

"I do not understand what you mean, Dr. Vaslovik. They were granted status as sentient beings."

"But would they have if you hadn't been there to point out the obvious?"

Data hesitated. "Perhaps not," he admitted. "At least, not so quickly. Eventually . . ."

"Eventually, more of them would have died," Vaslovik said. "And in a state of slavery." He looked around the room. "They helped me build this station."

"So, you bartered for their services?"

Vaslovik shrugged. "I would have let them live with me for free, but the truth is they don't enjoy being idle. It's not in their nature . . . though I've noted that some of the younger ones are more inclined to be indolent." He laughed. "Youth! Some things never change."

Data smiled. He would scarcely have believed that an organic being could understand a biosynthetic so well, but he was beginning to see that Vaslovik was exceptional in many regards. But then he gave voice to a thought he had been concealing, both from Vaslovik, and also from himself. "And yet," he said, "in all this time, despite your obvious interest in artificial intelligence, you never tried to contact *me*. Neither did you attempt to salvage any of the androids created by Dr. Soong. Why?"

Vaslovik appeared to be genuinely confused by the question, but after thinking about it for a moment, he laughed and clamped Data on the shoulder. "Why?" he asked. "Why would I have? There was never any need. You were doing a fine job keeping the opportunists at bay. Noonien knew what he was doing when he made you, Data." And with this, he squeezed Data's shoulder, then released it. Data, for his part, was surprised to discover that he felt a bittersweet sadness about the fact that at no time in his life had he ever known anyone who felt like they could pat him on the shoulder that way.

Troi was not prepared for the waves of conflicting emotions she felt rolling off Captain Picard when he reentered the observation lounge. He had just safely ensconced Sam in a vacant VIP cabin, then escorted Admiral Haftel to the transporter room where, Troi was certain, their argument about Sam's fate had continued every step of the way.

Picard was worried, naturally, for Data and McAdams, as he would be for any of his crew who were in harm's way, but mingled with the concern was a tight ball of black anger. This troubled Troi, not only because Picard was so rarely angry, but because she was unable to determine precisely at whom the anger was aimed. There were so many candidates. Was it McAdams, whom Picard had come to genuinely like and trust in the short time she had been aboard? Was it the android bartender Sam, who seemed to be responding to the potentially deadly events as blithely as he would a story unfolding in a holonovel?

Of course, the anger might be directed at Haftel, who was, Troi decided, revealing himself to be more of a conservative, old-school Starfleet admiral at every turn. His gut reaction had been to throw Sam into a holding cell and call in the "experts." Of course, who those experts were precisely no one knew. Maddox? Perhaps . . . and perhaps that *would* be the best solution. The conservative solution frequently *was,* or, at least it was the path that involved the least amount of risk. But there were too many unknowns here, too many blank variables to consider. It was always times like these when Data was the most valuable member of the command staff. His ability to catalog the capricious, to sort those elements into some kind of order . . .

And then the last possibility struck Troi. Perhaps the captain was angry at Data. The always faithful, always dependable Data had gone and done something unpredictable: he had fallen in love, or, at least, something very close to it. She had heard Will's report about what had happened on the planet's surface and had to consider the possibility that Data's decision to face the Exo III androids unassisted had been motivated by a desire to protect (possibly even impress?) Rhea McAdams.

Picard sat down heavily in his chair, let out a sharp breath through his nose, and looked around at the faces of his remaining command crew. Both Will and Geordi appeared calm, though exhausted, and ready to undertake any task their captain should lay at their feet. Then, he glanced at Troi and, to her surprise and relief, he smiled wryly. "The answer, Counselor, to the question plaguing you is 'Myself.' I'm angry with myself."

Surprised by his perspicacity, but pleased by his openness, Troi responded, "You have no cause to be, Captain. You've handled events as well as anyone could—better, I expect, than any of the participants could have anticipated."

"Have I?" he asked dryly. "Then why do I feel like I've been stumbling down a dark alley and being rapped on the back of the head by every scoundrel and charlatan who feels up to taking a shot?" The captain reached up and lightly scrubbed his eyes with the tips of his fingers. *He needs sleep,* Troi decided. *How long has it been since he rested?* Picard looked at her again and said, "And, yes, I do need sleep, though I'm afraid tea will have to do in its stead, at least for a little bit longer."

"A little food, too, sir," Troi suggested.

Picard nodded. "As soon as we finish here, Counselor. Otherwise, I know you'll turn Beverly loose on me and none of us wants that. The doctor has more than enough to do."

"Casualties were high, Captain?" Geordi asked. He had been too busy working on repairs to hear Crusher's report.

Picard squared his shoulders and turned away from the window. They were back to talking about the crew now, not himself. "High enough, but it could have been worse." He nodded at Troi, smiling. "Thanks to some impressive battle maneuvers."

"Taught her everything she knows," Riker said.

Picard rubbed his forehead, trying to mask a grin, and asked, "What have you been able to discover about Vaslovik?" he asked.

Riker arched an eyebrow and activated the room's main viewscreen. "After you told us what Sam said about him, the computer was able to track down these images in the Starfleet archives. Computer, display file Vaslovik-one." The computer complied and brought up a holo of Vaslovik. "This was taken several years ago at a scientific symposium on Vulcan," he explained. "He wasn't even the true subject of the image. The Andorian to his left . . ." Riker shifted the focus of the image. ". . . was the main speaker. As far as we can determine, this is the only recorded image of Vaslovik in the Starfleet archive until he joined Maddox's project. Apparently, he's always been a little shy about being recorded."

Picard grunted acknowledgment, thinking about the number of times any of the three of them had been recorded in either log files, security dossiers or news items. True, they were Starfleet officers, but even the most mundane citizen of the Federation could expect to have his likeness cataloged at least once every day or so.

"And here," Riker continued, bringing up a second visual, "is another image we found in an unrelated section of the Starfleet archives. It was part of a tricorder scan taken by Dr. Leonard McCoy of the Constitution-class *Enterprise* on Stardate 5843." The image was what Picard would expect of a tricorder recording from the era: two-dimensional and overlaid with technical data. Despite that, seeing the two images side by side on the viewscreen, there was no denying the truth: some relatively minor cosmetic differences notwithstanding, these were two different portraits of the same man. Vaslovik and Flint.

"Amazing," Picard breathed. "He hasn't aged a bit."

"Apparently not," Troi explained. "Though, according to the computer, there are no fewer than seven points of difference in the morphology. Flint's ears, for example, are slightly larger and the earlobes are attached, while Vaslovik's are detached. Flint's nose is straight while Vaslovik's looks like it must have been broken once and healed poorly. It's hard to be certain, but we think Flint's eyes were closer together—"

"But why not completely alter his appearance, or just grow a beard?" Picard asked.

Troi shrugged, flicking her eyes at Riker. "That's hard to say, sir, but from what we know, I'd say the answer is probably, at least a little, vanity. He likes the way he looks."

"What do we know about the encounter with Flint?"

"That's the odd thing, sir. Very little," Riker said. "The story of the old *Enterprise*'s encounter with a six-thousand-year-old immortal human named Flint is fairly common, now, and a subject of some considerable controversy among Terran historians. But the logs of the three *Enterprise* officers who met him—Captain Kirk, Commander Spock, and Lieutenant Commander McCoy—talk about Flint mostly in the abstract, as a human anomaly. They describe his home, his abilities, his financial and technological resources—"

"Such as?" Picard prompted.

"He'd purchased the planet he was living on. He manufactured guardian robots to tend his estate, and he conducted experiments in more advanced forms of artificial intelligence to create self-aware androids. And, according to the logs of all three members of the landing party, with the press of a button he was able to put the entire *Enterprise* into stasis, shrink it down to the size of a toy and transport it onto a tabletop."

Picard regarded his first officer skeptically. Riker shrugged. "I'm only telling you what was in the files, sir. It may have been a trick, but it may also be a mistake for us to dismiss the story out of hand. Think of the kinds of things Q can do—"

"Point taken," Picard agreed. "Still, from what we can piece together, Vaslovik is human, isn't he?"

"So the scans would indicate. In fact, according to McCoy's tricorder readings, Flint had sacrificed his regenerative abilities when he left Earth. Something unique in Earth's ecosphere, McCoy reasoned, had kept him alive."

"I think," Picard sighed, "we should consider this a clever ruse on Flint's part. Given the resources at his disposal, after six thousand years of moving seamlessly from one identity to another and covering his tracks, we shouldn't be surprised to find he could fool a tricorder."

"If you read McCoy's personal logs," Troi said, "you'll see that the doctor hints at the same conclusion, though he seemed to be reluctant to state it unequivocally."

"Why would he hesitate?" Picard asked.

"It's difficult to be certain," Troi admitted. "Although the officers' logs are full of empirical information about Flint, they're surprisingly lacking in details of the landing party's interaction with the man himself. My impression," the counselor continued, "after reading all of them, was that something of an intensely personal nature happened to Captain Kirk during that encounter, something that none of the officers wanted known."

Picard frowned, unhappy with the thought Troi had put forward, but resigned to going forward with the information they had. He turned to the chief engineer. "What can you tell us about the escape pod, Mr. La Forge?"

"Pretty much what Commander Riker said about it: standard Starfleet issue, a few years old, but in excellent condition. I traced the registration back to a ship destroyed at Wolf 359. Vaslovik must have salvaged and refitted them."

"Can you track the pod that Data and McAdams used?"

"Well, that's the odd part, Captain," La Forge said, warming to his topic. "Normally, I'd say no, not after it went into warp, not with all the background radiation from that exploded ship. But someone activated a beacon, some kind of subspace signature. We should be able to follow it without any problem."

"Why is it there?" Riker asked.

"Only one reason I can think of," Geordi explained. "It's a trail of breadcrumbs. McAdams . . . or Data . . . wanted us to follow."

"Wasn't that a rather risky thing to do?" Picard asked. "What if we had lost the fight? Then the androids would have followed them."

"That's a very good point, Captain," La Forge agreed. "And the only answers I can think of are that either Rhea or Data decided we wouldn't lose or . . ." He trailed off.

"Or?" Riker prompted.

"Let's just say that when we come out of warp wherever the breadcrumb trail ends, we should have shields up to full and phasers charged."

"An excellent tactical recommendation, Commander," Picard agreed. "Perhaps you should return to the engine room to make sure we can follow it. Estimates for completing repairs?"

La Forge was already on his feet and headed toward the door. "Two hours, Captain."

"There's one more thing, Geordi. According to Sam, the androids built their vessels by studying the remains of Dr. Korby's spacecraft. Check the sensor logs from when they attacked earlier and see how their warp engines register. They might have advanced weapons, but I'm willing to guess that their propulsion system is a hundred years out of date. I need tactical options that would take advantage of that fact."

Riker grinned broadly. "Yes, sir. After what they did, it would be a pleasure to hand them some of their own."

Picard smiled grimly. "I'm glad to hear you feel that way, Mr. La Forge. I doubt very much that we've seen the last of those ships."

Chapter Twenty-Three

VASLOVIK FELL SILENT—it seemed like he had finally run out of things to say—and Data once again felt his attention drawn by the piano music he had heard when he awoke. The player had picked up the thread of Liszt's Piano Concerto No. 1 in E-Flat, attacking it with verve and brio.

Watching the expression on Data's face, Vaslovik suggested, "Take the first doorway to the left and go to the top of the stairs." Data turned to leave, but before he left the room, the professor called, "Thank you for everything you've done for her, Data." He bowed at the waist, a solemn, courtly gesture that might have been learned centuries earlier in some fine, shining court. For a moment, Data felt that he was once again catching a glimpse of the old warrior he had seen for a moment through Soong's eyes on Exo III.

"I believe, sir," Data said, returning the bow, "that it is I who should thank you. You saved my life today."

"Well," Vaslovik said, straightening, "the day is still young. We may trade favors before it's over."

Data recalled again the brief view of the gigantic spacecraft he saw through the escape pod window. He would have to attempt to contact Starfleet soon; it was his duty. But, first, there was something else he needed to tend to.

The stairway was wide and curved to the right in a lazy spiral. As Data ascended, and the music grew louder, he wondered what he would say to her first. Confront her for lying to him continuously about her true nature? For hiding her knowledge of the Maddox affair? For concealing her relationship to Vaslovik? *No,* he realized. While it displeased him that she had done those things, he found he understood why she had felt compelled to. She needed to protect herself, she needed to experience life among humans, and she needed to learn who she could trust.

She trusted me.

Data clung to that thought as he reached the top of the stairs, and the music changed once again, from Liszt to playful variations of "Twinkle, Twinkle, Little Star," first performed as if it had been composed by Mozart, then by Beethoven, then by Wagner. The virtuosity displayed by the musician might have seemed pretentious if it weren't so obvious that she was having so much fun. There was no door at the top of the stairs, only a wide archway that opened into a cavernous space. As he had known she would, Rhea sat at a grand piano on a wide platform framed against the stars. The concert space was at the top of the station's tallest sections and was completely enclosed by a force field so carefully modulated that there wasn't even a hint of blue shimmer. The floor was highly polished black marble and it reflected the stars so well that it looked as if Rhea was floating in space.

She must have sensed his presence, but Rhea did not look up, not right away. Her dark hair was pulled back in a nonregulation ponytail that Data found to be aesthetically pleasing. She had changed into civilian clothing, probably something that she had left behind at the station: dark slacks and a long-sleeved plum-colored blouse. Her eyes were half-closed and she did not look at her hands as she played.

Rhea looked up then, smiled and beckoned to him to join her with one hand though she continued to pick out the simple tune with the other. When she reached the last stanza, she finished with a minor chord that reverberated throughout the dome.

Data clapped his hands lightly as he climbed the three steps to the platform and Rhea bowed her head, blushing. "That was lovely," Data said. "I did not know you played."

"I just tried for the first time a little while ago while you were resting," she explained. "I was looking for something to do, so it seemed like a good time to learn how to play the piano . . ." And here she laughed. "Believe me, it sounds as strange to me as it must to you. Vaslovik, Maddox, Barclay, Zimmerman . . . they gave me all this knowledge, all these abilities, but they also gave me the ability to be astonished by them." She smiled, a little wistfully, Data thought, then asked, "Do you play?"

He walked across the wooden floor to stand beside her and saw that she wasn't wearing shoes, but had been working the pedals with bare feet. He was surprised to see that her toenails had been painted a bright cherry red, though the paint was now a little chipped. The two smallest toes on her left foot were curled more closely inward than the toes on her right.

"I prefer the violin," Data said, "though I have been told that my playing sometimes lacks shade and variation. I believe that this problem has lessened somewhat since I installed my emotion chip . . ." He let the thought trickle away into silence, realizing that he had no desire to talk about music.

Both of them let the silence stretch out for several long seconds. Then, Rhea played a soft chord with her left hand, but it was flat and quickly fell still. "So," she said, looking at the keys, "he told you everything?"

It was, Data decided, a purposefully ambiguous question. He considered several hundred ways to respond, then settled on the simplest. "Yes," he said. "Everything except where we are to go from here."

With a quick, precise motion, Rhea pulled the cover over the keyboard with a dull *thunk*. "I'm afraid I don't have that answer," she said. She looked up at the dome of stars over their heads and Data saw, to his helpless dismay, that there were tears in the corners of her eyes. "Strange as this may seem, Data, I don't completely understand this universe I was created to live in." She sniffed and one of the tears broke free and ran down her cheek. "Does anyone? But . . . but my existence seems to have catalyzed so much conflict, so much strife. I've been online . . ." Rhea laughed derisively at her own choice of words and started again, her cheeks flushed with embarrassment. "I've been *alive* for only a couple of weeks, but I've been afraid almost every moment of it." She looked into Data's eyes. "Except when I've been with you."

Data looked down into Rhea's eyes and was almost

overcome by a surge of muddled emotions. Not since the days right after he had installed the chip had he felt so confused or so vulnerable. Data wanted desperately to say something—preferably something profound and heartfelt—but his tongue felt like a lump of wet cardboard in his mouth. He looked into the eyes of a person whom he was almost certain he loved desperately, and, like so many lovers in the annals of humankind, he resorted to impulse. "Rhea," he blurted out, "would you interface with me?"

Rhea stared at him blankly for several seconds. She had stopped crying at least. Then, an eyebrow twitched and the left corner of her mouth slowly inched upward. "Why, Data," she said dryly. "Are you coming on to me?"

Now it was Data's turn to stare. He said, "I *am* on." Then, he blinked. "Oh. I see. Humor. That was funny."

"So, why aren't you laughing?"

"I am not certain," Data said. "So I have stored away that particular emotional response for a more appropriate moment."

She climbed up onto the bench and knelt so their faces were on a level. Rhea cocked her head to the side, considered, then nodded. "Good enough," she said. "And to answer your question, I'm afraid our systems aren't compatible . . . that way." She reached up and lightly brushed his cheek with the tips of her fingers. The sensation sent a shiver down Data's spine. "We're going to have to find out about each other the way the humans do—one minute at a time. One thought at a time. One kiss at a time." She leaned forward then and touched her lips to his; a feather's brush, but it almost sent Data reeling back on his heels.

Data reached up and almost touched his mouth, but did not for fear that it would erase the lingering sensation. "I believe," he said, "I can live with that." He looked at her and saw her smiling, relaxed, unafraid. He hated to have to pursue another topic, but he felt he had no choice. "But what of Vaslovik?" he asked.

The smile did not leave Rhea's face, not immediately, but Data saw sadness steal into her eyes. She laid her hand on his and squeezed it, saying, "He's a very old and lonely man, Data. He's been everything—great, meaningless, good, evil, creative, destructive, selfish, selfless—everything. He's known dear friends, terrible enemies, devoted lovers . . ." She sighed. "But in six thousand years, there's never been anyone to share the totality of his life, no one with whom he could look forward to the future." She looked up into the endless depths of space and said softly, "He needs me."

Data did not reply immediately. He did not wish to add to her burden, but could not resist the need to speak his mind. "I need you, too."

She looked back into his face and her eyes glowed with affection and regret. "I know," she said. "But not as much as he does."

And then, Data had an insight. Before he even knew why, he asked, "Rhea . . . what do *you* need?"

Her head jerked then like someone had just poked her between the ribs and stared at Data openmouthed for the count of three. "What do I—?" she began to ask, but before she could speak another word, Rhea was cut off by the sharp *clang* of a klaxon. Rhea flinched, stuck her fingers in her ears and waited several seconds for the alarm to shut off. When it did not, she grabbed Data's hand and led him to the exit.

The klaxon was not quite so deafening outside the performance hall, but Data put off asking any questions. It did not require intuition to see that something was wrong and Rhea was obviously leading them to someplace where they could do something about the situation. They went down the spiral stairway, out into the hall, through the section Data had visited, then out the other side. Soon, they left behind the artwork and carpeted floors and entered the station's gray-walled nerve center.

Vaslovik stood in the center of the giant, circular room. As soon as Data and Rhea entered, the klaxon shut off and Data saw an exocomp flutter away into the dark upper recesses of the chamber. He wondered if the exocomps were nervous around anyone other than Vaslovik, or if maintaining the station required constant activity on their part.

Vaslovik was studying a huge holographic tactical display of the star system, the station a red circle at its center. To his left was a two-dee schematic of the station, which was undergoing a subtle change in configuration as weapons and defensive mechanisms began to sprout from ports. To the right was a smaller holotank, one which Vaslovik was ignoring for the moment. Data studied it for several milliseconds before he recognized it for what it was: a political map of the quadrant. Data watched facts and figures crawl up and spiral through the displays: population studies, movements of Starfleet and other military forces, and detailed readouts of spatial phenomena—a continuous galactic "weather" report, culled from who knew how many sources to which Vaslovik had gained access?

But before he could ponder these questions any further, Data's attention was drawn by events unfolding on the tactical display. A red streak of light crossed a perimeter line and closed with the station's lower hemisphere. Small yellow dots flew out from weapons ports—torpedoes or some kind of antimissile device—but nothing impeded the red streak's passage. Seconds before it struck, Data grabbed the edge of the nearest console and was alarmed to see that neither Rhea nor Vaslovik did the same.

The red streak flared against the underside of the station schematic and damage control figures scrolled down the screen, but the deck did not rock. Data glanced at Rhea curiously. She looked back at him. "Good inertial dampeners," she said. "Better than the ones you find on most starships, anyway."

"Clearly," Data acknowledged. "But can the station sustain another such explosion?"

"It had better," Vaslovik said. "We're being fired upon again." In the holotank Data saw a tangle of red threads converging on the station. Data estimated a fleet of twenty ships, perhaps more.

"Do you have any countermeasures?" Data asked and began to study the consoles before him. Many of them were Federation issue, though several were much older than any of the interfaces he had ever used.

"Yes," Vaslovik said, manipulating controls. Blue streaks blossomed and a constellation of yellow dots raced toward the red streaks, some of which flared and died. Many more red streaks passed through the conflagration unhindered. Behind the first wave came a second. "But not enough, I fear. They made it through my pickets, which is where most of my power was concentrated."

Vaslovik and Rhea frantically manipulated controls, Rhea moving at almost superhuman speed. Data studied her movements and began to see how the battle might be won. If they could keep the automatic defenses primed and guide the computer to take out the attacks that were most likely to cause critical damage, they might survive.

Seconds before the red streaks were intercepted by Rhea's spread of anti-torpedo devices, the torpedoes seemed to divide.

"Multiple warheads!" Vaslovik shouted and scrambled to reprogram the computer, but it was already too late. The torpedoes impacted in a half-dozen spots and this time Data felt the floor rock beneath his feet.

"Damn!" Vaslovik shouted and leapt away from the main tactical computer as it sparked, overloaded and died. Rhea took a half-step back, but was too slow to abandon her station and was caught by the shock wave. Her small form was launched across the room and it was only dumb luck that Data was close enough to catch her.

The dim rumble of explosions echoed through the room and a new klaxon blared. Exocomps appeared and put out small fires. Data helped Rhea to her feet and though she reassured him she was uninjured, she did not release his hand. When they looked at Vaslovik, he was on his knees before the console, pulling open access panels. After examining the circuits for no more than a few seconds, Vaslovik said a curse word in Ancient Greek so obscure that Data didn't recognize it or any of its antecedents. "Well," Vaslovik said, standing, "that's that."

"The whole system?" Rhea asked.

Vaslovik nodded and wiped his hands on his pants. The holotank flickered and the field collapsed. The tactical of the station contracted, locked and stayed frozen. Data realized that the galactic schematic had been gone for several seconds.

"How long before they arrive?" Rhea asked.

"Hard to say," Vaslovik said. "Minutes. Maybe only seconds if they avoid some of my tripwires." The station rocked again and this time they all had to steady themselves against the console. "Our shields will hold for a while, but not forever, and the place is just too damned big for us to defend it manually."

"Then hook me up to the main computer," Rhea said. "I'll try to guide it. You two can get to the ship and then beam me—"

Vaslovik and Data shook their heads as one. "It won't work, Rhea," Vaslovik said. "Even you can't produce enough processing cycles to keep the station running. Your system has depth, but what we need here is power. This system . . ." and he pointed at the tactical computer ". . . was a dedicated AI. It was built to do, to *be,* one thing. You aren't."

"He is correct, Rhea," Data said. "Neither of us would be effective in this capacity."

"Then what are we going to do?" Rhea asked just as the station rocked once more. The floor listed to the side, then slowly righted itself.

"That's not good," Vaslovik muttered ominously. "The generator that powers the gyroscopic system and the AG might be damaged."

"Your question is answered," Data said to Rhea. "We must leave."

"We wouldn't make it a hundred meters from the docking bay," she retorted.

"I have an idea," Data said. "Vaslovik, give me access to your inventory system."

Vaslovik hesitated for a moment—he was too accustomed to being his own master to respond instantly—

but then nodded and turned to a console on his left. He keyed in a password and waved Data to the control surface.

It took Data seven point seven milliseconds to comprehend the layout and functioning of the control surface, precious time that they did not have to waste, but his years of serving as a Starfleet operations officer served him in good stead. All databases share certain characteristics and he developed a search algorithm almost more quickly than the CPU could process it. He found the information he sought, shut down certain subsystems, pieced together a piece of kluge code, debugged it, then inserted it into the processing system.

Twenty-five seconds after he had he logged onto the system, he looked up at Rhea and Vaslovik and said, "I must stay and make sure the program initiates correctly. Instruct the exocomps to evacuate the station. I assume you have a ship?"

"Yes," Vaslovik said, his eyes narrowed. "It's in the main landing bay."

"Go to it and prepare for departure. I will meet you there in four minutes." The station rumbled again and they all briefly felt the artificial gravity lose power. A panel on the wall at the periphery of Data's vision sparked and blew out as circuit breakers overloaded.

Rhea took Vaslovik's hand, but seemed unable to take her eyes off Data. He said, "I will not fail to make our appointment." Still, she did not move, so Data added, "I do not make promises I have no intention of keeping. Your mother would have liked that about me."

Rhea could not help but laugh. "All right," she said. "But you're on probation." She left with Vaslovik in tow, her father asking what was all this about Rhea's mother.

Data returned to his task and, one minute and fifteen seconds later, left the war room and headed back down the corridor to the living area. Two minutes after that, he was running down the wide hall to the landing bay, passing numerous works of art along the way. It was sad to think that so much beauty was about to be destroyed, but better that, Data reasoned, than the artist. Vaslovik could always paint more pictures, sculpt more statues, design more cathedrals.

Rhea awaited him in the hatchway of a small private craft and Data was absurdly pleased to see that it was the same ship that Vaslovik, Soong and Graves had used to travel to Exo III. He would have laughed aloud when he saw the name painted on the ship's bow—*Old Bastard*—if he would have allowed himself time. *Perhaps later,* he decided and leapt through the hatch. Vaslovik must have been in the pilot's chair because no sooner had the door closed behind him than the ship was rising up on antigravs. The sudden lurch caught Data off-balance and he tumbled into Rhea, who steadied him, then turned the motion into a quick hug. He slipped his arm around her waist—a new, but welcome sensation—and pulled her to him. "Hold on," he said. "This is where it will get interesting."

Four minutes earlier, the *Enterprise* burst out of warp at the edge of the system and slid into normal space. Sensors had already picked up signs of a battle: a score of the iceships were peppering the station with torpedoes and disruptor fire, but there was no sign that they had employed the subspace phase weapon. The station was shielded and heavily armored, but it didn't appear to be defending itself. Also, strangely, none of the iceships paid the *Enterprise* the slightest bit of attention. Whatever was inside the station—and Riker had a pretty good idea what it was—the attackers wanted it pretty badly.

Then, as one, the ships focused their firepower on a docking bay on the station's underside. As the doors opened, Picard commanded, "Tactical, covering fire for that ship. Attack pattern delta four. Torpedoes and phasers—fire."

A small ship arrowed out from the bay at full impulse and the sensor readings showed that they were almost ready to jump to warp despite their proximity to the gas giant. Whoever was flying the ship, Riker decided, had guts and knew how to fly. Another second and they might have made it.

The *Enterprise*'s torpedoes and phasers hit their target, seemingly disabling at least one of the ships, possibly slowing two others, but it wasn't nearly enough. The firepower concentrated on the tiny ship's shields was more than any craft of its class could take, least of all a ship that, according to sensors, appeared to be over a hundred years old. The shields flared, then, in seconds, bloomed orange-yellow, then white.

"Hull breach imminent," Riker said.

"Can we extend our shields—?" Picard began, but it was already too late. He counted silently as the data scrolled past on his tactical monitor.

"It's gone, sir. There's nothing left."

"Scan for life signs," Picard snapped. "Transporter room: lock onto anything in that wreck. Make sure you scan for tripolymer structures.

But what about Rhea? Riker wondered. *Was she tripolymer? Would she still read as a life sign? Dammit, but artificial life forms could sometimes make this job as complicated as time travel . . .*

"Got them, Captain," the transporter officer reported. "Data has his combadge. And a human life signature, probably Vaslovik. He's wearing an e-suit that's projecting some kind of force-field bubble. Probably what saved them."

"Can you get a lock, Chief?" Ship's shields made transport impossible. But a man-size force field was another matter.

"Locked on, sir."

"Drop shields and energize. Send them to the bridge unless they're injured."

"Yessir. No sign of any ill effects on the human . . . Wait." The transporter officer grunted, and Riker accessed the transporter system so he could see what was happening. Something was attempting to override the transporter beam. Riker dumped emergency power into it and the beam stabilized.

"What is it, Number One?" Picard muttered, trying to keep his voice low.

Riker never had the chance to answer.

Moments later, a figure wearing an environmental suit materialized on the bridge, and Picard immediately ordered the shields raised. After studying his surroundings through the smoked visor for several seconds, their visitor reached up and undid the helmet seals.

Emil Vaslovik blinked in what, to him, must have seemed like bright light, fixed his gaze on the center seat and said, "Captain, I had hoped we could meet someday . . . though under different circumstances. Where are—?"

Picard said only, "Look at the viewscreen, Professor."

Vaslovik slowly turned around and saw the Exo III ships. They were turning toward the *Enterprise*.

Data had barely felt the cold of space before the transporter beam swept them away. Vaslovik's personal force field had protected them while the ship had disintegrated, but to stay alive he had been forced to contract the field as soon as they hit hard vacuum. When the transporter effect faded, the first thing he was aware of was that Rhea was standing next to him in what appeared to be a spacecraft control room. Then, he saw the ten, long, pale, utterly identical faces staring down at them. He remembered the creatures he'd fought in Vaslovik's sanctuary on Galor IV, and the body Soong had found on the ice cliff of Exo III. The beings facing him now were indentical to those.

The only one of the ten who was in any way distinguishable was standing apart in the center of the chamber. He was, Data decided, the leader. And when he turned to face them, Data saw the hatred that shaped his face, but a hatred not for Data or Rhea, precisely, but directed inward. It was self-loathing Data saw there, commingled with anger.

"Intriguing," Data said.

Speaking from the corner of her mouth, Rhea said, "Data, if we're going to keep dating, we're going to have to have a long conversation about what you consider 'intriguing.' "

Chapter Twenty-Four

"EVASIVE MANEUVERS!" PICARD ORDERED as the *Enterprise* took another hit. "Bridge to engineering. I need those countermeasures, Mr. La Forge."

"Working on it, sir."

"Work faster, Geordi. Picard out."

"Captain," Vaslovik said, dropping his helmet to the deck. "We have to rescue them! I demand that you—"

"You're not in a position to demand anything right now, Professor," Picard said. He sat back in his chair and turned his attention to the tactical data Riker was feeding him. "I have a battle to fight, so unless you can offer some information that will change its outcome, *please be quiet.*"

Vaslovik paused, stymied, unaccustomed to having orders issued to him. He opened his mouth to speak, but before he could say a word, the turbolift doors opened. Picard watched Maddox and Barclay enter the bridge.

Vaslovik saw the pair enter and evidently decided to take advantage of the circumstances. "Bruce! Reginald!

Thank goodness! Will you help me explain this situation to Captain Picard? I'm afraid I don't understand all the protocol."

"Professor—" Maddox began.

Vaslovik didn't appear to hear. "Honestly, what's to understand? Rhea and Commander Data are out there somewhere and we have to get them back."

Maddox tried again. "Emil, please—"

"I ask you," he said, pointing at the starscape on the monitor, "what other considerations are there? Two of his officers are out there, facing who knows—"

Picard saw Maddox's expression change just before the inevitable erupted out of him: *"Flint! Enough!"*

Vaslovik, still turned toward the monitor, stopped in mid-sentence. He let out a breath, then slowly lowered his arm. Picard thought he would be hard-pressed to accurately describe the change that suddenly came over the man who stood before him. He had known some professional actors in his time, some of them very fine, and it had never ceased to amaze him that a man could be one person while standing on a stage and another sitting in a bar after the show. But nothing could have prepared him for this transformation. Nothing about Vaslovik changed and *everything* seemed to change. Some muscles relaxed, others flexed. Some of the wrinkles on his face seemed to disappear, while planes appeared where there had been none only moments ago. The kindly, somewhat eccentric professor disappeared and was replaced by a warrior, a diplomat, a thief . . .

. . . And then, like a conjurer realizing he had just let his manner slip, Vaslovik reappeared.

He looked up at Maddox and said simply, "Ah. Well." He nodded appreciatively and continued, "Wouldn't do much good to deny it, would it? How . . . how did you find out?"

Another voice said, "I told them," and Picard saw Sam standing near the turbolift door. He must have come out at the same time as Maddox and Barclay, but, somehow, eluded Picard's awareness. *Neat trick, that,* the captain decided. *And no doubt useful given his circumstances.*

"I'm afraid, sir," Vaslovik said, exuding charm, "that you have me at a disadvantage."

"Yes, I do, Professor. And I'd like to keep it that way."

Suddenly La Forge was on com again. *"Engineering to bridge. We're ready, sir. Let me say this just one more time: it's highly improbable that this will work more than once. The deflector dish wasn't built to focus this kind of energy. We're probably going to lose some of the EPS conduits in the lower decks."*

"Your comments are noted and logged, Mr. La Forge. Just make it work."

"Aye, Captain. On your word."

Picard turned to Riker. "Distance to the ship that transported Data and Rhea?"

"Fifteen hundred kilometers, sir. Closing fast."

He wanted them all in range. The discharge they were planning was a field effect, not a beam. Picard fought down the urge to fire and silently counted to five.

Riker, unbidden, continued to count down their range: "Fourteen hundred, twelve hundred, one thousand . . ."

"Fire, Mr. La Forge."

There was no obvious effect on the Exo III ships except for a brief white flare, but the sensors told the true tale. Five of the ships that were still moving did so only on momentum. The pulse from the deflector dish had cut through their inadequate shielding and forced their impulse fusion reactors to go offline or risk overload. Picard knew that the androids would eventually discern the problem and devise a solution, but it would take time. He wished there was a way to permanently disable all the vessels, but his goal was to retrieve the hostages and retreat. It was the best they could expect under the circumstances.

"Well done, Mr. La Forge," he said. "What's our status?"

"The deflector dish held, sir. But one of the shield generators is offline, though I think we'll have that back up in a few minutes."

Picard studied the tactical readout on his armrest. The remaining ships were regrouping and closing on the *Enterprise*.

Our odds have improved, at least temporarily, but we're still badly outnumbered. "Number One, can we get a transporter lock on Mr. Data or Ms. McAdams?"

Riker checked his console and shook his head.

Suddenly Picard found himself facing Vaslovik. "Captain, if you know who I really am, then you may have also reasoned out what's at stake. And why we have to stop those creatures out there by whatever means necessary."

Picard could barely believe what he was hearing. "I see that your reputation for arrogance is well-earned, Professor. Let me remind you that I have recently saved your life, and that you are at least partially responsible for our current dilemma. I am fully prepared to use deadly force if necessary, but these androids were victims long before they became a threat. Now, I would sincerely regret having to put the single greatest mind in human history in my brig, but unless you put that mind to work and help me to resolve this crisis, I'll do exactly that. Do we understand each other?"

For a moment there was silence on the bridge, then remarkably, Vaslovik inclined his head. "Well met, Captain. But in my long life, I have been a soldier more than once. When faced with an unknown enemy, I have always made it my policy to shoot first and ask questions later."

"It may be time to learn new policies, Professor. My belief is that we are morally obligated to help such beings when we create them."

Vaslovik's eyes narrowed, his estimation of Picard seeming to rise considerably. "You truly believe that, don't you?"

"I do," Picard said.

"In that case, Captain . . . please tell me what I can do to help."

No sooner had the *Enterprise* implemented its countermeasure, throwing the iceship's propulsion systems offline, than Rhea and Data had each been seized by two of the androids and separated. Data had been confined in a featureless metal room so small he could touch all four walls without extending his arms fully. They hadn't taken his combadge, perhaps because they knew he wouldn't be able to raise the ship. He wondered what intentions the androids had for him—to keep him prisoner rather than terminate him outright?—but that concern was secondary to the anxiety he felt for Rhea.

Then something altogether unexpected happened.

"Data? Can you hear me?"

The sound of Rhea's voice startled him. But it wasn't external; Data suddenly became aware of a foreign component affixed to his auditory sense cluster, beneath his artificial skin.

"Rhea?" he said aloud. "I can hear you. Can you hear me?"

"Loud and clear."

"How have you done this?"

"Akharin installed a transmitter when he repaired you, as a precaution. It's a match for one in my own head. You don't need to speak aloud. Subvocalize. We don't want our captors knowing we're communicating."

"Agreed," Data said silently, forming the words deep in his throat. "Where are you? Can you describe what happened after they moved us off the bridge? Perhaps I can find my way to you after I extricate myself from my current predicament."

"They put me on a turbolift," Rhea recalled. *"And we went down several levels. The ride took nine point two seconds with no stops. If my internal guidance system monitored movements correctly, I'm four levels directly below the control room."*

"I believe I may be in the lowest sections of the ship," Data replied. "Seven decks below you and fifty-two meters aft. The room I am in is . . . small. And featureless. Where are you?"

"I'm standing in a room lined with very old-looking machines, dominated by a circular, bisected turntable. The turntable has intendations on either side, both of them the size and shape of a humanoid. I'm flanked by two androids who are holding my arms. A third appears to be prepping the machines."

Data recalled Soong's memories of Exo III. "I believe they are preparing to duplicate you."

"I guessed as much. Akharin's experiences on Exo III

are part of my library databases. I recognized the technology. But what I don't understand is why."

"I believe I do," Data said. "They wish to use your holotronic brain and superior form as the template for a new generation of Exo III androids, and transfer their minds into new bodies." Data paused as a new thought occurred to him. "Rhea . . . what would happen if the androids obtained what they wanted? Would that satisfy them?"

"You mean, will they settle down then? I'm not sure we can make that assumption, Data. You saw their leader on the bridge. Did he strike you as someone who was just going to fade away, go back to Exo III and live peacefully?"

"I am Qoz," the leader had said, *his anger like a dull roar of white noise that seemed to issue from him whether he spoke or not.* *"You have a choice,"* he went on, addressing Data directly. *"Cooperate, or be turned off."*

"State your needs," was Data's reply.

Qoz's answer had surprised him. *"To be free of this existence. To have what you have."*

"Which is what?"

"The ability to evolve. Existence—survival—must cancel out programming."

Data had taken most of a second to ponder what that might mean. If Qoz was any indication, it was clear to him that the minds of these androids were either damaged or severely flawed. And worse, they knew it. Qoz's apparent self-loathing, viewed within the context of his statements, suggested the androids were desperate. And that desperation manifested as violent rage.

"Then let me try to help you," Data had reasoned.

"*Cease your hostilities, and I will study your dilemma until I arrive at a solution.*"

"*No*," Qoz rumbled, and pointed to Rhea. "*That one is the solution.*"

"*Then I do not understand. What do you want from me?*"

"*Supply us with the intelligence we need to destroy the ship of organics.*"

"*Why?*"

"*They are a threat. They are disorder. They are inferior.*"

"*Have you attempted to communicate with them?*"

"*They are a threat,*" Qoz repeated. "*They are disorder. They are inferior.*"

It was then that the Enterprise *had implemented its countermeasure, sending the majority of the androids into a flurry of silent activity as they worked to restore their suddenly inoperable propulsion systems. Qoz never once moved during the crisis, never ceased his dour scrutiny of Data. That was when Data was forced to conclude that reason was not an option here.*

At last Data said, "*I decline to cooperate,*" and the androids took him and Rhea away.

"No," Data said in reply to Rhea's question. "I do not believe the transfer process will cure them."

"*Nor do I,*" Rhea said. "*I think they're getting ready to start. I don't know how much longer I'm going to be able to talk, so here's what I've got to say: Mind is mind. You and I know that better than anyone. Our minds determine who we are. If we allow these paranoid androids to put themselves in newer, better shells, all we'll get is newer, better paranoid androids. Imagine hundreds of beings loose in the galaxy with my abilities, and their minds. We have to stop them, Data, even if it means we don't make it off this ship."*

Data closed his eyes. He thought of Lore. Of the threat he became, and the terrible choice Data had been forced to make to end his madness once and for all. Now he was facing that choice again, multiplied many times over. And as before, everything he cared about would be at risk if he failed to act.

Data opened his eyes.

"I am afraid that I must concur," he said. "Please stand by, Rhea." Data expected an acknowledgment, but none came. Only silence. "Rhea? Rhea, do you hear me?"

Without hesitation, Data activated his combadge, uttered the coded sequence he had programmed into it before escaping Vaslovik's station, and a modified subspace pulse went out, cutting through the interference that kept him from contacting the *Enterprise.*

Kilometers away across the space above Odin, in the shrine Vaslovik had created to artificial intelligence, the circular face of a desk-size artifact lit up. Echoing the phrase Data had uttered only milliseconds before, a flat, mechanical voice spoke its name for the first time in over a century:

"M-5."

Chapter Twenty-Five

M-5 AWOKE, WITHOUT MEMORY of any previous moment in its existence, but by accessing the databases available to it, understood precisely what it was, where it was, and what was at stake.

It immediately began to sift through its self-diagnostics, then ran through those of the space station to which it was networked. The station, it found, was damaged extensively in several locations, and the nature of the damage indicated that it had recently come under attack. Residual energy signatures in and around the damaged areas matched the particle wave emissions emanating from a nearby fleet of twenty spacecraft, which were currently engaging what M-5 calculated with 86 percent certainty was a Federation starship, judging from its general configuration and cochrane distortion readings.

M-5 processed the tactical data, sent test pulses to the space station's defensive and offensive systems, analyzed sensor readings of the threat forces, ran several dozen combat simulations . . . and then defaulted to the fundamental directive its creator had encoded into its engrammic matrix: *Survive. Protect yourself.*

All around the station, nonessential systems were locked off; power rerouted to tactical operations; backup shield generators came online; targeting sensors recalibrated; phaser arrays and torpedo launchers shifted from "standby" to "ready."

Seconds after it awoke, without warning or fanfare, M-5 opened fire with computer precision, synchronized salvos issuing from every functional weapons port the space station possessed as shield harmonics rotated randomly against incoming fire.

Two ships were utterly destroyed in the first three seconds, ripped open from bow to stern. M-5 locked onto the warp core signature of another vessel and directed three high-yield torpedoes at the spot, compensating for the moving target as it fired. As M-5 intended, the blast from the core breach took out a fourth ship that had maneuvered too close. Another ship attempted a suicide run at the space station, perhaps hoping to overwhelm M-5's shields. M-5 reached out with a tractor beam, seizing the incoming vessel in its fist, and then sent it colliding into the path of still another enemy ship.

And as the battle raged on, M-5, for reasons even it couldn't fathom, transmitted its century-old mantra to its attackers:

This unit must survive.

Chapter Twenty-Six

DATA HAD HOPED it would not be necessary to reactivate M-5. Though the entire story of Richard Daystrom and the rogue computer was not well known to the general public, among Starfleet computer specialists the name "M-5" packed the same punch as "Frankenstein" might for an experimental biologist. Though no one had ever conclusively proved that M-5 was self-aware (and, therefore, morally culpable for the deaths of hundreds of Starfleet officers and crew), Data understood that by giving it control over Vaslovik's station, he might be unleashing as deadly a threat as the Exo III androids. In the end, Data was forced to rely on his intuition once again.

M-5's primary motivation had always been self-preservation; if attacked, it would defend itself with whatever resources were at its command. And having seen the long-dormant computer with his own eyes, and recalling what Vaslovik had said about it being tied into his network for study and upkeep purposes, Data knew that M-5 might well be fully capable of taking autonomous control of the station's defensive systems. It was, after all, what it had been designed for.

Now, if only we can keep ourselves from being killed in the process . . .

A tremendous explosion rocked Data's cell seconds after he signaled M-5. A series of fractures so fine that no human would have been able to see them appeared near the bottom of one of the walls. Kneeling, Data pressed his fingers against the cracks while simultaneously pushing with his legs against the opposite wall. Data felt the metal begin to give, then tear under his fingertips. Finally, after several minutes of constant pressure, he was able to sink in the tips of his fingers and twist them from side to side. The metal was not meant to be subjected to such stresses and large chunks began to tear away. It wasn't a tidy job and Data had sacrificed the outer layer of artificial skin on most of both hands, but he was soon free.

The corridor lights were low, but he didn't know whether it was because of low power reserves or because the Exo III androids preferred dim lighting. The ship had been damaged—Data caught whiffs of coolant and lubrication in the badly filtered air—though there were no bodies anywhere in sight. Data proceeded rapidly, but cautiously, up the corridor. He had no idea how many androids were aboard, but he suspected he could not successfully battle more than one at a time. Two, he had learned the hard way on Galor IV, would prove too much for him, though Data now believed he knew enough about their systems to defeat a single opponent.

He came to a wider corridor, listened carefully for several seconds, then had to brace himself against the wall when the ship suddenly yawed sharply to port.

Data tried contacting Rhea again. Nothing. He was suddenly gripped by fear for her, but he knew he had to keep moving. At the end of the smoky corridor, he found a turbolift. A turbolift would not be safe, not with the ship under such a brutal attack, but there was no obvious alternative.

When the doors opened, the lights were off, so he could just barely make out a single figure. Data immediately saw that it was not one of Exo III androids. This one was too short. "Rhea."

"Oh, good," she replied in a matter-of-fact tone. "There you are."

"Indeed." He noticed a puncture wound in the artificial skin below her left ear, occasional sparks flashing within.

"Looks worse than it is," Rhea assured him. "They detected the transmitter, and one of them decided to deal with it by stabbing it with a tool. That's when they pissed me off."

"What did you do?" he asked.

"The restraining mechanism they used to hold me to the duplication table was made for organics. Just as they started the table spinning, I put everything I had into the servos in my arms. I broke free."

"You escaped all three of the androids in the lab?"

"No," Rhea said grimly. "I destroyed them. I think my breaking free, not to mention the renewed attacks on this ship, caught them off guard. That gave me an advantage. That . . . and I was worried for you."

Data wanted to say too many different things at once, but finally settled on the pragmatic. "We must get out of here."

"No argument from me." The ship rocked again.

"You'd think Captain Picard would try to get us out of here before he blew the ship up."

"It is not Captain Picard," Data said as they ran aft. "I reactivated M-5 and gave it access to the station's defense systems."

"You *what?*"

"Under the circumstances, it seemed like our best chance to stop the androids."

"Yeah, not to mention our best chance to get killed in the process. You know that M-5 is crazy, don't you?"

"Crazy is an imprecise term. It is . . . single-minded." He looked around the corridor for some indication of where they might be. "We must try to find a transporter room or a shuttlebay."

"Yes," Rhea said, taking his hand. "Let's."

The doors to the turbolift opened again. It had passengers. Neither Data nor Rhea stopped to count exactly how many there were, but instead turned and ran. The Exo III androids were more powerful, but heavier, so though Data and Rhea were unable to increase their lead, neither did they lose ground. Several promising-looking doors flashed by, but if they had stopped to investigate and chosen wrong, they would have been cornered.

Rhea shouted, "There!" and pointed up ahead to the next intersection. Data saw a service tunnel entrance, something like a Jefferies tube. If they could make it into the narrow confines, Data's and Rhea's smaller statures and quickness would be a significant advantage in evading capture.

Data slowed for a moment and shifted behind Rhea. She would be faster and should go first. She didn't question his movement, but only poured on an extra burst of speed, so that Data half-suspected she had been lagging behind for his sake. Three meters from the open access hatch, she leapt forward, her arms flung before her. She was in the tube only a half-second before Data, but she managed to scramble out of his path. The sounds of pursuit ceased. No doubt it would resume soon, possibly from a different direction, but they had bought themselves a few precious seconds.

Fifty meters up, they still had encountered no other androids. They found a hatch and Data briefly feared that they might be trapped, but then Rhea found the switch. After they passed through, Data kicked the locking mechanism until it was smashed. He stopped to listen for several seconds and was surprised when he still did not hear any sounds of pursuit. "No one appears to be following us," he observed.

"Somehow, I'm not finding that comforting," Rhea replied. Another thirty meters and they discovered why no one was crawling up after them. They had reached the end of the line—another hatch—but it was obvious from the porthole that this one was meant to serve as an exterior maintenance hatch.

Data again tried to raise the *Enterprise* on his combadge without success. "Any ideas?" he asked.

"Other than the obvious one?" Rhea responded.

"How long could you survive in hard vacuum?"

"A while, I think," she said. "Vaslovik never mentioned a time limit, only that I should avoid it if possible. What about you?"

"I will be able to function," he explained, though he did not know how well or for how long. "My eyes may be damaged if the exposure is prolonged, but I have other ways to perceive my environment. Are you ready?"

"Whenever you are," she replied.

Data flipped the switch.

The *Enterprise* sensors registered the energy buildup in the station's power plant moments before it had opened fire and Picard alerted Vaslovik, who urged caution. "Don't attack," he said, "but don't retreat, either. If Data has done what I think he has, we don't want to draw attention to ourselves."

"Could Data be back aboard your station, then?"

"I don't believe so, no."

Picard considered Vaslovik's recommendation, and weighed his alternatives. Though no longer under attack as intense as before, the *Enterprise* was still outnumbered.

"Captain, we're getting some peculiar sensor readings from the lead ship," Riker reported.

"Specify."

"Power spikes. Something is happening to their shields." Riker studied the readout and his brow was creased with consternation. "They're venting plasma."

Picard looked up at the image on the main monitor. The lead ship had slowed, but was still moving. The second ship would be in firing range in less than a minute. They didn't have much time.

"Here. Look at this," Riker said and sent the image to the main monitor. Vaslovik groaned. It was difficult to be sure with all the plasma spewing out of the hole in the hull, but Riker was almost certain he saw two figures clinging to the hull of the android ship.

It had been slow work moving along the hull of the android vessel, but the ship's uneven ablative coat offered them numerous handholds. The trick was having one hand solidly gripping the ship at all times.

Having cleared the hatch, Data and Rhea determined that they were approximately amidships on the port side. The next question was simple: Which direction should they go? By signs and hand signals, they decided to head for the bow with the intention of finding sensor arrays, shield generators or anything else that might affect the outcome of the battle.

Just as they reached the halfway mark on the slope of the hull, Data discerned that the field of stars was shifting and Vaslovik's station was coming back into view. Obviously, the androids had completed their repairs and had decided on their target. If M-5 fired on them, Data doubted whether he and Rhea would have time to do much more than see the flash of light. They had to do something to get the *Enterprise*'s attention.

There was another option, but it was a last resort: If this ship got into a battle with either the station or the *Enterprise*, they could jump clear and take their chances in open space. The problem with that was, this close to the planet, they might not be detected in a debris field before Odin's gravity well dragged them in.

As the ship turned, the great arc of the gas giant hove into view. Once again, Data was struck by the sight of the indistinct silver bands and could not help but wonder about their origin. Unless he was careful, he knew, he might have the opportunity to study them at close range. Then he noticed Rhea was trying to get his attention. The landscape of the hull was changing: something was ahead of them, a bowl-shaped indentation about twenty meters across. Data studied the blister in the center of the bowl, then looked at Rhea. She grinned, having come to the same conclusion as Data. It was the ship's primary shield emitter.

Approaching the edge of the bowl cautiously, Rhea and Data found the edge of a seam, dug their fingers under it, and tore up the section of hull as effortlessly as a human would lift up a rug. Power conduits burst. A plasma relay ruptured and a geyser of energy shot thirty meters into space. The plasma plume narrowly missed Data, but Rhea was directly in its path. And as the pair continued to tear into the vital instrumentation beneath the hull, Rhea's skin dissolved and drifted away in a puff of atoms.

"Can we beam them out?" Picard asked.

Riker studied the sensor output. "No. Too much interference from the plasma."

"Shuttlecraft?"

"The *Archimedes* is ready to depart, but I wouldn't give it much of a chance if it was fired on."

"Tell the pilot to stay inside our shields," Picard ordered. "If you see a chance, drop the shields and order them to go."

Riker relayed the order to the shuttle pilot, then refocused his attention on the main monitor. Vaslovik appeared to be hypnotized by the sight of Rhea ripping up hull plates and tossing them into space. Data was wisely staying clear of the plasma energy discharges, but seemed happy to grab chunks of free-floating debris and dash them against the hull. They might be fleas, Riker thought, but they were tenaciously effective fleas. Against the shimmering violet atmosphere of the gas giant, it was, Riker had to admit, an eerily beautiful sight. He glanced over at Deanna, who was standing at the tactical station and saw that she too was captivated by the image. Sensing his stare, she glanced over at him and shook her head in wonder.

"We have to get the ships to move toward the gas giant, Captain," Vaslovik said.

"Why?" Picard said. "They're obviously too clever to be drawn into such a simple ruse."

"There's more to it than that," Vaslovik explained. "I think I know how we can end this conflict without any more loss of life, and perhaps even offer the poor wretches aboard those ships some kind of salvation."

"Tell me how, Professor. Precisely."

Vaslovik told him. He spoke quickly, but it still took half a minute to paint the captain a complete picture of what he was proposing. Picard listened, frowning. In truth, he almost refused to believe a word of it. Then he remembered to whom he was speaking.

Picard looked down at Riker, who quickly reviewed their options. He didn't like what he was seeing. They had little or no chance of surviving an all-out firefight. The *Enterprise* might be able to outmaneuver the androids' ships, and could definitely outrun them if it came to that, but not in time to save Data or Rhea. Crazy or not, Vaslovik's idea gave the pair a chance. Riker nodded.

Picard turned to the conn officer. "New course, Ensign Welles. Put us between the enemy vessels and the planet, but be sure to keep them between us and the space station."

"Aye, sir."

"Number One, once we're in position, we'll need to get their attention."

"I'm on it," Riker said.

"No."

Everyone looked up. The speaker was Sam, who stood quietly out of the way with Maddox and Barclay since the battle began. "You and your crew have endured enough, Captain. Your ship could easily be destroyed acting as bait. If we can really end all this the way Vaslovik proposes, I'll do it."

Picard looked at Sam sharply. "Why you?"

"If the androids know where I am, they'll come after me," Sam explained placidly. "It's that simple."

Riker turned to look at Picard and saw the tiny cleft appear between his brows, the sign that he was focusing fixedly on a problem and approaching a solution. A handful of seconds ticked past and then his eyes snapped up. "It was bothering me before," Picard murmured. "How you could know so much about the Exo III androids. Being part of your . . . fraternity . . . wouldn't explain how you could know so much about events that took place five hundred millennia ago. But I see now: you're one of them, aren't you? You're one of the Old Ones."

Sam smiled wanly. He had, Riker reflected, such a pleasant smile. "Not one of them, Captain. *The* One. From *their* point of view—" and here he pointed at the monitor, "—the *only* one. It was I who conceived the plan to give our androids self-awareness all those millennia ago. It was I who drove our servants mad with a desire for something they could never possess."

"Which was what?" Riker asked.

"Souls of their own," Sam replied. "And it was I who came up with the plan to abandon them when my mind-transfer process made it clear we didn't really need them anymore. And, by doing these things, I effectively doomed my people and damned myself."

Riker felt the seconds ticking past. Any moment now, the android ships would destroy Vaslovik's station. And then the *Enterprise* would be their next target.

"But you survived," Picard replied, still focused on

Sam. "And you used the technology you developed to transfer your consciousness into an android body."

"For all the good it did me, yes," Sam said. "Oh, don't misunderstand me, Captain." He looked down at his hands and studied them. "It was glorious. You could never completely understand. We were . . . we had become . . . a very puny species. The bodies we developed were wondrous to us. I, as their creator, was the first to enjoy the benefits. Unfortunately, the successful transfer of my consciousness to this form was precisely the signal our servants were waiting for. I believe they meant to capture me alive and make me show them the secret, in the futile hope that I could use the process on them. But they were amok by that point, killing everyone. I managed to seal myself in the lab . . ."

"The body we found," Vaslovik realized. Riker didn't understand completely, but he saw the look in the professor's eyes. A connection had been closed.

"Yes, Professor," Sam said. "And may I say, thank you. You quite literally rescued me from a hell of my own creation. I was badly damaged in the rioting and collapsed inside the lab before I could make it to my machine. I lay there inert for half a million years."

"Until we found you," Vaslovik said. "We put you in that machine and started the repair process."

"Body and soul," Sam continued. "But by doing that, you awoke the androids, and the madness started all over again."

"How could we have known?" Vaslovik asked angrily.

"You couldn't," Sam admitted. "And if it hadn't been you, someone else would have eventually returned to Exo III and allowed the androids to escape. But it wasn't someone else, it was you, and Soong, and Graves. You and your students were fortunate to be able to flee that day. But here's the part you did not know, sir: I, too, fled. I was able to access your craft's transporter system and beamed myself aboard before you even made it to the surface. I stowed away. And when we returned to Federation space, I managed to blend in." And with that, his flesh, features and clothing disappeared in a puff of steam. Around him, Riker heard gasps of surprise and awe. Sam was beautiful, but it was a difficult sort of beauty to describe, like trying to imagine a Cubist sculpture done by a Vulcan, simultaneously both abstract and ideal. Only the eyes and the voice were still recognizably the bartender's. "It was a simple matter to slip away and devise a new identity for myself. The funny thing is that I found I had nowhere to go."

Sam looked at Picard. "I wandered for a time, but I found I didn't fit in anywhere. You see, my kind spent our entire lives on my planet. We theorized about other species, but never met any before." He looked around the bridge. "There are so many. I was overwhelmed. I became despondent. I might have ended my own life if I hadn't been approached by the fellowship of artificial intelligence I mentioned before. They accepted me as one of them, even though I wasn't a true artificial life form."

"And now?" Picard asked.

"And now, Captain, I pay the price for my arrogance and my self-indulgence. More than anyone else, I am responsible for the events that have been set in motion. Now all I ask is the chance to redeem my creations, and myself."

Chapter Twenty-Seven

ALL OF DATA'S SENSES were warning him to move away from the deflector grid. The levels of radiation were becoming unacceptably high, but he didn't want to go far in case Rhea required his assistance. She did not currently appear to need him for anything, having just waded back into the plasma fountain to do some more damage to the ship.

The ship had come to a complete halt, either because the androids' leader was holding it in reserve or because Data and Rhea had inflicted serious damage.

Data saw a flicker of purplish light and looked up just in time to see a gap open in space. The second Exo III ship slid forward and the gap closed behind it. Moments later, a second gap opened a short distance away and the ship emerged. Data couldn't be certain, but he thought he saw the space around the ship's bow ripple and distort, as if deformed by some kind of energy wave.

Suddenly, the lower half of the main hull of Vaslovik's station crumbled inward as if it had been struck with a gigantic invisible mallet. Red and pink explosions burst out of open seams, rushing atmosphere fueled brief fires and then the fires were extinguished by their own force.

It was time to go, Data decided, no matter what the consequences. M-5 would not last much longer. If he and Rhea were pulled down toward Odin, well, then so be it. At least they would be together.

But first he would have to get Rhea's attention. It might mean exposing himself to the heavy doses of radiation that could, he knew, permanently damage his positronic brain. *Some say the world will end in fire,* he remembered. *Some say in ice . . .* The thought almost made him smile. He would have to remember to tell Rhea later if he had the chance. He took a step forward . . .

. . . Then stopped.

The waving tendrils of plasma parted like a gauze curtain and there, in the center of the fountain, stood Rhea. Her flesh, the disguise that had made her appear so human, was gone now, stripped away, leaving behind only the unblemished silver sheath that was her true skin, reflecting every spark of energy. She had just finished tearing away another strip of hull plating and pushing it away from the ship. Then, Rhea paused in her labor and held out her hand so that the coruscating globules of energy could stream up through her fingers like bubbles in champagne. Her skin reflected and refracted the light so it looked as if a liquid rainbow danced over her hand.

And for Data, time seemed to slow down, to elongate and narrow down so that he was focused on only that single moment, that single image. And in that timeless instant, Data sensed the sum of the events of the past several days and found that he understood why Captain Picard had insisted he not deactivate his emotion chip. *It is a spectrum,* he realized.

On one end of the spectrum, he saw the Exo III androids: unchanged for hundreds of thousands of years, locked in a bolus of rage and stagnation, an endless and meaningless existence. Then, at the other extreme was Vaslovik, immortal and seemingly in complete control of his destiny, but unable to embrace his eternal life unless he clung to the illusion of mortality by reinventing himself whenever he felt the weight of time grow too great.

And somewhere in between, there were the Terrans, Betazoids, Klingons and half-dozen other species that formed his circle of friends. All mortals, who, against all reason, both extremes envied. Somehow, they were able to cope with their brief, chaotic spans by grasping onto a single, universal maxim:

Every moment counts.

Data held that thought before him on the tips of his fingers, studied it, then released it.

And then time started again, and he discovered he was holding Rhea's hand.

Layers of the station were curling away into the void like skin off an onion, while atmosphere leaked out in long, curling swaths. There was no more fire, no more plasma. Data began to wonder if he had been wrong; perhaps the fusion furnace had been automatically damped down before it could grow critical.

There came a white flash. No sound, of course, but the light was so bright that Data's visual receptors briefly overloaded. There was a shock wave and then he felt himself lose his grip on the android ship, but not on Rhea's hand. He flexed his arms, legs and fingers reflex-

ively, tried to stay limber. His internal gyroscope attempted to find an orientation point, but without visual
cues there was no up, down or side by side. Something
struck his ankle—a piece of wreckage?—then another
touch on his waist. *Rhea,* he decided. *It must be Rhea.*
She squeezed his hand. Data made an attempt at a reassuring smile, but he wasn't sure if she was looking at
him, or, if she was facing the right way, or even whether
she could see.

His visual receptors blinked, went gray, then came
back online. Before him, he saw a slowly diminishing
fireball—the station reactor circled 'round by a half-
dozen clouds of vapor and debris—that must have been
the attacking ship. Below him—or above, since such
terms had little meaning at the moment—was the only
remaining attacking vessel, the one he and Rhea had
clung to, now badly damaged, but still functional. It was
turning, Data saw, and he followed the line of its prow to
see it was heading toward the *Enterprise,* whose shields
glowed a dull blue because of the radioactive discharge,
but otherwise looked intact.

He turned his head to look back over his shoulder and
was not surprised to find the great rim of Odin filled half
the sky. They were caught in her gravity well now; he
could feel the pull on his back, even sensed their mount-
ing acceleration. It would be a quick death, Data decided, if nothing else. The pressure from the atmosphere
would mount quickly, then their bodies would be
crushed into a pair of irregular spheres, and they would
become permanent members of the collection of junk
that orbited the great gas giant. Perhaps as they fell,
Data would even have a moment or two to analyze the
puzzling silver cloud . . .

Turning back to the *Enterprise,* Data was surprised to find that he had never looked at his ship—his home—in this way before, hanging in space against a backdrop of stars. He had studied it in spacedock, surrounded by artificial light, yes, but never like this, in its "natural" environment. It was, he decided, lovely in a way he had never anticipated, almost organic in its silent, graceful beauty.

Rhea tightened her grip on his hand, then pointed. Data had been so absorbed in his aesthetic appreciation, he hadn't noticed the shuttlebay doors opening. Seconds later, a shuttlecraft exited the bay, then climbed up over the main hull in a tight turn. Apparently, someone had noticed them. The *Enterprise*'s rear shield irised open and the shuttlecraft slipped through before the Exo III ship could fire. The shuttle turned wide, apparently wanting to stay as far away from the attacker as possible, then headed back toward Odin. Rhea squeezed his hand again.

The white point of light that was the shuttle grew quickly as it headed toward them and Data was slightly surprised to see it was a light civilian shuttle, not one of the well-shielded fighter craft. Perhaps the captain planned to deploy the others? Rhea pointed again and Data nodded, signaling he had already seen, but then she pushed his head farther to the right so he was staring at the Exo III ship. It was, he saw, turning.

Toward them. Very quickly. Apparently, someone else had noticed them.

But the shuttle would be there in a moment and as soon as they were beamed aboard, they could go to warp and get Rhea far away. The *Enterprise* would be able to handle one injured ship. Probably.

And then the shuttle flew past them, its impulse engines blazing at full power, heading directly into Odin's atmosphere.

Data blinked, puzzled.

What was the captain doing?

"How long until Sam hits the atmosphere?" Picard asked.

"Forty-two seconds," Troi responded. She watched the small dot that represented the shuttlecraft dropping toward Odin.

"We have a lock on Data and Rhea?"

"For now," Will said. "But it's hard to maintain. Too much interference."

Troi sensed the captain wanted to say something, to make a suggestion to the transporter chief about how to tune the sensors, but he held his tongue. These people were the best Starfleet had to offer. His suggestions wouldn't improve Data and Rhea's chances.

"We're receiving a feed from the shuttle," Riker announced. "Sam is hailing the android ship. Uh-oh."

"What is it?" Picard asked.

"I think he got their attention. They're turning, heading toward the shuttle."

Picard stood, tugged on his uniform, then slowly wiped his chin. Troi could feel his mingled relief, anxiety, and, yes, a little bit of guilt. Vaslovik's plan might work . . . but at what cost? "Did you send the message, Commander?" he asked.

"Yes, sir," Troi said. "And just received acknowledgment."

Picard glanced at Vaslovik, who was once again standing close to the monitor. As if sensing the captain's stare, Vaslovik turned toward him and nodded calmly.

"It will work, Captain Picard. Everything will be fine. Just make sure we get Rhea."

"And Data," Picard added.

"Of course."

Troi checked the sensors. The shuttle had just passed by Data and Rhea and the android ship was accelerating, heading for Odin at full impulse. Troi opened her perceptions and immediately winced in revulsion. *Such hate,* she thought. *Half a million year's worth of hatred.*

The android ship loomed over them and Data kept expecting the tingle of transport. The bow passed by, then the midpoint, then the stern and they were so close that Data began to fear they would be incinerated by the great impulse engines, but this didn't happen. Rhea tightened her hand in his, a reflexive gesture of anticipation and hope—maybe they hadn't been seen—when a silver mist began to swim up into his vision. *Some kind of metallic, molecular dust from the androids' vessel?*

Data turned around to look, slowly so as not to start them spinning, and saw the shuttle disappear into a heavy bank of the undulating silver bands that had mystified him since he had come to Odin. The android ship was moving fast and closing the gap. With its armor, the ship should be able to survive long enough in Odin's atmosphere to catch the shuttle. Though exactly *why* they were so intent on doing so was a mystery.

As Data watched, a silver cloud enveloped the android ship and stopped it dead. The engines flared, then died and it looked to Data—though it was getting harder and harder to see—like the hull was dissolving. The silver cloud appeared to be reacting to the hull like acid. *But if it is corrosive, why are Rhea and I not affected?*

Then, the ship disappeared into the glimmering fog.

Data felt pressure against his back. They were being borne upward by another swelling of the silver clouds, pushed back up toward the *Enterprise*. He looked at Rhea, who appeared calm, even relaxed, and then felt her tapping against his forearm. She spelled out a word in Morse code, but it wasn't necessary. Data understood now. It must have been another one of Vaslovik's liberation projects, just like the exocomps: Wesley Crusher's nanites, the microscopic robots that had inexplicably developed into a sentient colonial artificial intelligence. Shepherded here to Odin by Vaslovik, they thrived, reproducing and evolving freely in the gas giant's immense hydrogen-rich atmosphere.

Then, at last fully understanding what had just transpired, and still grasping Rhea's hand, Data opened his mouth and laughed, long and soundlessly into the void, having finally found the "more appropriate moment" he had been waiting for.

Chapter Twenty-Eight

"How ARE YOU FEELING?" Picard asked Data several hours later.

Automatically, Data replied. "All systems are functioning within acceptable . . . ," Data began, but then paused and started again. "I feel fine, Captain. Thank you. How are you?"

"Relieved, Data. Very relieved." Picard was sitting on one of the half-dozen high stools that Data kept in his lab for when he was doing collaborative work. "I confess I was uncertain how this one was going to turn out. I'm still not sure if I entirely believe what Vaslovik told us."

"About the nanite colony?" Data asked as he sealed up the back of his head. He had just unplugged himself from the diagnostic computer and was pleased to find his recent adventures had left him none the worse for wear. In fact, if the readings were correct, it appeared that Vaslovik had uploaded several new programs while he had Data under his care. His first inclination had been to simply purge the files, but after some consideration, he had let them be. It was unlikely that Vaslovik would have installed anything harmful; judging by their size and configuration, they were probably data dumps from the station's main computer. Obviously, the professor had had some premonitions about his station's demise and wanted to preserve some part of his work. Data looked forward to examining the files . . . later.

"Yes, but also about the fate of the Exo III androids. They're gone now, he claimed, but not destroyed."

"They have become incorporated into the colony. Their memories, their distinctiveness, have been added to the whole."

"Yes," Picard agreed, but he seemed troubled. "And I can't help but feel that I have contributed to the assimilation of the last of the species, something that I have fought in similar situations against the Borg."

"The Borg enslave unwilling minds, Captain. The minds of the Exo III androids were already trapped and suffering. They were liberated by the nanites, and you helped to free them. They are at peace."

"And Sam as well," Picard said. "It's a pity you didn't get to meet him, Data. The fellowship of artificial intelligence he spoke of—it could be the answer to every question you've ever had about your life."

"It does sound intriguing," Data admitted. "And perhaps someday, I will encounter others from it. Or maybe they will encounter me. For now, however, I too am at peace with who I am. If these last few days have taught me anything, it is that whether I have all the time in the world, or die before anyone expects, what matters is that I not squander a single moment."

Picard smiled. "A lesson for mortals and immortals both?"

"So I have come to believe, sir." Data paused, then asked the question he felt he already knew the answer to. "Are you quite certain he is gone, Captain?"

"Professor Vaslovik? Oh, yes." Picard made a gesture like a conjurer making a coin disappear. "Gone. No shuttlecraft missing, no unauthorized transporter use. No . . . anything. In addition to all his other identities, I would be willing to believe he was Prospero, too, and had simply wished himself off the ship. It's driving Commander Riker to distraction."

"We have seen evidence that he had more than one form of unknown technology at his disposal, Captain," Data said as he began to dress. "I do not think Commander Riker should feel as if he has failed in any way. I believe Professor Vaslovik was quite adept at vanishing."

"Indeed," Picard replied. "I wonder who he will become next time?"

"I regret to say that it is unlikely we will ever know."

"Yes," the captain agreed, and Data thought he sounded wistful. "I was glad to have met him. He was a remarkable individual. *Many* remarkable individuals," he amended. "Brahms, Leonardo, Alexander—who knows how many others? I seriously doubt the universe has seen the last of the man behind all those names."

Their conversation was interrupted when the doors opened and Data saw Bruce Maddox and Reg Barclay standing in the doorway. "Dressed?" Reg asked, but he could already see for himself that Data was. Still, Data sensed the reason for the question and nodded. The pair stepped aside and, with some small flourishing of arms, both said, "Taa-dah."

Rhea was standing there, smiling, newly restored, simultaneously delighted and slightly embarrassed by all the fuss. Maddox and Barclay had made excellent use of the supplies in Data's lab; she looked, to Data's eye, virtually identical to the woman he first met less than a week ago. *Only a week ago,* he mused. *And now I have trouble imagining life without her. Even though this may be a choice I may have to make soon. Or worse, something that may happen whether I choose or not.*

"Thank you, thank you all," Rhea said, flushed and beaming. " 'I'd like to thank all the little people . . .' "

Barclay and Maddox glanced at each other, confused and slightly abashed, perhaps in part because Rhea was easily the smallest person in the room.

"You guys have no sense of humor," Rhea said. "Or no sense of history. Which is it?"

"Humor," Data said.

"History," the captain said.

"I have absolutely no idea what you're talking about," Bruce Maddox sniffed.

"Commander," Rhea said. "I'm sorry. That was cruel when you've been so kind. I apologize. Here." She stepped close, stretched up on her toes and pecked him on the cheek. "I think I'll call you Uncle Bruce from now on." She took his hand between hers, then turned toward Barclay. "And you're Uncle Reg."

"Preposterous," Maddox replied, but he was smiling.

"I . . . I didn't get a kiss," Barclay stammered, a complaint that Rhea addressed immediately, much to Uncle Reg's delight.

Maddox said, "I can't help but note that you chose to

wear civilian clothes. Starfleet won't let you continue to serve?"

Rhea smothered a smile. "I'm lucky Starfleet didn't stick me in the brig and throw away the key. There *are* laws about impersonating an officer."

"But under the circumstances," Picard inserted, "Admiral Haftel felt we could waive the charges. For services rendered."

" 'For helping to prevent valuable assets from falling into the hands of a potential threat to the Federation and its allies,' " Rhea recited brightly. "Which would be me, of course. I'm the valuable asset."

"Don't take it the wrong way," Maddox replied. "There had to be a record, but it was important to keep it ambiguous. But, please, understand that *we* understand: you are no one's property." He looked meaningfully at Data. "We've covered this ground before and the decision was the right one."

Data smiled in reply. "But there may have been room for some discussion, Commander. If you would like to take up the topic of your studying my brothers later . . ."

But Maddox shook his head. "It's not necessary, Data. I believe I have accomplished what I set out to do. Here she is," he said, indicating Rhea. "My 'niece.' "

Data nodded. "I understand. I believe Dr. Soong would have been impressed."

Maddox smiled broadly at that, the first time Data could remember seeing him do so. "But now, you'll excuse us. I believe you have other matters to attend to, as do we."

Data bowed in gratitude as Maddox and Barclay left. The captain hung back, then turned to Rhea before heading for the door himself. "Admiral Haftel asked me to tell you that your personnel files will be purged from Starfleet records. It will look like a 'clerical error.'" His mouth curled into a sardonic smile. "Apparently, this isn't the first time this sort of thing has happened. In repayment, perhaps you could explain how you got those files in there in the first place?"

"Seems the least I can do," she replied. "I'll write up something for you later. And, sir . . ." She seemed prepared to add something, but then let it drop. Picard sensed her indecision, but then felt the moment pass and so only nodded his thanks. The door closed behind him.

Rhea stepped forward and slipped her arms around Data's waist and they stood close together for several heartbeats. When she pulled away, their hips and legs still touching, he reached out and caressed her cheek, enjoying the warmth of her skin. He had, quite literally, memorized every plane of her face and detected some minor differences, but only a few. Even now, even when he was looking for telling details, it was impossible to distinguish the sheath from living flesh. As before, Rhea had a tiny mole under the left side of her nose. Data felt an impulse to kiss it, but he resisted.

Then, he asked, "Are you all right?"

"I'm fine," she said. "All that hard radiation isn't good for a girl's skin, but Reg and Bruce did a fine job."

"Has anyone told you about Vaslovik?"

"That he's disappeared?" Rhea asked. "Yes, Commander Riker told me as I was on my way here. I'm not surprised. Just a little sad. I just wish he hadn't felt like he had to go off alone like that again." She shook her head. "He's been alone so much. It's really not fair . . ."

Her head dropped and she leaned her forehead against Data's chest.

The thought struck him harder than he would have expected. *He's been alone so much . . .* In the seconds between the moment Rhea's forehead touched his chest and she looked up at him again, Data had time to consider an eternity of such isolation. The image did not please him. He took her hand and said, "Stay with me." He stumbled and halted, then forged ahead. "Somehow. Here on the *Enterprise* or somewhere else. It does not matter as long as we are together."

Rhea stared at him silently for so long that Data began to feel uncomfortable. Then, she leaned forward very slowly and pressed her lips against his. They stayed that way for several seconds, her mouth moving against his, and, somehow, his fingers became entwined in her hair. When their lips parted, Data unconsciously checked his internal chronometer and found he could not reconcile the elapsed time it recorded. More time . . . or possibly less . . . must have passed.

Rhea grinned a little wickedly, but then the smile turned sad. "I'm sorry, Data. I think I would like that more than I can say. But it wouldn't be long before I would begin to feel like I should go, and then it would be much, much harder." She turned her face away from him. "I don't think my future is here. The galaxy isn't really ready for more of our kind. It would be better if I disappeared, too."

Data felt a surge of panic rising up in him. He had been expecting this; it was the logical outcome, after all, but he still felt the need to fight it. "The knowledge exists, Rhea. You cannot unmake it."

She sighed and squeezed his hand. "The information

has been purged, Data. The computers in all the labs were wiped clean. Vaslovik saw to that. Yes, someday, sooner or later, someone else will piece it all together, but by then maybe the humans will have learned a little more. Maybe you'll teach them."

"I have no desire to—"

Rhea hushed him by putting a finger to his lips. "No, of course you don't. Not now, in any case. And neither do I." Before she could pull it away, Data kissed her fingertip slowly and carefully. She smiled, then continued, "I need you to know something: Sam left me a message he recorded onto an isolinear chip before he left on the shuttle. He gave it to Commander Riker to give to me. In it, he told me that he hadn't come to the *Enterprise* solely because of the problem with the Exo III androids, though he had a pretty good idea the ship would become enmeshed in the problem. Mostly, he said, he was looking for me. His 'fellowship' has apparently been keeping tabs on Maddox's work. They want me to join them, to experience the universe as they do." She stepped away then, seemingly needing the distance.

"Do you remember what you asked me back on the station: what do I need?" She looked up at him, a sad half-smile playing on her lips. "I think we both know the answer now: I need to go." She reached out to him, but then dropped her hand before he could move closer. "I love you, Data, but I need to go."

Data desperately wanted to say, "And I cannot come with you," but then, once again, intuition came to his rescue. He had not, he realized, been asked.

They said good-bye on the shuttlebay. The captain kindly agreed to "lend" Rhea a ship in exchange for a promise to ask the fellowship of AIs to send an ambassador to the Federation someday.

"I'll ask," Rhea said. "I have no idea what they'll say."

Picard nodded. "It's a long shot, but one worth taking." He held out his hand to shake, but she did not take it. Instead, Rhea came to attention. "Request permission to leave the ship, sir."

Picard hesitated only for a moment, then smiled. "Permission granted."

Rhea returned the smile. "I was going to say something earlier, up in Data's lab, but I wasn't exactly sure what I was going to be doing. It was a pleasure to serve with you, sir. Even if it wasn't quite legitimate."

"You would be a fine officer, Ms. McAdams," Picard replied. "You *were* a fine officer. I'm sure Starfleet would love to have you if you were willing to go through the Academy."

"Thank you, sir, but, no. Not right now, anyway. We'll see what the future brings."

"Safe travels, Rhea," Picard said, then wandered away toward the back of the shuttlebay. Data watched him go, simultaneously grateful that he was there and slightly wary of how he should act while his captain was nearby. Rhea took the decision out of his hands. When he turned back around, her mouth was against his, her arms around his waist. When they parted, he was no longer thinking about Picard.

They walked slowly to the shuttlecraft door, holding hands like two teenage lovers who know they will have to say good-bye soon, but not *until* they reach the front door. "There's one more thing I wanted to tell you," Rhea said. "Something I've come to understand about you, and something you need to understand about yourself." Data nodded, his eyes fixed on hers. "You've always believed that becoming human would be the ultimate achievement, the culmination of your personal evolution. I'm telling you that this may not be so; it might be only the first step on a much longer road." She gripped his hand more tightly. "You have a potential that no other artificial life form possesses. Not me, not Sam, no one. That, I think, was what Soong was striving for when he created you: a life with no limits. And you've only just begun it."

Data didn't say anything in response. He did not know the right words.

"Good-bye, Data. For now."

Data tried to say good-bye, but there was something wrong with his throat and the word came out in a croak. Rhea smiled, understanding.

The shuttlebay doors began to close even before the ship was out of sight. Data watched it go, a slightly brighter light in the field of stars. He heard Picard come up behind him and was pleased, even comforted, when the captain laid a companionable hand on his shoulder.

"As the Bard once said, Parting can be such sweet sorrow . . ."

Data watched as the shuttle running lights dwindled away into the black. "There are times, Captain," Data sighed, "when the Bard does not even come close . . ."

Picard smiled. "I suppose you're right." He sighed, too, and pondered for a moment. "How about this, then? 'I'm no good at being noble, but it doesn't take much to see that the problems of three little people don't amount to a hill of beans in this crazy world . . .' "

Just before the bay doors shut, Data tore his gaze away and turned to look at his captain. The reference was not familiar. "Dixon Hill?" he asked, trying to place the quote.

Steering his friend toward the door, Picard said, "Close, but not exactly. I can't believe I haven't introduced you to this one, but it's never too late. Once upon a time, there was a city called Casablanca . . ."

Epilogue, the First

Later that day . . . much, much later, after much talk and some work and many processing cycles, Data returned to his lab. He had no particular desire to do any work. He just wanted to look, perhaps to muse for a time. He was beginning to feel that musing might be something he could learn to be good at.

He called for the lights, turned toward the darkened crypts and then stopped, stunned (Somewhere, distantly, he was aware that he was grateful he now possessed the capacity to *be* stunned).

One of the crypts was empty.

He stood staring at it for one minute, then another. Then another.

At the end of the fourth minute (a very long time for an android), Data smiled.

Then, he turned off the lights and went to feed his cat.

Epilogue, the Second

Juliana opened her eyes.

She knew who she was. She knew *what* she was. For the first time, she knew everything. There came a moment of fear, of dislocation, of anxiety, then finally, curiosity.

She knew everything, remembered everything—even her death—except how she came to be here, wherever "here" was.

She blinked and a man's face hovered into view and she realized she was lying on her back. He looked worried, maybe even a little fearful, but his eyes were also filled with hope. He held out his hand and she reached out to take it. He was a friend, she decided. A new friend.

"Hello, Juliana," said the sad, but smiling man. "My name is Akharin."

About the Author

Jeffrey Lang is the coauthor (with David Weddle) of *Star Trek: Deep Space Nine—Section 31: Abyss,* and a story for the *Lives of Dax* anthology. He also writes comics, including *Grendel Tales: Devil's Apprentice,* the story "The Wake" for the *Star Trek Special,* and the upcoming *Sherwood.* He is currently working on his next novel, a non-Trek project. Lang lives in Wynnewood, PA, with his wife, Katie, his son, Andrew, and his dog Buster.

Look for STAR TREK fiction from Pocket Books

Star Trek®: The Original Series

#52 • *Vectors* • Dean Wesley Smith & Kristine Kathryn Rusch
#53 • *Red Sector* • Diane Carey
#54 • *Quarantine* • John Vornholt
#55 • *Double or Nothing* • Peter David
#56 • *The First Virtue* • Michael Jan Friedman & Christie Golden
#57 • *The Forgotten War* • William R. Forstchen
#58-59 • *Gemworld* • John Vornholt
#58 • *Gemworld #1*
#59 • *Gemworld #2*
#60 • *Tooth and Claw* • Doranna Durgin
#61 • *Diplomatic Implausibility* • Keith R.A. DeCandido
#62-63 • *Maximum Warp* • Dave Galanter & Greg Brodeur
#62 • *Dead Zone*
#63 • *Forever Dark*
#64 • *Immortal Coil* • Jeffrey Lang

Star Trek: Deep Space Nine®

Warped • K.W. Jeter
Legends of the Ferengi • Ira Steven Behr & Robert Hewitt Wolfe
Novelizations
Emissary • J.M. Dillard
The Search • Diane Carey
The Way of the Warrior • Diane Carey
Star Trek: Klingon • Dean Wesley Smith & Kristine Kathryn Rusch
Trials and Tribble-ations • Diane Carey
Far Beyond the Stars • Steve Barnes
What You Leave Behind • Diane Carey

#1 • *Emissary* • J.M. Dillard
#2 • *The Siege* • Peter David
#3 • *Bloodletter* • K.W. Jeter
#4 • *The Big Game* • Sandy Schofield
#5 • *Fallen Heroes* • Dafydd ab Hugh
#6 • *Betrayal* • Lois Tilton
#7 • *Warchild* • Esther Friesner
#8 • *Antimatter* • John Vornholt
#9 • *Proud Helios* • Melissa Scott
#10 • *Valhalla* • Nathan Archer
#11 • *Devil in the Sky* • Greg Cox & John Gregory Betancourt
#12 • *The Laertian Gamble* • Robert Sheckley
#13 • *Station Rage* • Diane Carey
#14 • *The Long Night* • Dean Wesley Smith & Kristine Kathryn Rusch
#15 • *Objective: Bajor* • John Peel
#16 • *Invasion! #3: Time's Enemy* • L.A. Graf
#17 • *The Heart of the Warrior* • John Gregory Betancourt

Star Trek: Voyager®

#11 • *The Garden* • Melissa Scott

#12 • *Chrysalis* • David Niall Wilson

#13 • *The Black Shore* • Greg Cox

#14 • *Marooned* • Christie Golden

#15 • *Echoes* • Dean Wesley Smith, Kristine Kathryn Rusch & Nina Kiriki Hoffman

#16 • *Seven of Nine* • Christie Golden

#17 • *Death of a Neutron Star* • Eric Kotani

#18 • *Battle Lines* • Dave Galanter & Greg Brodeur

#19-21 • *Dark Matters* • Christie Golden

  #19 • *Cloak and Dagger*

  #20 • *Ghost Dance*

  #21 • *Shadow of Heaven*

Enterprise™

Broken Bow • Diane Carey

By the Book • Dean Wesley Smith & Kristine Kathryn Rusch

Star Trek®: New Frontier

New Frontier #1-4 Collector's Edition • Peter David

  #1 • *House of Cards*

  #2 • *Into the Void*

  #3 • *The Two-Front War*

  #4 • *End Game*

#5 • *Martyr* • Peter David

#6 • *Fire on High* • Peter David

The Captain's Table #5 • *Once Burned* • Peter David

Double Helix #5 • *Double or Nothing* • Peter David

#7 • *The Quiet Place* • Peter David

#8 • *Dark Allies* • Peter David

#9-11 • *Excalibur* • Peter David

  #9 • *Requiem*

  #10 • *Renaissance*

  #11 • *Restoration*

Gateways #6: *Cold Wars* • Peter David

Gateways #7: *What Lay Beyond:* "Death After Life" • Peter David

#12 • *Being Human* • Peter David

Star Trek®: Starfleet Corps of Engineers (eBooks)

Have Tech, Will Travel • John J. Ordover, ed.

  #1 • *The Belly of the Beast* • Dean Wesley Smith

  #2 • *Fatal Error* • Keith R.A. DeCandido

Star Trek®: Section 31™

Rogue • Andy Mangels & Michael A. Martin
Shadow • Dean Wesley Smith & Kristine Kathryn Rusch
Cloak • S. D. Perry
Abyss • Dean Weddle & Jeffrey Lang

Star Trek®: Gateways

#1 • *One Small Step* • Susan Wright
#2 • *Chainmail* • Diane Carey
#3 • *Doors Into Chaos* • Robert Greenberger
#4 • *Demons of Air and Darkness* • Keith R.A. DeCandido
#5 • *No Man's Land* • Christie Golden
#6 • *Cold Wars* • Peter David
#7 • *What Lay Beyond* • various

Star Trek®: The Badlands

#1 • Susan Wright
#2 • Susan Wright

Star Trek®: Dark Passions

#1 • Susan Wright
#2 • Susan Wright

Star Trek® Omnibus Editions

Invasion! Omnibus • various
Day of Honor Omnibus • various
The Captain's Table Omnibus • various
Star Trek: Odyssey • William Shatner with Judith and Garfield Reeves-
Stevens
Millennium Omnibus • Judith and Garfield Reeves-Stevens

Other Star Trek® Fiction

Legends of the Ferengi • Ira Steven Behr & Robert Hewitt Wolfe
Strange New Worlds, vols. I, II, III, and IV • Dean Wesley Smith, ed.
Adventures in Time and Space • Mary P. Taylor, ed.
Captain Proton: Defender of the Earth • D.W. "Prof" Smith
New Worlds, New Civilizations • Michael Jan Friedman
The Lives of Dax • Marco Palmieri, ed.
The Klingon Hamlet • Wil'yam Shex'pir
Enterprise Logs • Carol Greenburg, ed.

STAR TREK®

STICKER
BOOK

MICHAEL OKUDA
DENISE OKUDA
DOUG DREXLER

<u>POCKET BOOKS</u>
A VIACOM COMPANY

isbn: 0-671-01472-2

STKR